About the Author

Brett resides in beautiful British Columbia, Canada, with her husband, three kids, five dogs and hobby farm inhabitants. Outside of being a mom, Brett loves to read books, scrapbook, play sports, train in long-distance running, beer tasting, catch up with friends, and hang out with her pets. Brett has a serious love for chocolate and will hide it in the cupboard from her kids, so she doesn't have to share. Be sure to follow Brett on Instagram: *@brettneythompsonauthor*. Don't forget to leave a review on Goodreads or wherever you purchase your book!

I Knew You Would Be Trouble

Brettney Thompson

I Knew You Would Be Trouble

Vanguard Press

A CIP catalogue record for this title is
available from the British Library.

ISBN 978 1 80016 848 0

*Vanguard Press is an imprint of
Pegasus Elliot Mackenzie Publishers Ltd.*
www.pegasuspublishers.com

First Published in 2023

**Vanguard Press
Sheraton House Castle Park
Cambridge England**

Printed & Bound in Great Britain

Dedication

For Austen, Adalyn, and Lachlan
   You were made for us.

Acknowledgements

Writing this book was something that I wanted to do for a long time, and I'm extremely proud of this accomplishment. This story is sentimental to me in many ways, and I'm glad that I'm able to share a story about real love. I want to thank my publishing team, *Pegasus Publishing* for all your support and encouragement along the way. Thank you for allowing me to keep my book authentic, as well as all your hard work in helping me bring my vision to life. Thank you, Eric for supporting my dream of becoming a published author. Thank you for always encouraging me and my ideas. Thank you for all the books you bought me on how to be a successful writer, and for the countless hours you spent listening to me talk about this book. Thank you for taking the time to read through my book, and for always being honest with your thoughts and opinions. I couldn't have written this book without you. Thank you, Mom, and Matt, for being my number one cheerleaders, pumping my tires, and excitedly supporting me throughout this process. Thank you for always reminding me that the sky is the limit, and whatever I want to put my mind to, I can achieve it. Thank you for your kind, warm, loving, and helpful feedback, support, and encouragement. I appreciate you both. A special thanks to my best friend, Sam, for your unwavering support. It's heartwarming knowing I have someone who always has my back, who wants to see me succeed, and who finds happiness in my happiness. I've never known a best friend love like yours, and I wouldn't trade it for the world. Thank you for taking the time to read my book and provide honest feedback, constructive criticism, and encouragement, all with the intention of seeing me succeed. Thank you. Last, but certainly not least, thank you to anyone who took the time to read this book. It means a lot to me knowing that you took the time out of your life to read my book, so thank you. I would love to hear your thoughts so be sure to leave a review! I plan to have more books in the future and would love for you to check those out as well! Thank you. XO, Brett.

Blake Taylor: Fall, 2014

The sun was shining, and it was a perfect day to spend at the beach rather than moving furniture and unpacking boxes in my new home. My parents, Dean and Kara, had decided to move to a more central location of Victoria, British Columbia, as they were wanting to save time on their commute to their respective jobs. The house was located in downtown Victoria, only one block away from Beacon Hill Park. The location was perfect, as I have a golden retriever named Merc who I know will just love spending time at the park.

I decided to bite the bullet and move back in with my parents to save some money. Thankfully, the home that they bought has its own private basement suite that I will be staying in. With summer almost being over, September meant the commencement of my 3rd year of nursing school at the University of Victoria. I was so excited two years ago when I was accepted into the program that I had moved out to live on my own and start my life as an independent adult. Little did I know, Victoria is extremely expensive, especially on a student's budget and only working part time at Urban Garage, a furniture store. So, when I heard that my parents were moving to downtown Victoria, which had a suite with my name on it, I couldn't pass up the free accommodations. My parents had always had a rule that myself, and my two sisters, Audi and Brenna, could live at home rent free as long as we were attending university.

I was in the middle of carrying a box of clothes into my suite when I heard Audi shouting, "Blake, come here I have to show you something, now!" I put my box down on my kitchen island and made my way to the front yard. Audi was standing next to the moving truck empty handed.

"What's up Audi, what did you need?"

"Oh, nothing!" Audi pointed in the direction of a few of her personal items spread out on the front lawn. "I just needed your help carrying my mirror into my bedroom, it's way too heavy and Trevor is busy helping dad."

Audi was a typical twenty-year-old female living in a big city. She loved to party, dress up with pretty makeup and nice clothes, hangout with friends, spend time with her boyfriend Trevor, and avoid all types of physical labour. It didn't really surprise me that she had tricked me into coming to help her. I jokingly rolled my eyes, grabbed her mirror, and made my way to her room.

Audi followed closely behind with one of her Audrey Hepburn paintings that I knew she was just dying to hang up. Even though Audi was only two years younger, we couldn't be any more opposite. She loved the glitz and the glam of being a girl, the clothes, the makeup, the boys. I, on the other hand liked to *be* one of the guys. I was athletic and grew up playing hockey, whereas Audi did gymnastics and dance. I was more of a ripped jeans, hat on backward, no makeup with wet hair type of chick, and Audi wouldn't be caught dead leaving the house without looking like she was ready to pose for Vogue magazine. Despite our polar opposite personalities, we were best friends and got a kick out of each other's quirks.

I placed the mirror down on her already perfectly made bed, and jokingly said, "Isn't it funny how everyone is busting their butts hauling in furniture and boxes, having nothing personal unpacked yet, and your room is basically all set up?"

"Well Blake I have Mariah's Birthday dinner tonight so I need to hurry up and unpack so that I can get changed and get ready to go out," Audi rebuked. "Plus, I don't want to be all hung over tomorrow trying to set up my bedroom. I'm pretty sure dad won't care if I'm not bringing in dining room chairs. That's why I brought Trevor."

"How are things going with Trevor anyway?" I asked, genuinely curious.

"Oh, you know, same old same old. One week we're madly in love, the next week he's being an ass," she said matter-of-factly.

"Right, well you know my thoughts. Anyway, I'm going to finish bringing in more stuff. Have Brenna help

13

you with the rest of your stuff if you need someone. Have fun tonight!"

As I exited Audi's bedroom and made my way to the moving truck, I couldn't help but wonder if I've been too hard on Audi in accepting her relationship with Trevor. Trevor is a nice guy and fun to be around, but when he drinks, he becomes a completely different person, and unfortunately, my little sister has been the one to take the brunt of his actions for the past two years. It's hard being the person that Audi comes to when she needs to vent about Trevor, because then I know all the mean things he says and does, and it really persuades my personal opinion of him. But I have to be supportive and kind, because they're happy together and that's what sisters do.

I got outside and the sun was beaming down. It was a beautiful day in Victoria, not its typical cloud covered drizzling rain type of day. I grabbed a box labeled 'Kitchen' and brought it inside. Mom was busy unpacking dishes and glassware that she didn't notice me enter the room.

"Oh! Goodness Blake, you startled me. What have you got there?"

"I don't know some box that's meant for the kitchen. I actually came in here 'cause I wanted to grab a beer. Where's Brenna, Dad and Trevor?" I asked as I raided the fridge.

"Brenna was just bringing boxes down to the basement, she said there's only a few heavy dressers left in the moving truck, but the movers were handling them. We made good time having unloaded pretty much everything by early afternoon. Thank goodness we hired those movers to help otherwise it would have been a long and tiring day! Oh, and the boys are in the back yard hauling the patio furniture. I'm sure they'd appreciate a beer in this heat," mom responded.

"Yeah, I'll grab them one and then see if they need a hand, otherwise I'll just keep unloading the small things in the truck." I grabbed two more Coors Light and walked out the large French doors that led off the kitchen onto our outdoor deck.

I stepped onto the deck and realized this was the first time I had even seen the back yard. I took a second to look around. The yard was gorgeous. The deck that I stood on was enormous, it was probably big enough to be a dance floor at a wedding reception. I could imagine how pretty it would be if we strung twinkle lights from the overhead pergola. The entire green grassed yard was fenced in with trees and flowers surrounding the perimeter of the yard. I guess one of the upsides to living in a rainy city is that it sure does nourish beautiful landscaping. Merc had already made himself at home sprawled out in the shade chewing on his favourite ball.

In the back right hand corner of the yard was where dad and Trevor were setting up the fire pit. I walked over with the beers in hand.

"How are you guys making out? I brought you a cold one."

"Thanks!" Dad and Trevor both exclaimed. "It's so hot out here that this is exactly what I was needing" continued dad.

"No problem, mom had suggested it. Did you guys need a hand, or do you mind if I continue unloading the truck?"

"No, go ahead, Trevor and I can manage. Hey Blake, where's Colin? I thought he was coming by the house today?" Dad asked.

"He's at the hospital until six p.m. then he said he would pop by and see how we were making out."

"Right, I couldn't remember what you had told me earlier. Alright, thanks for the beer, catch ya later."

Colin and I have been together for about a year now. We met through a mutual friend, Abby Scotts. Abby and I work together at Urban Garage. She and her husband James moved here from Australia a year and a half ago. They met Colin through their beer league softball team and unintentionally set us up. Colin will be starting his second year of medical school at the University of Victoria in September. Because he is still in school for a few more years, he decided to move out of his friend Wyatt's place and move back in with his parents to save money. He has the basement to himself, and it's nice that they let him live there rent free so he can just focus on school. This summer he has been working and completing a practicum at the hospital for extra experience. His schedule is super demanding and between lectures, studying, and practicum, I'm surprised he even has time for a girlfriend.

"Yeah, no problem!" I shouted as I made my way back to my suite. I quickly glanced over at the moving truck in the driveway and could see the movers wrapping things up. Looks like they're all done. I have a separate entrance on the side of the house that is locked and unlocked by a code. I still haven't set up my own personal code so I'm using the one the previous homeowners had left: 4041. I entered my basement suite and did not realize how much work I had ahead of me. Although everything was perfectly packed and sorted accordingly to each particular room, there was still a lot that needed to be done.

My suite was very modern, consisting of a beautiful kitchen with white cabinets, white quartz countertops, and stainless-steel appliances. The kitchen was an open concept with the living room which was painted light grey with floor and ceiling crown moldings. The floors were a dark engineered hardwood which provided a lovely contrast to the bright kitchen. There was a small den area that would be perfect for my desk and laptop for the late-night study sessions ahead. Off of the living room was a four-piece bathroom, also painted grey, however a few shades darker. The bathroom had a stand-up tiled shower with glass doors, a soaker tub, a toilet, and a large vanity. I couldn't wait to have my first bath in this luxurious spa like bathroom. My bedroom was a good size. I assumed it would be big enough for a queen-sized bed, two-night stands, and a stand-up dresser. Although the bed wasn't set up yet, the mattress and furniture were already placed in the room, and it seemed roomy enough.

My microwave read two-fourteen p.m. I took a sip of my beer and decided to start in my bedroom and set up my bed, that way I at least have somewhere to sleep tonight. After three hours of unpacking, I received a phone call from Colin stating he was finished early at the hospital and was going to quickly shower at his place and then he would be over. I was pleased with my amount of progress I had made in that short amount of time. For the most part, my entire suite was unpacked, I just had to decorate and get rid of all of the empty boxes. One of the benefits to working at a furniture and décor store is that I get an amazing discount and can make my suite look like a magazine at a very low price.

I made my way up to the main house to await Colin and help the rest of the family settle in. Brenna was sitting on a bar stool concentrating intently at her phone.

"Hey Bren, what are you up to?"

"Just on the school website looking at the elective options. I'm torn between visual arts or pottery. I've never taken pottery, so I sort of want to try something new, but I absolutely love visual arts. Ugh, why does grade eleven have to be so tough," Brenna exclaimed.

Brenna was not your typical sixteen-year-old. She was very smart, loved school, and was extremely passionate about her art. She wasn't your typical teenager who was experimenting with drugs, alcohol, and sex. Instead, she was academically focused and working very hard in the hopes of getting a scholarship to the University of Victoria after she graduates.

"Well, it might be cool to have one more skill on your resume. You're already fantastic at visual arts, and you can continue that as a hobby, and I'm sure the teacher would let you go in there after hours to work on things for fun if you wanted. That way you get the best of both worlds and get to learn something new by trying out pottery."

"That's true. Thanks," Brenna replied. "Should we order a pizza? I'm getting hungry and I doubt anyone feels like cooking?"

"Good idea. Maybe order three larges… You know how the boys like to eat. I'll run outside and see what kind they want, and you can look up some specials." I made my way to the deck. Mom, dad and Trevor were sitting on the newly arranged patio furniture.

"Brenna's about to order pizza, what kinds do you guys want?"

"Maybe a meat lovers and something else," dad responded.

"I'm actually heading out here soon. Audi just texted me saying she would be ready to leave in fifteen minutes. I swear I have no idea what she does in there when she says she is getting ready…Takes her three hours some days," Trevor expressed, slightly annoyed.

"Here Blake, you can put this toward the pizza when it arrives." Mom handed me a couple twenty-dollar bills.

"Sounds good, I'll let Brenna know so she can order. Patio furniture looks great you guys!"

Brenna was still sitting at the island when I entered the kitchen. "So, dad wants a meat lovers. I know you'll want vegetarian, then we can just order a plain cheese or something."

"Done. I overheard the conversation through the patio door, so I basically had the whole order put through on my phone," Brenna explained.

I sat at the island next to Brenna and we talked about how her summer has been and how she has been enjoying spending time with her friends. She explained that her best friend just lives two blocks over, so she is looking forward to having someone to carpool with to and from school.

As we were catching up, there was a knock at the door. Merc let out a quick bark to inform us that there was in fact someone at our front step. I grabbed the cash mom had given me, with the assumption that it was the pizza delivery man at the door.

As I approached the door, I could see out the side window that it was not the pizza man, but it was actually Colin.

"Hey! Glad you got off early, you're just in time for pizza" I exclaimed as I welcomed Colin into the new house.

"Hey, looks like I have perfect timing then, eh" Colin replied as he greeted me with a quick hug and kiss.

"Hey Brenna, how's moving day?" Colin asked, as we made our way into the kitchen.

"It's good! We got a lot done today, no thanks to you. Typical Colin, showing up at the last minute when all the work is done and can sip on beers and eat pizza:" Brenna joked.

"Hey now! Sorry that I have an extremely busy schedule and can barely find time to even sleep or eat meals" Colin retorted.

"Bren, I'm going to leave the cash on the table so you can pay the pizza man, I'm just going to give Colin a tour of the house and of my suite" I expressed.

We toured the house room by room, Colin stating that he liked the layout of the home and that overall, it was a great house. We talked about how nice it was to be close to downtown and that we would have to take advantage of the tennis courts at Beacon Hill Park. We then made our way to my suite.

Colin was impressed with how much I had accomplished stating, "Wow Blake, it looks great, you did an awesome job."

"Thanks, time sort of flew by once I got on a roll." I motioned toward the corner of the living room, "I still have to get rid of all of these boxes but that won't take long, and then I'll be pretty well settled in. How was the hospital today?"

Colin made himself comfortable and grabbed a seat on my charcoal linen couch. I grabbed us some cold water and then joined him on the couch as he began to tell me about his day.

"It was good. I was shadowing Dr. Kipp and just observed him all day, learning how to interact with patients and properly assess and diagnose. Definitely learned a lot. Being in the hospital makes me excited for next year when I'm a second-year med student and will actually be doing clinical rotations," Colin explained.

"Oh, that's good that you're getting some experience in beforehand. Have you bought all your books for school yet?" I inquired.

Colin took a sip of water then proceeded, "Pretty much. I have one lab book I'm just waiting for but other than that I have everything. Classes start in a week and a half, and the bookstore said it would be in next week."

Before I had the chance to respond, I received a text from Brenna stating the pizza had arrived, and that everyone was eating on the back deck. I informed Colin of the same and we made our way to the yard.

We joined my parents and Brenna on the deck, as Trevor and Audi had left for their friends' Birthday celebration. The sun was still out but the summer air had a slight breeze which made it comfortable to sit outside. Dad looked exhausted from all the lifting and maneuvering he had managed today, and mom looked relaxed as she finally had a back yard she could enjoy.

"So, Colin, how was the hospital? You must be getting antsy to jump into second year," Dad questioned.

Colin managed to gobble down the last bite of his pizza before responding. "Yeah, it was good. I'm only there a few times a week and I'm just shadowing one of the hospitalists. Basically, just trying to gain as much experience in the hospital setting as I can to prepare me for next year."

"Good for you Colin. My girlfriend Lisa is a nurse in emerg, she's really nice, keep an eye out for her when you're there" mom added.

We sat around socializing and eating until we were too uncomfortable to move. Colin didn't stay too late as he had an early morning tomorrow spending Sunday fishing with his dad. They planned on doing a day trip and wanted to leave before the sun came up.

After Colin left around eight p.m. I took Merc for a walk around our new neighbourhood, and over to the park as I wanted to check things out. Beacon Hill Park was gorgeous. It was filled with lush vegetation including plants, flowers and trees, and the entire park was so well kept. Park benches, pathways, and garbage bins were dispersed throughout the park. We walked around for half an hour only covering about one fifth of the park. I would have to come back and tackle other portions of the park the next couple of times.

When I got to my suite, Merc was pretty exhausted and retired to his bed. I had bought him a nice comfy dog bed a few months back and placed it in the corner of my room so we could sleep together. Occasionally he would jump into bed with me, but he typically would get too warm and retreat to his bed after about an hour or so.

I made myself a mint tea and then ran a warm bath. I bought lavender bath salts at the store yesterday so I couldn't wait to test them out. I filled the tub with my favourite coconut scented bubble bath and submerged myself in pure relaxation.

Alec Kohl

"Alec, I'm not going to ask you again. Wake up! We are supposed to be at brunch in twenty minutes and you still haven't showered" Heather shouted.

I groaned before tossing and finally rising out of bed. I stumbled my way, with my eyes half shut into the ensuite bathroom that my girlfriend Heather was occupying as she finished up her makeup. I turned on the shower and stepped in when the temperature was warm enough.

"It's really frustrating when I'm having to ask you three times to get out of bed and shower. Now we're going to be late, and I hate being late" Heather complained.

It's not that I didn't care, but I struggle getting out of bed in the morning on a normal day, let alone on a Sunday when it's my one day to sleep in. Mornings are not my cup of tea, and I'm definitely known to be quite the 'night owl.' Typically, I plays men's hockey on Friday nights, but yesterday evening I got asked by a friend to step in and play in another league as they were short players. The ice time started at ten p.m. so by the time I got off the ice, showered, had a beer or two in the dressing room and then got home, it was nearly one a.m.

Of course, I couldn't just jump into bed right away because I was wide awake and hungry. So, after making a midnight snack and playing a few rounds on the Xbox, I didn't even realize that it was nearly three a.m. I made my way quietly up the stairs and noticed that Heather was sound asleep. Attending a brunch at ten a.m. with my girlfriend's friends was the last things that I wanted to do, but here I am, showering and now I'm grumpy.

I quickly brushed my teeth and got dressed and Heather and I made our way to the restaurant to meet up with everyone else. I was dreading this brunch as I found it difficult to socialize with Heather's friends. They were all either weird, or socially awkward and it was challenging to find common ground. We were the last to arrive and I knew I would hear about it on our way home.

There were two chairs left at the table and it was nice to see a familiar face. It looks like Heather's friend Brooke had started dating someone new, which so happened to be one of the guys at hockey last night, Jason. I was pleased to at least have someone to talk to at this stupid brunch.

We said our hellos to everyone at the table and grabbed our seats. I sat next to Jason and Heather sat opposite me on the other side of the table next to Brooke. We made small talk amongst the four of us, occasionally expanding and speaking with others from the other end of the table. It's always difficult being able to connect with everyone at a meal like this because everyone is so spread out and everyone is talking at once.

Jason asked what was new as he didn't stick around for beers after hockey last night, so we didn't have a chance to catch up then.

"Oh, not much, work is busy, as per usual. Trying some new techniques for training the dog so I've been really busy with that," I explained.

I've been a member of the Royal Canadian Mounted Police (RCMP), for ten years now, and have specialized in drug detection for the past eight. My partner is a German Shepherd named Chip, in which he is able to sniff out and indicate on several types of drugs. It is my job to ensure his skills are up to par so I'm constantly having to train with Chip and test his capabilities.

"Oh man, that does sound busy. How is Chip doing? You've only had him for a few months now right" Jason asked.

"Yeah, Guinness my old search dog, who is a yellow lab, retired last year and then the RCMP decided to have all searching dogs be of the same breed, so they gave me a shepherd, and so I got Chip. He's a great dog, very intelligent and has the drive to want to please. He's settling in well and is a great worker."

As I was explaining and speaking to Jason about Chip, I could see Heather glaring from across the table. She wasn't too pleased that we had to get *another* dog. It's not that she isn't a dog person, but she felt as though one was enough. Heather is also a member of the RCMP and feels as though between the two of us and our long shifts, the last thing she wants to do when she gets home is deal with dogs and having to exercise them. She's starting to come around though, because Chip comes to work with me every day, and I still bring Guinness along as well. The dogs are never left at home alone and I walk them every day either before, during, or after work. I don't consider spending time with my dogs a chore, but Heather seems to think it is.

"Well, that's awesome, I'm glad he's settling in," Jason replied. "Did that house next to you ever end up selling? As a cop it must be nerve racking getting new neighbours…You never know what sort of people you'll get?"

"Uh yeah, it sold…It's definitely something that is important to me, 'cause I find it important to have good neighbours, so hopefully these folks will be nice. I was thinking of stopping by there in a few days after they settle in and welcoming them to the neighbourhood."

"That's nice." As Jason was about to continue, the waitress came by asking for our order. We placed our orders and then he continued, "So is it an old couple that moved in, or a couple youngsters or what?"

I glanced across the table and noticed that Heather was deep in conversation with Brooke, so I quickly responded, "I was only outside briefly. I saw the moving truck pull up and saw a family exit. The husband and wife look nice, and they had three daughters. When I was in the back yard, I saw someone moving around in their basement suite. A twenty something year old blonde with tattoos up her arm came out, and I thought to myself, 'great, she's gonna be a pain in my ass'."

Jason laughed and both Heather and Brooke looked over. They resumed their conversation after giving us the "quiet down" looks.

"Why is she going to be a pain in your ass?" Jason questioned.

"Are you kidding?" I replied.

Jason looked quizzical wanting more of an explanation. I didn't want to explain too loudly so I leaned slightly closer to him before saying, "A young, attractive blonde moves into the basement suite next door…You know Heather, she's practically jealous of my own mother."

Jason let out another laugh and this time the girls just ignored us. He was smart enough to drop the conversation there and talk about pre-season NHL hockey instead as we awaited our meals.

Brunch was good, very filling and I felt like I was going to explode by the time we got the bill. We said our goodbyes and Heather and I made our way to the vehicle. We weren't in the SUV for thirty seconds before she started asking what Jason and I were laughing about at the table.

"I don't even remember."

"How can you not remember? It wasn't even an hour ago. What did you guys talk about then," Heather persisted.

"Work, training Chip, the new neighbours, and hockey."

"Sounds hilarious," Heather responded sarcastically.

"What can I say, I'm a pretty funny guy. Speaking of the neighbours, I was thinking of introducing myself and welcoming them to the neighbourhood. Were you wanting to join?"

Heather thought to herself before responding. "That's okay, if I see them out, I'll say hello but I'm not going to go over to their place."

"Alright." We drove the rest of the way home in silence. When we got back to the house, both dogs greeted us with slobbery kisses and loud over-exaggerated whines. I wanted to take advantage of the nice day, so I told Heather I would be in the back yard doing some yard work and then I would be taking the dogs for a walk. Heather grabbed a book and made herself comfortable on the couch.

I took the dogs outside with me and looked for the rake. I started gathering fallen leaves and branches and assembling them into piles. Guinness and Chip were busy running around and playing with the ball.

I heard a door close next door, so I peeked over the fence. It was a man; I'm assuming the father of the household. We made brief eye contact and I waived, making my way over to the fence to say hello.

"Hey there, I'm Alec Kohl. Welcome to the neighbourhood."

"Hey, thank you. I'm Dean Taylor. Beauty day, isn't it?"

"Sure is. You guys picked a great weekend to move in. Couldn't have asked for better moving weather. Where did you and your family move from," I asked, genuinely curious.

Dean took a sip of his water before replying, "We were living in Sidney, over by the ferry station and wanted to be closer to downtown for travel purposes. Both my daughters, Blake and Audi are attending U of Vic, and my youngest daughter Brenna is in high school a few blocks from here, so it made sense to move closer."

"Sound like you've got your hands full with three daughters," I joked. Hopefully, Dean wouldn't take offense to my sense of humor.

"Yeah! You got that right" Dean chuckled back.

"Well, if you're ever looking for a break from all the girls, I play hockey on Friday nights, and we're always looking for extra players."

Dean let out a long exhale then stated, "Oh jeeze, I haven't played hockey in over ten years...But my daughter Blake plays. I know she would love to go out."

Shit. Heather would be pissed if she knew the neighbour girl was coming out to play hockey. I decided to be polite and reached for my wallet, pulling out one of my RCMP business cards, as this was all I had on me. "Cool, well give her my card and let her know it's Friday at nine-fifteen p.m. She can text me for the details if she's interested."

"Right on. Thanks. I'll let her know for sure." Dean grabbed the business card and looked it over. "RCMP eh? How long have you been a member?"

"Ten years now." I replied. It's always awkward when people ask me about my job because people are either pro police or hate them. I quickly looked up at Dean and could tell he was genuine with his questioning and was interested to hear more. I continued, "But I've only been a dog handler for the past eight of those ten years.

"Sounds like a good job, can't complain when you're working with a dog every day" Dean expressed.

"It's great. I'm pretty lucky to be working my dream job already." I looked at the yard and thought about the work I had ahead of me. "Well Dean, it was great to meet you, I should get back to the yard work."

"Yeah, right back at ya. I should do the same. I know the wife wants this yard set up right away so we can enjoy it. When we're all settled in, Kara and I would love to have you over for a barbeque. Have a good one!" Dean exclaimed as he made his way over to his deck.

I tossed the ball for the dogs for a few minutes before picking up my piles of leaves. I ran inside to quickly grab a soda before starting to mow the lawn. Heather was still reading on the couch.

"Neighbour was nice. His name is Dean. Has a wife and three daughters. Seems like they're a nice family," I explained to Heather.

Heather took a moment before responding. She must have been engrossed in her novel. "That's great Alec. Hopefully, the kids aren't annoying."

"Sounds like they're older" I replied, sort of annoyed with Heathers' attitude. "Two of them go to U of Vic, and the youngest is in high school."

"Gotchya," Heather responded without looking up from her book.

"Anyway, I'm gonna mow the lawn." I made my way to the back yard and fired up the lawn mower. I don't understand why Heather was acting so immature and annoying. Maybe she was still mad with me about brunch, but whatever it was she better get over it, because she's making it difficult to want to be around her when she's in a mood like this.

Thirty minutes later I was done with the yard. It was starting to cool down and I thought it would be a great time to take the dogs for a walk through the park. When I entered the house, Heather was in the kitchen looking through the fridge. I asked her to join me, but she explained that she was going to get dinner going. I told her I would be back within the hour.

The best part about this house is the close proximity to the park. There is a trail behind the house that takes you to the park, so the dogs can walk off leash the whole time, which they love. The off-leash dog park area is ten minutes from my back yard. When I arrived, it wasn't too busy. The dogs ran, played, and sniffed the other dogs that were running around.

In between throwing the ball for Guinness and Chip, my phone buzzed. I pulled it out of my pocket and saw that I had a text message from an unknown number,

Hey, it's Blake, your new neighbour. My dad gave me your number and mentioned the hockey on Friday. I'd love to go! Thanks for the invite. What arena?

Great. I didn't think she would actually take me up on it. I hate being friendly, look where it gets you. I quickly typed up a reply,

Yeah, no worries. It's at the ice box at nine-fifteen p.m.

Shortly after I received a response,

Okay... I've never played there, and I have no idea where it is. Mind if I get a ride with you?

What the hell? She's pretty bold. Doesn't even know me but would take a ride with me... Sort of ballsy. I don't really have an excuse, so I guess I'll have to give her a ride. It would seem rude if I said no, especially since she will most likely see me leave for the rink anyhow. I texted back,

No problem. Meet me at my truck at eight-thirty.

A minute later, a reply came in,

Great thanks! See you then. Have a great week.

Perfect. She seems nice. I have no idea how I'm going to explain this one to Heather. She is going to be pissed that I'm driving a girl to hockey. I love Heather, but her jealousy drives me nuts and it's only been getting worse the past month or so.

Blake Taylor

They say that you will start off your day in a better mood if you set your alarm clock to an uplifting song that you enjoy. Every morning I wake up to *Happy* by Pharell Williams and even though it startles me, it sure does start my day off in the right mind set. This morning was no exception. I was excited to be waking up in my new basement suite and was looking forward to this upcoming week. Although I would be busy working Monday to Friday, nine to five, I had Colin's sister Allie, Birthday dinner this Wednesday night. Colin is five years older than me, and Allie and I are only two years apart, so we have really grown to be close friends. Allie's best friend was planning a dinner for her family and closest friends, then all of the girls would be going out for drinks afterward. I felt honoured to be included in the post-dinner drinks.

This week was also exciting in the sense that I was secretly looking forward to playing hockey on Friday night. I grew up playing organized competitive hockey and since having graduated, I would play the odd pickup game with friends. I haven't played anything consistently in a while, so it will be interesting to see how I do. It's one of those things you don't grow out of though…I think I'll always love it and have a desire to play.

The neighbour guy seemed nice. It was kind of him to even offer for my dad and I to join him on Friday night, and also nice to agree to give me a ride. I sort of figured that him being a cop, I could trust taking a ride with a complete stranger. Who knows, he could end up being a total weirdo.

I was just finishing up brushing my teeth and getting ready for work when I realized the time. I'm running a few minutes behind, so I guess I'll be grabbing breakfast on the go. I quickly check my schedule and see that my girlfriend Abby was opening the store this morning, so I know that if worst came to worse, being a few minutes late wouldn't be the end of the day.

I speedily dialed her number, and she picked up after the first ring.

"Hey Blake, what's up?"

"Hey! I'm just running a few minutes behind and have to grab breakfast on the way. Did you want anything from Starbucks?"

"Oh no worries, mate. Umm, yeah, a Grande green tea would be nice, thanks! See you soon," Abby replied in her little Australian accent.

"See you soon!"

The Starbucks drive through was surprisingly quick, and it's so incredibly convenient that it is across the street from Urban Garage. Because of this, I actually made it to work with two minutes to spare. Abby was just starting to open all the blinds to the store when I came in through the back door.

"Aw, thank you so much for the tea, Blakey!" she exclaimed.

"Was no trouble at all. Plus, I thought I was going to be late, so I had to make it up to you somehow," I joked.

The morning went by sort of slow. Mondays are always slow as nobody seems to want to shop for furniture as soon as the weekend is done. Abby and I caught up on our regular gossip in between folding blankets, putting away new stock, and assisting the odd customer.

"So, how's your new place? All settled in," she asked.

"Yeah, it's great. I'm basically all unpacked, I just have a few photos and art pieces that need to be hung but for the most part it's liveable. It's nice being so close to my family in case I need anything, and at the same time so nice to have my own space. It's totally like living on my own because they respect my privacy."

"Aw yeah, that sounds lovely. Has Colin been by to see it?"

"Yeah, he popped in briefly on move in day. He was at the hospital, so he wasn't able to help actually move anything, but he came to check things out. He's been pretty busy getting ready for second year...I don't know how he does it," I explained.

"Yeah, Colin has always been like that. Well as long as James and I have known him. He has always put his career and education first, and has a good head on his shoulders, that's why we thought you two would work well together. And look at that, a year later and you're still together! I guess it's all thanks to us!" Abby teased.

"Yeah, yeah, I owe our whole relationship to you and James. Will you ever let me live that down?"

"Oh, I'm just kidding Blakey!"

The morning was filled with small chat and the odd customer coming in to browse. No major purchases were being made, so by the time lunch came around, Abby and I both could not wait to take a break from the floor. Abby took her break first, she went across the street to get a wrap, so I mindlessly folded blankets on couches, and hung new artwork on the walls.

I couldn't help but notice a text I received from Colin stating that he would be at the hospital for an extra hour this evening so asked to push our date until seven p.m. instead. Colin and I were planning on going to a local brewery for supper and have a few beers. By now, I was used to him having to reschedule or push plans because I know how important his schooling and career is to him, but still, I couldn't help but feel a tad annoyed. It would be nice for just one night, to be the priority. I was going to respond to his text message with a simple, "K", but then I realized that would be pretty immature of me. I know that it isn't his decision, or it's not his fault that he has to stay late, so I responded that it was okay and that I was looking forward to seeing him.

After work I made my way to the university to pick up my last couple of textbooks for my upcoming semester of school. The bookstore is open year 'round as some students are still taking classes throughout the summer. Thank goodness I have the summer off and I'm able to enjoy my free time. I love nursing school, but I'm not looking forward to school and practicums being my whole life, leaving little to no time for friends, family, Colin, and sports.

After grabbing my 700-page Medical Surgical Nursing textbook, I made my way to the whole foods store by my house to pick up some chicken and veggies to throw together a quick meal before meeting up with Colin. The whole foods store is a little hidden gem. They have all local meats, fruits, vegetables and even some baked goods. It's hard to go back to a chain grocery store when you have all this delicious fresh produce that is sourced locally. I decided on siracha chicken breasts, and all the fixings for a Greek salad. This is definitely my go-to meal in the summer.

Once home, I pre-heated the oven, tossed my salad, and quickly applied some makeup while the chicken was cooking. Colin likes that I'm plain and not into a lot of makeup (a typical day consists of mascara and bronzer, or no makeup at all), but this morning before work, because I was running late, I didn't have time to put any make up on. After the quick five-minute makeup application, I decided to go to the main house to quickly say hi to my parents, as the timer for the chicken still read twenty-five minutes.

Dad was out on the BBQ and mom was inside mixing up some sangria. As I entered the kitchen my mom offered me a glass, and I couldn't resist.

"My God, is this not the perfect drink for summertime?"

"Totally! I love it with red wine and oranges best. I've been experimenting with different recipes, so hopefully you like this one," mom responded.

"So far so good! How was your day? Busy at work?"

"Yes, same old, same old. But Mondays are typically busy for us. What about you, what are you up to this evening?"

"Colin and I are meeting at this new brewery that opened up on Granville Street around seven, so I have to make this visit quick 'cause I have chicken in the oven and then I'll have to make my way over there," I explained to my mom.

Mom was putting the big jug of sangria back into the fridge while asking, "Well that sounds like fun. How is Colin doing at the hospital? He seems so busy; we really don't see him much."

"Tell me about it," I said with a sigh. "He's so busy, I barely get to see him. Tomorrow he is at the hospital until eight p.m. and then Wednesday I have Allie's Birthday dinner, and then Friday I have hockey with that neighbour guy. So, unless we make plans to see each other on Thursday evening, I won't see him until the weekend. Oh wait, I can just stay at his place after Allie's Birthday."

"Sounds like you're a busy lady. Hey, I meant to ask, are you actually going to play hockey with the neighbour? I was surprised you actually took him up on it," mom asked.

"Yeah! Well, it was sort of a no brainer for me. I love hockey, I love meeting new people, and I love a good exercise outlet especially since I quit the gym. I figured he was trustworthy to drive me since he's a cop and all, and at the end of the day, if he's a weirdo, I just won't go back."

"Yeah, that makes sense, well I'm sure you'll have a good time. Dad met him over the weekend and said he was really nice, he liked him a lot."

"Good to know, anyway mom I should head back, I'm sure my oven timer will go off any minute." I gave my mom a hug before leaving for my place.

I checked the clock and realized it was already six-thirty p.m. I wolfed down my supper, jumped in my little beat-up Honda Civic, and made my way to meet Colin. Sometimes the Victoria traffic can be so congested, so I always leave early to make sure I'm on time. Hopefully, Colin was able to leave the hospital on time, so I won't have to wait too long.

By the time that I parked and got us a table, it was five past seven, so I figured Colin wouldn't be too much longer. When the waitress came by, I just ordered us two waters and asked for a drink menu and just one dinner menu.

Thankfully, Colin did leave on time, and he arrived as soon as our waters came to the table. Once seated, I leaned in for a quick peck. Colin has never been much for PDA, so a quick kiss is enough for him. It's not that I'm huge into PDA, but if onlookers observed us and hadn't seen that quick kiss, people would just assume that we're friends. We never hold hands, we never cuddle on the couch at friends' houses, we very rarely kiss in public, all of the cuddling and kissing is saved for when we are alone, and even then, we don't kiss an awful lot. If I could change anything, it would be that 'cause I love to kiss. When I asked him about it before he would just say something along the lines of, 'our friends don't want to see us all over each other' and I just left it as that. Colin and I have a sort of unique relationship. We connect deeply on an emotional level, we can talk about anything, and support each other no matter what, and help encourage each other to follow our dreams. We also love to spend time exercising whether it be going to a hot yoga class, going for hikes, or even rock climbing. We both get along well with each other's families, I'm just not sure why he can be a bit distant. I know that his last girlfriend cheated on him, and it took him a few years to get over that, so maybe he is just afraid to fully commit, and doesn't want to get too attached. I'm not sure, but for now I'm enjoying the ride and I absolutely love being with him.

Colin ordered a citrus type of beer, and I ordered an amber ale. I love red beers, and Colin likes hoppy, fruity beers. Colin took a few minutes to browse the menu. "Blake, you're not getting anything?" he asked.

"No, I was hungry when I got home from work, and I knew we weren't meeting until seven, so I just ate before I came, you go ahead though, I'm sure it was a while since you ate last," I encouraged.

"Yeah, you said it, my day was so busy, so the last that I ate was at lunch. We had to stop by Emerg and be the hospitalist for the morning, and then after lunch we did our daily rounds checking in on our patients we have been dealing with for the past week. It's been awesome though, I'm learning so much, and Dr. Kipp is sweet. He's this young, hipster type of doctor. He's only like thirty-five, he dresses like all the young adults now a days with the super trendy clothes and hairstyle, he always loves to crack a good joke, yet he's so knowledgeable and professional, he's definitely the kind of doctor I want to be," Colin gushed.

"Wow, he seems like the ideal role model, I'm so glad you get to shadow him. I'm sure you will learn a lot just by observing him."

We continued to talk about Colin and the hospital, and how we're both dreading going back to school full time, when Colin actually suggested a "last hoorah" camping weekend with all our friends. He explained

44

that although it's last minute we should organize a camping trip for this weekend as he has the weekend off before starting school on Monday.

"Oh my gosh Colin! That's a great idea! After Allie's Birthday dinner, I can mention it to a few of the girls and see if they can come. But oh shoot, I forgot to tell you, my neighbour invited me to play hockey on Friday night, so I'll just come meet up with all of you on Saturday morning."

Colin took a long pull from his beer before responding, "Oh okay, that's awesome you're going to get back onto the ice. What's your neighbour's name, that was nice of her to invite you out."

"His name is Alec, I guess it's a mixed league. I don't actually know many of the details. He came by the house to introduce himself and actually invited my dad out to play. Long story short, dad said that he doesn't play any more but suggested me instead. Alec left his business card and said if I was interested to text him for details, so I did" I explained.

"Okay cool, you'll have to let me know how it goes when we meet up on Saturday morning, I'm sure you'll have a great time."

We each ordered one more beer and talked about our camping trip, where we would go, and who we would invite. I told Colin that I would take the reigns in booking everything, inviting everyone, and putting together a grocery list, as I knew he had a busy week.

We left the bar in our separate vehicles, but Colin didn't have to be at the hospital until nine a.m., so he decided to come and spend the night at my place. We popped in a movie, and both ended up falling asleep by eleven p.m.

Happy by Pharell Williams went off at seven a.m. and alarmed both Colin and I, as we were sound asleep. It was so nice waking up next to Colin, as it doesn't happen often because he usually has early mornings at the hospital, so this was a nice treat.

We jumped in the shower, and as I was finishing up getting ready for work in the bathroom, Colin made us each a mug of coffee to take in our thermoses. It's so great when you get to that point in your relationship where you know how your spouse takes their coffee. As we made our way to our vehicles, we wished each other a great day, shared a kiss, and Colin said he would call me when he was done for the day. I jumped in the car, turned on the radio and sang my heart out all the way to work. I was in a great mood.

Abby was at work again this morning, greeting me with her big, beautiful smile. Abby is one of those people that everybody loves. She exudes this type of energy that makes people want to be around her. She is so positive, uplifting, fun, and kind. She doesn't have a mean bone in her body, she wouldn't judge a soul on this Earth, and she would never share any of my secrets. I'm grateful that although we started out as co-workers, we were able to become great friends.

"Hey Blakey! Boy you've got a skip to your walk this morning," Abby shouted from across the store. Abby and James are the only two people to have ever called me Blakey…I think it's an Australian thing, but I secretly like it.

"What can I say, Colin and I had a great evening, we went to that new brewery on Granville, then he spent the night, and it was nice to sleep in and wake up next to him this morning, so it was a great way to start my day."

"Aww, that sounds so lovely, I'm glad you had a nice evening. Hopefully, this doesn't ruin your mood, but we got an e-mail from management saying that they're putting on a huge sale this weekend, so we need to prep all the price tags, so we will have a busy day ahead."

"That's alright, just turn the music up a bit and we'll just buckle down and get it done," I responded.

The day actually passed quite quickly as we were so busy and only a few customers came in. We told them about the upcoming weekend sale, and all the customers appeared to be excited and stated they would be back this weekend.

By the time five p.m. came around I had barely noticed that it was time to go home. I decided to head home, make a quick wrap from the dinner leftovers and go for a jog with Merc. We strolled through Beacon Hill Park and stopped to let him play at the dog park with the other dogs. By the time I got home it was nearly seven p.m. so I decided to curl up on the couch, read for an hour, catch up on my favourite TV show, *Big Brother*, and then head to bed for an early night.

When I woke up Wednesday morning, I couldn't help but feel excited for Allie's Birthday dinner. Last week I picked out a nice, scented candle, the new issue of her favourite magazine, and a new Lulu Lemon workout top, so I'm really excited to give her her gift. Before leaving for work, I packed my going out outfit, and a change of clothes for tomorrow morning as I knew I would be sleeping at Colin's place tonight. Work dragged because Abby had the day off and because I was so excited for my evening, it seemed as though time was standing still.

I made my way to Colin's house as soon as I finished work. Colin moved back in with his parents to save money while going to school. Allie invited me to go over and get ready with herself and her mother, and the three of us would go together. Allie isn't a high maintenance girl, so I was surprised to see that she had a bottle of champagne with cut up strawberries for us girls while we got ready, but hey, it's her day, and you only turn twenty-four once.

Before heading out, Colin surprised all three of us and walked through the front door.

"Hey, I forgot you were gonna be here Blake," said Colin.

I walked toward Colin and greeted him by the front door. "Yeah, Allie invited me to come over and get ready so we could all go to the restaurant together."

"Oh, that's awesome! Why don't you text me when you girls are all done dinner, and I'll come meet up with you at whatever bar you're at downtown. I have an article I have to read to prep for class on Monday, so I'm going to do that and then head to the rock-climbing gym, and I figure you'll be done by then. Dr. Kipp gave me the day off tomorrow so I can actually sleep in, head to the bookstore to get my lab book and relax. My last day with Dr. Kipp is on Friday, but I'm sure it'll be pretty relaxed" Colin said excitedly.

"That's awesome babe, I'm so excited that you can come meet up with us later. Tonight, will be so much fun. Allie! Are you almost ready? We should get going!"

Alec Kohl

"Yeah, I'll head there right now. Thanks for letting me know" I said drowsily as I hung up my work cell phone.

"Who was that, and why are they calling at five a.m. that's so annoying," Heather asked bitterly.

"That was my boss, I guess he pulled some guy over and they think there's some drugs in the back compartment, so they need me to head over there to put the dog on it to confirm." I started to roll out of bed before I continued, "Whatever, I'll just start my shift now and then I'll be home earlier."

"Well, I made plans tonight with Steph because I didn't think you would be home until like nine, so we're going for drinks and I can't really cancel on her this last minute, so I'll just see you when I get home."

I was used to Heather being bitter about my job, which is surprising because she is a member too. But her shift is a set schedule, five on, four off, and she had a hard time realizing that my work never stopped. I was constantly on call and unfortunately that meant that my schedule was quite unpredictable. Heather would try to have conversations asking me to try and make more time for her, and although I would sincerely try, if I got a call in the middle of one of our dates, I would just have to go.

Over the past few months, Heather had stopped asking to hang out, and started becoming busier. She always had plans and had this newfound attitude like *well if he's always going to be at work, I'm tired of waiting around so I'll just always have plans.*

It's not that I minded that Heather was making plans, but I sure have noticed that she's been quite distant. Maybe I should talk to her about it when I get off work tonight.

I quickly brushed my teeth and got dressed in my uniform, and as I looked in the mirror, I noticed I had a bad case of bed head, so I put on my RCMP baseball cap, and made my way outside to grab my work dog, Chip. Chip was a four-year-old German Shepherd who was able to detect eight different types of drugs. Chip loved to work, and he was extremely loyal to me.

I didn't have time to stop for a coffee because my boss, Gordon, was waiting for me, so I felt quite groggy by the time I arrived on the side of the highway where they were waiting with the pulled over vehicle.

I got a quick run down from Gordon and then grabbed Chip to have him walk around the suspected vehicle. After walking from the hood of the car to the trunk, Chip sat down with his nose pointing to the rear right hand side of the trunk. Bingo.

Gordon arrested the suspect and thanked me for coming out so early. I made my way to the detachment after grabbing a quick drive thru coffee and started on my leftover paperwork from my files from this past week.

By the time lunch came around, I had finally finished two of my files and was able to hit the road. Most of the time when I'm working, I patrol the highways and often come across drug traffickers. It's really easy to become complacent so it helps to have a fresh coffee, some candy, and music.

Because I had started my shift early this morning, I was able to make my way home around four-thirty p.m.

I quickly dialed Heather's number as I made my way to town. Her phone went straight to voicemail, so I hung up and continued to make my way home.

Ten minutes later, my phone buzzed, and my Caller ID showed that it was Heather phoning back. After two rings, I picked up.

"Hey! Sorry, I didn't even feel my phone buzz, and then I noticed that you had phoned," Heather explained, sounding sort of winded.

"That's okay, weird how it went straight to voicemail. I was calling to say that I'm on my way home. What time are your plans with Steph? Did you want me to pick something up for supper so we can eat together quick before you go?"

"Ummm, sure. Our plans are at seven, so you can just grab something to throw on the barbeque, that way we can eat and then I can get going. Hot dogs and hamburgers are fine with me. I have stuff at home, I can toss together a salad. I just have to pee babe so I gotta run, but I'll see you when you get home!" Click.

That was weird. I wonder why she had to run so quickly. I've been in the bathroom with her when she has gone pee, it's not a big deal, I wouldn't have even known if she was peeing while still talking to me on the phone.

I made my way to the local market to grab fresh meat and buns from the butcher and bakery. While I was waiting in line to pay, I heard someone call my name. As I turned to look, I noticed it was Dean, my new neighbour."

"Hey! Looks like we have the same idea" I said to Dean.

"Right on! Great day for a barbeque. Kara loves when I barbeque up the chicken, it's her favourite," Dean explained, making friendly conversation as we stood in line to pay for our meat.

"Yeah, we're just cooking up a quick dinner tonight, Heather has plans with a girlfriend later this evening," I answered.

"Well, you can't go wrong with hot dogs and hamburgers. Blake was telling me that she took you up on your hockey offer. She said she's looking forward to playing, I think she will have a lot of fun."

"Yeah, it's a good group of guys that I play with. They're all mid thirties to early sixties so it's a lot of fun. They're all really nice and welcoming so she'll like them." I was just finishing up paying for my bill when I continued, "Anyway Dean, I hope you and Kara have a good evening! I'll see you around."

Dean gave me a quick wave and then was next in line to pay for his chicken.

When I got home, Guinness greeted me with a nice slobbery kiss and a rapid tail wag. Chip immediately grabbed his favourite ball and laid down on his dog bed by the fireplace to relax after a long workday. Heather was just finishing up in the shower. I told her that I would start on the barbeque.

By the time everything was cooked and being served it was nearly six p.m. Heather and I sat on the deck to eat our meal and we caught up on each other's day.

"It was so nice to have the day off and do nothing today," Heather said while shoving a sloppy hamburger into her mouth. "How was your day, you must be tired after being up so early?"

I finished chewing my hot dog before replying, "Yeah I was tired this morning but after a coffee or two, and once I finally got out of the office and hit the road, the tiredness went away."

"Yeah, I've got a file to finish when I go back to work tomorrow. I should have finished it before my days off. I hate when I do that," Heather said sounding annoyed.

It seemed like all we spoke about lately was work. As I ate my dinner, and spoke with Heather, we rarely made eye contact, (and that could be because we were both eating) but I was thinking to myself, what is it that we have in common anyway. As I was daydreaming, Heather was waving her hand in my face.

"Earth to Alec, hellooooooo," Heather said impatiently.

"Shit sorry, I was sort of in the moon there. Yeah, that sucks that you have a file to finish when you go back. So where are you and Steph headed tonight?" I said before having a drink of my coke. I continued before Heather had the chance to respond, "Sort of sucks you're going out, I have hockey tomorrow night, so we won't get to spend any time together."

"I'm sorry, I figured you would still be at work, so I made plans. And yeah, I know, you have hockey every single Friday night, so I tend to keep that in mind and those are my 'me nights.' Steph is busy tomorrow; this was the only night she could do. She wants to go to that new karaoke bar that opened up downtown. I don't know, I'm sure it'll be fun."

"Well why don't you see if Steph's boyfriend wants to go, and we can all go out," I asked.

"Sorry babe, girls' night!"

Heather went out, and I took the dogs for a walk-through Beacon Hill Park, stopping at the dog park to let them play and socialize with other dogs. While there, it was hard not to be slightly annoyed with Heather. I don't mind her having girls' nights, but it seems that lately she has no time for me, or she couldn't be bothered to spend time with me. I'm finding myself becoming more and more independent, and because I'm so stubborn, it makes me think, *okay, you don't want to spend time with me, I'll do my own thing then.* At least I have hockey tomorrow, that's always the highlight of my week. I know this is spiteful, and I'm just acting in the moment because I'm still annoyed at Heather, but I'm actually looking forward to driving that neighbour girl and meeting someone new. Not that I'm looking, or on the prowl, I'm not like that at all, but I'm always open to having new friends if they're the right kind of person.

After spending a half hour at the dog park, we made our way home, the dogs got a nice bone to chew on, and I played video games. By the time eleven p.m. came around, Heather still wasn't home. I sent her a quick text to see if she needed a ride. It took her about twenty-five minutes to respond when she finally said that she was on her way home.

I made my way up to our room and threw on Family Guy to settle in before she arrived home.

Blake Taylor

"Oh my gosh I'm stuffed. That was such a good meal, I think I might have to undo my top button on my jeans, or I might explode," I joked pointing to my mid section.

"Right! At least we can dance it off" Allie said jokingly.

The restaurant that the Birthday dinner was held was very loud and busy. The restaurant is called *The Zebra*. It's this new wine and whiskey bar that also serves fancy appetizers and entrées. All the décor is strictly black and white, and they use mirrors to make the restaurant look bigger than what it is, which adds an intricate depth to the lounge. There are no tables in the center of the restaurant, instead there is a long sleek black bar with short white stools, which runs from one end of the restaurant to the other, and the perimeter of the restaurant is booths. Each individual booth has a chandelier, with leather seating and an all-white high gloss table. We chose one of the larger booths which comfortably fit all eight girls.

"Allie! What club are we going to tonight? I hope it's somewhere we can find cute guys," Stacey said giggling. Stacey was one of Abby's friends from high school. She was the exact definition of *single and ready to mingle.*

"We're heading right around the corner to this pub for some pre drinks, and then we're heading to the Sugar Nightclub after that," Allie replied while sipping from her appletini. She then continued, "I think some of us will be inviting our boyfriends out to meet up with us at Sugar though, so it's only a half girls' night."

We finished at The Zebra and made our way around the corner to have some pre drinks. By the time eleven p.m. came around, everyone was feeling pretty good. I was at the point where my head felt a little bit lighter than it normally would, and I knew that I was in no position to drive. Stacey was ready to get her dancing shoes on, so she suggested we make our way to Sugar which was only two blocks away, so a quick walk.

During the walk to the club, I sent Colin a quick text to let him know we were on our way and for him to come meet up with us. He quickly responded stating he would make his way down.

Once arriving to Sugar, we grabbed a corner booth which was off to the side of the dance floor. The club was already quite busy. I had never been here before, and it was basically all red décor, and all their fruity drinks were rimmed with sugar.

I sat down at our booth waiting for Colin as I didn't really feel like dancing with all the single girls and random guys. A waitress came by, and I ordered their signature drink, which was some sort of a strawberry flavoured martini, with of course, a sugared rim.

I was halfway through my martini when I saw Colin arrive, I waved him over and he joined me at the booth. Colin was dressed casually in burgundy chinos and a black V neck tee shirt. Colin was very handsome in a sort of rugged way. He was very well built, with chiseled arms and defined abs. He spends so much time doing yoga and rock climbing that he's in excellent shape. He's also sporting a five o'clock shadow that really suits him.

Colin ordered a beer and we socialized with some of the other couples that ended up joining for Allie's Birthday. Both Colin and I aren't really the dancing type, so we spent the rest of the evening in the booth hanging out with the other non-dancers.

By two a.m. when the club was closing, we decided to call it a night. A few of the others were heading to one of the girl's downtown apartment to continue the party, but Colin and I were tired, so we went back to his place.

Thankfully, Colin only had two beers, so he was okay to drive us. My car was back at his place anyhow as Abby' and Colin's mom, Sandra drove us to The Zebra. We went to bed as soon as we got to his place, and morning came all too quickly. I knew I would be extra tired at work today.

I always kept shower supplies at Colin's place and having the change of clothes made getting ready before work less of a hassle. Colin had the day off today, so he was headed to run some school errands. Colin had his last shift with Dr. Kipp tomorrow, and I reminded him as we were heading out the door that I had hockey tomorrow evening. Colin didn't seem too bothered, he told me he was going to have a low-key evening at home anyhow.

I made it to work five minutes before the store was supposed to open and it was so nice to see Abby's bright smile when I arrived, I absolutely loved working with Abby.

"Hey darlin' don't you look like a tonne of bricks hit you upside the head," Abby said with a smirk."

"Easy, it was a late night, and just be thankful I'm in clean clothes and had a shower," I replied while taking a long sip from my extra-large coffee.

"I'm just kidding, you look wonderful. I think it'll be a good day; we have some fun little jobs to do."

Abby was right. The day passed fairly quickly, and we chatted the entire shift. I told her that I was going to play hockey tomorrow and my neighbour was taking me.

"Have you met him before? How do you know he's not some crazy dude or something," Abby said half jokingly, half concerned.

"He introduced himself to my dad when we first moved in. My dad said he was really nice. Plus, he's a cop, so I feel like he would be somewhat trustworthy." I hesitated before continuing, "Either way, if he does end up being a total weirdo, then I just won't go back, simple as that."

"Yeah, except you'll be living next door to him and still have to see him regularly," Abby responded chuckling.

"Whatever, I'm sure it'll be fine."

We closed the store at five p.m., and I made my way home. I spent the evening walking Merc and catching up on laundry. I made myself a lunch to be able to take with me to work tomorrow.

Work went by quickly as Friday's seemed to be busy with customers. I love meeting new people and I'm not shy, so I always manage to strike up conversations with customers, however I was happy when my shift came to an end.

I had a few hours to kill before I would have to meet at Alec's truck. I couldn't help but feel a bit anxious about going to play, for a few reasons. First of all, from getting a ride from a complete stranger...What if Abby ends up being right and he's such a weirdo and the car ride is almost unbearable, and then also the fact that I haven't played hockey in a few months, so I'm sure I'll be rusty out there.

I got home, whipped together a quick meal, had a couple glasses of water, and turned on the TV. I put on the sit com *Friends*, as it's one of those shows I've seen a million times and don't need to focus on what I'm watching. I packed and re-packed my hockey bag as I anxiously waited for eight-thirty p.m. to come around.

Alec Kohl

Eight-twenty-five came quicker than usual. I packed my hockey gear and put a six pack of beer in my bag, then tossed it in the cab of my truck. I looked next door and saw no sign of Blake. Maybe she was backing out. I checked my phone for a text from her. Nothing. I sat in the driver's side seat and turned on some music. I always love to listen to some pump-up tunes on the way to hockey, so I shuffled my all-time favourite band, *The Offspring*. As *Pretty Fly For A White Guy* started, I heard a little bang come from the back of my truck and noticed Blake throw her hockey bag next to mine. She closed the tail gate and made her way to the passenger side door.

She jumped in without warning. She was wearing a backwards black ballcap, a black v neck tee shirt, and a pair of jeans. I've never seen such confidence radiate from a single person. Not in a bad way, it was sorta cool. I felt a spark of excitement pass through me, but I dismissed it as excitement to play hockey.

"Hey, I'm Blake. Thanks for giving me a lift. This is a great song."

I was suddenly taken aback. She was so outgoing, not shy at all, so comfortable, *and* she liked my music!?

I couldn't even make eye contact with her as I was so nervous. I don't even know why I was nervous, but I quickly mumbled, "Yeah, no problem."

We made small talk in the truck and occasionally she would ask me about my family or where I grew up, and in return, I would ask similar questions. At one point I looked over at her, she didn't notice that I was looking as I made it seem like I was checking my right-hand side mirror, and noticed how big and beautiful her hazel eyes were. *Why was I looking at her eyes?* I snapped out of it and focused on the road.

"Hellooooooooooo, Earth to Alec, I get that you're driving but are you going to keep ignoring me until we get to the arena?" Blake said jokingly.

I must have been preoccupied in my own thoughts that I didn't even hear her say anything. "What? Sorry I was lost in thought there. What did you say?" I asked quickly.

Blake adjusted her seated position and outstretched her legs before continuing, "I said that I haven't played in a few months, so I feel like I might be rusty."

"These guys are pretty chill, go at whatever pace you're comfortable, no one is out here to make it to the NHL. Just have fun with it."

"What! We're not here to make it to the NHL, well then you better turn around and bring me home if that's the case," Blake said half laughing.

I laughed too, just as we pulled into the arena's parking lot. We grabbed our bags from the cab and walked into the arena. Blake followed me as she hadn't been here before. We entered the dressing room and took our seats. I made room for Blake so that she didn't have to sit by herself.

"Hey guys, this is my neighbour Blake, she's gonna come out and play with us tonight," I said, introducing Blake to a dressing room filled with all males except one other woman. I'm sure it must have been a tad intimidating for her.

"Thanks for having me out, if I'm a bit rusty I'll blame it on the big meal I just ate," Blake said with a smile.

We cracked a beer and started getting dressed. It's always a bit awkward when a girl sits next to you because you have to discreetly slide off your boxers and slide on your jock without revealing the good stuff. I grabbed my towel and through it over my waist as I put my jock on. Blake was already chatting to a few men next to her and didn't notice my vulnerable position.

I could overhear some of the guy's teasing Blake, but she sure held her own. She's quite witty and can defend herself on the spot. I think this added fuel to the fire as some of the guys were trying to embarrass her but weren't succeeding.

I've always been a respectful guy so when I could tell that she was getting dressed and removing her tee shirt to reveal a sports bra, I quickly turned my head. I didn't want to get caught looking, and I didn't want her to feel uncomfortable by me. I felt a small tap on my shoulder and was hesitant to turn, but Blake was already wearing her equipment and jersey, so no need for it to be uncomfortable.

"Got any more beer? I'll bring it next time and get you back, that last one went down pretty quick," Blake asked politely.

I reached into my bag and tossed her a fresh can, and she thanked me with a smile. A sudden little shock ran through my body. I thought to myself, *I gotta get on the ice and separate myself from her, this isn't good.*

We got on the ice and skated a few laps, taking a few shots on net here and there and then stopping to stretch. Blake seemed quite comfortable, not rusty at all. After a few minutes, one of the guys whistled to announce that we would be starting.

Blake and I were both wearing black jerseys, so we sat on the same bench, and we actually ended up playing on the same line.

The game went by pretty quick; I was having a lot of fun and noticed Blake having a blast too. During one of our breaks on the bench she thanked me again for inviting her out as she was having such a good time.

I grabbed a quick drink from my water bottle before responding, "Anytime. Glad you're having fun. Tonight's been fun for me too. Most of the time I play goalie, cause it's harder to find people to play net, but tonight they were all set so I got to play out, and it's been a lot of fun. You don't look too rusty out there."

"Really!? I'm so exhausted, I feel so sluggish out there and I can't find my hands to stick handle for the life of me, but thanks."

Our line changed and we were back on the ice. Blake and I played well together. She always stayed on her side of the ice, and always did her best to get open if I had the puck. She was also a great passer. She didn't shoot as often as she could, she would try to make the pass instead.

After seventy-five minutes the game came to an end. We ended up losing, but it was still fun. We made our way back to the dressing room and cracked another beer. Sometimes one of the guys would crack a joke at Blake, making comments about how she was playing on the ice, or about how she was a girl who played hockey, and Blake sure knew how to stand up for herself.

"You're sure small out there Blake, could barely see you. You know there's a youth game that plays on Monday nights hey," laughed one of the old timers.

"Hah, good to know, thanks Fred. I've definitely heard the short jokes time after time, maybe come up with something a little more original next time. By the way, the reason you probably couldn't see me out there is because I'm so quick at skating circles around you. Do you typically just plop yourself in front of the net and never back check? Would suck to be your line mate, you seem quite lazy," Blake jabbed back.

Within seconds, the dressing room was roaring with laughter, including myself. No one ever stands up to Fred, however Blake just threw quite the jab at him. She didn't even seem nervous about it either. As we all laughed, one of the guys cheersed her, and she had another drink from her beer.

I discreetly wrapped my towel around my waist so that I could quickly jump in the shower before leaving. Blake was already back in her clothes but didn't mind waiting for me to shower. As we were leaving the dressing room to head home for the night, one of the guys invited Blake to come out and play more as she was actually fun to play with. Blake agreed.

The drive home was less awkward than the drive to the rink. We were already pretty comfortable with each other. It was as if this was our usual routine, as if we do this on a weekly occurrence. We chatted about our plans for the weekend and Blake mentioned she was going camping with her boyfriend and friends. Noted. Good to know that she has a boyfriend.

Blake Taylor

I woke up to a strange buzzing sound, as if a bumble bee was humming right next to my ear. It took me a second to realize that my cell phone was vibrating with a phone call. I quickly checked the caller ID and then answered.

"Hey Colin, what's up," I said half asleep.

"Hey, just making sure you're still going be here for noon. Everyone's heading up to the lake and we're all meeting at the Petro gas station on the way out of town at twelve-thirty."

I checked the time. nine-thirty, which meant I still had time to shower, get ready, pack my bag, and pack a cooler before heading to Colin's. "Yeah totally, I'll be there for noon. I must have forgotten to set an alarm, so I'm glad you called."

"Yeah, I figured since I hadn't heard from you yet this morning. What time did you get in last night?" Colin asked.

"I think it was just before midnight, by the time Alec showered and we had a quick beer in the room afterward, it was close to midnight when we left," I replied.

Colin took a moment before responding, I'm not sure if the shower comment made him uncomfortable or not. "I see. Did you have fun?"

"Yeah! It was so much fun. I actually played better than I thought I would, and everyone was really nice and welcoming. They actually invited me to go out more often. I think I will," I responded.

"Cool, well I'm glad it went well. Are you still going to bring a cooler full of drinks, and then I'll just bring a cooler full of food? Also, I can't remember, are you making us sandwiches for lunch, or should we just grab something on the way?"

"I'll still bring the drinks cooler, and yes, I can make us sandwiches. I'll make them on those good pretzel buns. K, I better go so I can get everything done on time. I'll see you at your place at twelve. Love you," I said quickly so I could get my morning going.

"Love you too," Colin said before hanging up the phone.

I jumped in the shower, shaved my legs, blow dried my hair, and threw on a dash of mascara. I quickly packed up my toiletries but doubted that there would be a shower for us to use. I grabbed my under-armour gym bag and threw in some warm PJs for at night, an extra hoodie, a bikini, a towel, and two changes of clothes. In a separate bag I packed Merc's dog bowls and his food along with his favourite ball.

I quickly grabbed two poptarts to eat on the way, said bye to my parents, and loaded the empty cooler, duffel bag, and Merc into the car. We stopped at the liquor store, and I left Merc in the back seat with the windows down. He's such a friendly dog that I don't have to worry about him barking at people walking by. I probably bought way too much alcohol for just one night of camping, but I'm sure other people will want the odd drink or whatever. Colin loves Keystone beer, and I love Bud Light, so I got us each a twenty-four pack of that, and then just some sodas and water bottles too. I put half the beer, a few waters, and a couple sodas into the cooler then ran back inside to buy a few ice bags.

Once the cooler was loaded up, I drove across the street to the grocery store to grab the stuff for the sandwiches. I looked at my phone to check the time, eleven-thirty. Perfect. I went to the deli and grabbed some meats, grabbed our pretzel buns, and grabbed some individualized mustard and mayo packets from the deli section.

As I was making my way to the till, I grabbed some beef jerky, M&M's, and sour patch kids for the road. I paid my bill and made my way to the car. I quickly made my sandwiches, threw them in the cooler and made my way to Colin's.

I pulled up to Colin's and parked in my little spot across the street. Colin was outside loading up the truck with all our camping stuff. Looked like he already had the tent in there, as he was just loading up some Tupper wear bins of supplies and the camping chairs.

I brought over the cooler and my duffel bag, and Merc accompanied me at my side. Merc greeted Colin with an over exaggerated tail wag, a puppy whine, and a few sloppy kisses. He then grabbed his ball and laid in the shade on the front lawn.

"Hey, thanks for grabbing all that stuff, I'm just about done and then we can hit the road," Colin said while lifting a bin into the truck.

"Sounds good." I stole a quick kiss from Colin, grabbed our sandwiches and two sodas out of the cooler and put them in the front seat. I made my way to the tail gate to load up the drinks cooler, but Colin already had it up and in the box.

"Merc, come!" I yelled. I opened up the back seat and Merc jumped in and sat on the floor. Our duffel bags were placed on the seat behind him. Colin and I jumped in the truck and started to eat and make our way over to the gas station.

After meeting with everyone at the Petro, we all left together to head to the lake. Some of Colin's friends knew of this little lake about forty-five minutes from town, that not many people know about and is pretty secluded, which is a bonus because it's nice to have privacy and not worry about being too loud.

The drive went by quickly, and once we arrived, I let Merc out so he could say hi to everyone and sniff all the other dogs that had come along as well. I got him a bowl of water and started helping Colin unload the truck.

two other couples, and two single guy friends of Colin's had all joined in, and three other dogs, so Merc was already in heaven running around with them all.

Everyone unloaded their vehicles, the guys were all working on setting up their tents, while the girls organized coolers and the picnic table, and one of the girls brought a kitchen tent, so we put that up around one of the tables. Joey (one of the single guy friends) came around handing out beers, as he was already done setting up his tent.

Colin was just finishing up setting up our tent as I went to the back of the truck to grab our lawn chairs. I placed them around the fire and then went to grab Merc's dog bed and our duffel bags out of the truck to pop in the tent.

Wyatt and Brie were setting up posts so we could play beersby, and Steph and Dillon were pulling out cups and balls for beer pong later. A few of us played beersby (I won both games that I played), and then we all went for a swim in the lake. The water was warm yet refreshing. The guys went back to play more beersby, but myself, the girls, and the dogs stayed in the water.

"So how are things with Wyatt?" Steph asked Brie curiously. Wyatt and Brie had been together for three years, but their relationship hadn't progressed much. They were living together, but I think Brie was ready to get engaged, or at least get a dog together.

"Things are good! Of course, I'm ready for the next step, but Wyatt just got promoted at work, so I think he's just focusing on his career right now. Plus, I'm graduating with my bachelors this spring, so I'm trying to stay focused too. But he's so great, I love him so much. What about you and Colin? And you and Justin?"

Justin and Steph had only been dating for about six months, so Steph was sort of 'new' to our group, but she was such a sweetheart. Personally, I think that Steph might be in over her head with Justin, because he's such a party animal, and she seems to be very structured, and a 'good girl.'

"You go first Steph, I'm actually curious to hear!" I responded.

Steph took a moment before starting, "Things are good," she hesitated. "But sometimes I just wonder if we want the same things. I know I'm young, but I'm done school already, I know what I want, I have a good career, and I'm looking to settle down, you know? I don't date just to date; I date to settle down with someone. Justin is six years older than me, but he seems like, a couple years younger, maturity wise. He has a great job, and he owns his own house, which is amazing, but he's not even ready for me to move in yet. I know it's only been six months, but like when will the right time be? I feel like all he wants to do is work and go out with friends and party. Don't get me wrong, I like him a lot, and I love spending time with him, I just wonder if he's serious about me, or if we're just hanging out. I don't know."

"That's tough. They do say that men mature later than women! I know Colin and I are a few years a part as well, and I feel like I'm in a similar situation as Brie and Wyatt, cause obviously, with med school, which has to come first, so Colin is completely submerged in school, and that leaves me second. Which is fine, as I knew it would be that way when I met him, but I also don't want to be thirty before I ever get married and think about starting a family," I added.

"Yeah, but Colin is so mature and thinks everything through," Brie responded. "I've known Colin ever since Wyatt and I started dating and he has always been so scheduled, and sticks to a plan, so I know that when it's meant to be, it'll happen for you guys."

"Same goes to you Brie," said Steph with a shy little grin.

Just then Merc came splashing into the lake chasing after the Frisbee that one of the guys tossed at us.

"Well, I guess that's our cue! I'll go set up the beer pong table," Steph said while walking out of the lake. Brie and I followed closely behind.

The rest of the night was so much fun. We made hot dogs and hamburgers over the fire, and Steph had made a huge macaroni salad to share. We played beersby until it got too dark to see the cans on the posts, and so then we switched to flip cup and beer pong. Colin brought a few of his head lamps that he rigged up so that they could shine down over the picnic table so we could continue playing. After everyone was feeling pretty tipsy, we all sat around the fire and had a few more beers before turning in for the night.

When Colin and I got into the tent, Merc immediately passed out on his dog bed. I guess all the running around with the other dogs really tired him out. We stayed up for about fifteen minutes chatting and then both fell asleep.

The one thing about camping that you never seem to remember about, is how early the sun comes up, which means, you're up early. I checked my phone and saw the time was five past seven, I rolled over and noticed Colin and Merc weren't in the tent with me. I pulled on some sweats and a hoodie as it was a bit chilly first thing in the morning to go out and join the boys.

Wyatt was also up and sitting at the table eating a left-over hot dog. Colin was adding some wood to the fire and Merc was laying down next to him.

"Morning. Have you guys been up long?" I asked.

"Just a few minutes, sorry if I woke you. I'm just adding another log to the fire so I can get some water boiling to make some coffee," Colin responded.

"You didn't wake me; did you have fun last night Wyatt? Seems like you kept getting your ass kicked at beer pong," I said with a chuckle.

"Yeah, yeah, yeah, whatever. I also had like ten more beers than you, so it's no wonder my aim was a little off by the end of the night. But yeah, it was a fun night. We have to try and do this more often," Wyatt responded.

"Totally. It's so hard for me to try and plan things with my crazy schedule. It's hard for me to commit to any plans, so I'm glad this worked out," Colin said as he placed the saucepan on the grill over the fire.

We had a lazy morning with some people only waking up around ten, and after packing up and having a quick lunch, we all made our separate ways back home.

"Wyatt was right," I said, as we were driving on the backroad to get back to town.

"About what?" asked Colin.

"About needing to do this more often. I mean, maybe not a camping weekend all the time, but just trying to get together, it's so nice hanging out."

"For sure. I'm hoping I'll have a better idea as to what my schedule is going to look like so I can try and actually have a life outside of school," Colin responded.

"Tell me about it. I don't even know the last time we went out on a date."

"Hah, yeah really hey," Colin replied.

The rest of the truck ride home was quiet. I think we were both tired from having such a late night and early morning. We got back to Colin's place and unloaded the truck at a snails' pace. Both his parents were home and they asked if I would be staying for dinner, so I said that I would join. I didn't have any extra clothes with me, and I smelt like a campfire, so I told Colin I would head home shortly after dinner, as I was exhausted and wanted an early night.

I put Merc in the back yard to run around with Colin's parent's two dogs while we laid in bed watching Netflix until supper was ready. His mom made a delicious pasta with a garden salad and some garlic bread. We ate and chatted about our camping weekend, and how we're both returning to school on Tuesday. I loved Colin's family. They were so welcoming and easy to talk to, and Colin had told me a few times about how much they loved me, so that was reassuring.

After dinner I made my way home and was ready to crash when I noticed Alec at his side garage door with his two dogs.

"Hey!" I yelled, rather enthusiastically.

"Hey. I'm just about to take them for a walk. Wanna come?"

I was super tired, but I figured Merc would have fun, and it would be nice for him to meet the neighbour dogs.

Alec Kohl

Blake told me she would be a minute grabbing a leash for Merc and that she'd meet me out the back gate on the trail. I threw the ball for Guinness and Chip while I waited. Blake approached a few minutes later. She was wearing a worn-out ball cap with her hair pulled back in a ponytail. Her jeans were dirty from a weekend of camping, and she had a tank top with a plaid flannel on over top. But what caught my eye most were these huge Dunlop rubber boots she was wearing. They were a shade of an army green colour, and they looked three sizes too big.

"Hey," I said as she made her way down the path toward me. "Are you wearing your dads' boots?"

"Hey to you too. Ummm no, these are my boots and I quite like them so shut up," Blake replied with a laugh. "I bought them when I worked up north. They were good for rain, snow, mud, everything really."

"I'm just joking. They just look huge on you, that's all. Chip, drop it," I referenced to the ball in Chip's mouth. He dropped it at my feet, and I threw it. Merc joined in and was chasing after the ball behind Chip. Guinness was slowing down and enjoying walking at a leisurely pace.

"Oh yeah, they are big, but I would have to wear super thick socks, plus my feet are small to begin with, so this is the smallest they had. Is this going to be a problem, did you need me to go home and change so that I can walk with you," Blake said with a grin sarcastically.

"Haha, no it's fine. How was camping?"

"It was good!" Blake said enthusiastically. "It was a lot of fun, when we left, we all said that we had to do it more often. Sucks coming to that realization at the end of the camping season but maybe we'll plan a winter campout or something."

"That's good. Glad the weather held out for ya. Was there a big group of you?" I asked.

"Yeah, me too, would have sucked if it had rained the whole time. Umm, not too big. Myself and Colin, two other couples, and then two single guy friends of ours. It was good, we played beersby, flip cup, beer pong, all those games."

"Oh yeah, nice. Colin's your boyfriend, right? What's he like? Does he work or?"

Blake grabbed the ball from Merc and threw it before answering. "Yeah, Colin's great. We've been together for just over a year now. We were introduced by mutual friends at a party and hit it off. Colin's actually just starting his second year of medical school at UVic. He's been busy with practicum at the hospital all summer, and now he's back at it full time. He's super busy, I'm surprised he even has time for a girlfriend to be honest. What about you? I thought I noticed a female cop living with you. Is that your girlfriend or something?"

"Yeah, that's Heather. She's a cop too. That's how we met," I replied before throwing the ball again.

"That's it? That's all I get. I gave you a pretty decent sparks' notes version of my relationship and you give me one sentence?" Blake said jokingly.

"Haha, yeah, I guess that's just how I am."

"Ahh…A man of few words."

"Yep."

"Oh my God, laaaaaame. Give me something! Isn't this what friends do, they get to know one another. How are we supposed to be friends if you won't even tell me anything?"

"Okay, okay! Heather and I have been together for about three years now. Like I said, we met through work. Things were great, but we seem to be in a bit of a funk at the moment. I don't even know what it is, that's why I didn't elaborate. She just seems to have a lot going on, seems to be wanting to go out with friends a lot more than normal, and we haven't really been connecting as much. There, that's it." I replied.

"Damn. That sort of sucks, I'm sorry. And sorry if I pushed you to share. I'm sort of a pain like that, I guess. I hope things get better with you guys. Maybe we can all go for a beer sometime and get to know each other," Blake suggested.

"Yeah maybe. Anyway, do you want to continue past the dog park, do that little loop and then come back? I typically don't stop there because most dog owners are idiots."

Blake laughed before answering. "Hah, totally agree, that's why I bring a leash as back up. Not that I don't trust Merc, but like you said, some people can't control their dog."

We continued to walk and talk about my work, Blake's schooling and her job, and just regular friendly conversation. She was actually super easy to talk to, and I'm actually surprised that I even told her anything about Heather, as I'm typically pretty private. She has this weird effect where she just makes you feel comfortable, like you can trust her.

We got back to our back yard gates, and I asked her if she would be coming to hockey again on Friday. She said she wouldn't miss it. I offered her a ride again, and she accepted, stating that it made no sense to take two vehicles when we're so close.

I gave her a wave and made my way in the house. I could hear the shower running, so Heather must have just gotten home from work. I pulled out the chicken from the fridge and preheated the oven to get a start at dinner.

Heather had finished her shower and made her way down the stairs. Before she had gotten to the bottom step she already started, "How was your date?" She asked bitterly.

"What?"

"I saw you out back walking with some chick, who looked like a hobo by the way."

"That's Blake. The neighbour," I replied.

"Gotchya." Heather made her way to the fridge and poured herself a glass of white wine.

"Seriously? Are you actually mad? Come on Heather, I was being friendly to the neighbour girl. She has a boyfriend. She's actually nice."

Heather rolled her eyes. "Does she know you have a girlfriend?"

"Yes, she actually suggested we all grab a beer sometime so we can all get to know each other," I responded.

"Yeah okay, like I'll have anything in common with a teenager."

"You're being ridiculous. She's not a teenager, and she's actually nice. She's a nursing student, and her boyfriend is a med student. If she and her boyfriend invite us out for a beer, I'll be going with or without you. Welcome home by the way." I leaned in for a kiss, but Heather was hesitant. She gave me a small peck and said thanks before taking her wine to the couch.

We ate dinner at the table with minimal conversation. Occasionally we talked about work, and then once we finished, we both tidied up the kitchen, and Heather stated she was tired and was going to watch a show in bed.

I grabbed the dogs a bone, grabbed my Xbox headset, and played Xbox until late into the evening.

Blake Taylor

The school year seemed to be going by quickly already. I know we were only six weeks in, but I couldn't believe it was already Thanksgiving. This year, my mom was having a Thanksgiving dinner on Sunday, and Colin's mom was having a meal on Monday because of her work schedule. Unfortunately, Colin had to be at the hospital on Sunday, but he invited me to his mom's Thanksgiving Monday so I would see him there. Our Australian friends Abby and James don't have any family here, and my family love them, so we actually invited them to join us for Thanksgiving.

I finished showering and getting ready at my place before heading upstairs to join the rest of my family. My mom was busy in the kitchen making thirty thousand dishes at once, dad was sitting on the couch with his Denver Broncos jersey on, his athletic pants, slippers, and beer in hand. Audi was supposed to be here soon as she was picking up Trevor from his place. Brenna was in her room; I'm assuming doing her makeup.

"Dad, I'm grabbing a beer, did you need a top up?" I yelled from the kitchen.

"Actually yeah, thanks B."

I sat next to my dad on the couch and looked him up and down and chuckled to myself. "So, this is the life hey. Thanksgiving and you really outdid yourself with the dressy outfit," I said jokingly.

"It's all about comfort. Football and food day, it's all about comfort," Dad responded, not peeling his eyes from the TV. "What time are the Scotts' coming?" He asked.

"I told them to come anytime after two. I wasn't sure what we had going on during the day. It's one now, so I'm sure they'll be here in a bit."

My mom brought over some meats, cheeses, and crackers, and rested them down on the coffee table in front of dad and me. We snacked and chatted and watched the game. It was actually nice to sit and watch the game with him alone and to be able to bond. Audi and Brenna both aren't really into sports, whereas I am, so it's something that my dad and I have always had in common. Although we cheer for different teams, we're always up for Sunday football, especially on Thanksgiving.

As I was just about to ask dad about the Bronco's number one running backs' ankle injury, Audi and Trevor walked in the door, both with arms full of baked goodies.

"Hey! Sorry we're a few minutes late. Time got away from me with all this baking, and I ended up just having to go to the store to pick up a pumpkin pie, 'cause my stupid crust didn't turn out. So yeah. It's store bought, but whatever. I still made cookies and sweet tarts," Audi explained, sounding rather stressed.

"That's okay! I'm sure it'll taste great, and it was the thought that counts. Thanks anyway. Hey Trevor, how are you?" my mom asked with a smile.

"Good. Yeah, sorry we're late. You know how Audi is when she's in the kitchen," Trevor said jokingly.

Audi put the desserts in the kitchen and organized them all pretty on separate plates. She put a bouquet of flowers in the background, a bottle of wine, and a Thanksgiving napkin next to the desserts. She took pictures of them and posted them to her social media page. She takes so much time to make sure the photo is just right before posting.

Audi is hoping to get into Vancouver's Art Institute, to study fashion and design, so she continuously likes to keep her social media page updated with super trendy content. Over the past year, she's actually gained quite the following, between her culinary photos, her fashionista photos, and her aesthetically pleasing design photos, she's built a following of just over 10,000 people!

Trevor had already sat down on the loveseat, grabbed a napkin full of snacks from the coffee table before Audi had come to join us.

"Blake check it out! I literally just posted that baking pic, and forty-five people already like it. It's only been up for two minutes!"

"Wow, that's actually really awesome. It seems like your page is really taking off. When will you find out if you get accepted to school?" I asked.

Audi also grabbed a napkin of meat and cheese and sat down next to Trevor before answering. "It's such a long process. My application isn't even completed yet. I'm only wanting to get in next fall, and they need so many different elements in the portfolio. I'm so busy bartending full time, and then I'm taking two evening art classes at UVic, so I'm hoping that'll help. I'll be submitting my application by November, so I'll find out by spring."

"Wow, that's super exciting. I'm happy for you."

The doorbell rang, and because Abby and James are practically family, they just walked in. Merc greeted them with a big wag of the tail, and a sloppy kiss for James.

"Hey guys! Man, thanks again so much for having us. It's so nice to spend the holidays with some family, you know," James said, handing my mom two bottles of wine and going in for a hug.

I got up off the couch and greeted Abby with a kiss on the cheek and a warm hug.

"Hey Blakey, thanks again. This is so nice," said Abby.

"Oh my gosh of course, it's no problem at all, seriously, you don't have to thank us. We wouldn't want it any other way."

Brenna came down to join in on the festivities a few minutes after Abby and James had arrived. Brenna was super preoccupied with a play that she was apart of in school and stated that she hated to be antisocial, but she really had to memorise her lines. She hung out with us for about a half hour before returning to her room to run her lines.

The smells coming from the kitchen were enough to make anyone's belly rumble. We were all practically drooling by the time my mom announced that dinner was ready. She yelled up the stairs to inform Brenna. Dinner was amazing as my mom always outdoes herself with far too many dishes, and an overly tasty turkey.

We finished the night with the late-night football game and some board games. Abby and James stayed until about ten p.m. before heading home. They thanked my parents' numerous times, and I hugged them both goodbye before heading down to my suite.

"Oh my gosh mom, I'm so full. That was so good. Thank you again. I think I'm going to head down to bed. I'm pretty tired, and I've got to do it all over again tomorrow at Colin's," I said before saying my goodbyes.

As soon as I got home, I changed into some PJs, washed my face, brushed my teeth, and jumped into bed to watch Grey's Anatomy on Netflix. Before I started the episode, I gave Colin a quick call to see how his day was.

The phone rang, and Colin picked up after two rings. "Hey! How was your Thanksgiving with your family? Good timing, I'm just walking to my car in the parkade. I got held up at the hospital," Colin said.

"Oh my gosh, did you ever! That's such a long day for you. Thanksgiving was good. It was nice to see Abby and James. I told them that you said hello. They mentioned they want to try and get together soon, maybe go for dinner or something. How was the hospital?"

"Oh yeah, I forgot that they were going, but yeah that sounds good. It was good. We just ended up having a patient whose bloodwork wasn't adding up, and I was too stubborn to leave before figuring out what was going on. He's okay though, but I'm exhausted. Think I'm going hit a drive thru on my way home then head to bed. I'm so looking forward to having the day off tomorrow," Colin said excitedly.

"Oh, I bet! What are your plans? What time is dinner?"

"Mom said to come over around four. I was going to sleep in and have sort of a lazy morning, then maybe go to the climbing gym, and then just chill at home. I can call you when I'm done at the gym, and I can just pick you up on my way home. I'm assuming you're sleeping over anyway?"

"Yeah, sure that works," I replied.

"Okay, awesome. I'm just at my car now, so I'll give you a shout tomorrow. Have a good sleep."

"Okay you too!" I hit play on my remote and watched about five minutes of the episode before having to turn it off and go to sleep.

It might seem crazy what I am about to say, sunshine she's here, you can take a break. I leaned over to turn off my phone alarm before too much of the song began to play and it would be stuck in my head for the rest of the day.

I set my alarm for nine-thirty so that I would have enough time to get outside and go for a run with Merc before showering and getting myself presentable before Colin would be here to pick me up. He didn't really say what time he would be going to the gym, so I was planning on being ready for early afternoon so that he wouldn't be waiting on me in case he was done early.

I made a quick peanut butter and banana toast, changed into my running gear, and grabbed a leash for Merc. We jogged at a decent pace and ended up running for an hour. By the time I got home, showered, blow dried my hair, and put a bit of makeup on, it was noon.

I got a text from Colin saying that he would pick me up in an hour. I realized that I couldn't really show up to his house for Thanksgiving empty handed, so I ran to my car and drove to the little plaza up the street.

I ran into the bakery to grab cinnamon buns, and a banana loaf. I walked next door to grab a rosé and red wine, and then I went to the grocery store to grab a bouquet of flowers.

By the time I got home, it was a few minutes shy of one, so I knew Colin would be here any minute. I quickly topped up Merc's water dish and let him out for a pee. I sent a quick text to my mom asking if she could feed Merc dinner, and if he could sleep at her house tonight, as I would only be home in the morning to feed him breakfast. As I was letting him back into the house, Colin's car pulled into my driveway. I quickly grabbed my wine, treats and flowers from the kitchen table and jumped into the passenger side seat.

"Those are pretty, mom will love those. What else you got there," Colin asked curiously.

"Just some desserts from the bakery and some wine," I replied.

"Well, that was nice of you. I'm going to shower quick when we get home, the gym was quite the workout today. I was only bouldering, but I haven't been in a while, so it kicked my ass."

"Yeah, I can tell. You're still sweating, and you stink," I said jokingly.

Colin's mom Sandra loved the flowers and put them in a vase right away. She put the rosé wine in the fridge and set the red on the table. She already had a bottle of red opened and poured me a glass while Colin made his way to shower.

Allie, her husband Adam, Colin's other brother Brandon, and Brandon's wife Mia were all playing Catan, (a board game) in the living room. They set up a little puzzle table to play games as the dining table was prepared for the meal. There was hooting and hollering between the four of them as they tended to get quite competitive with most games. Colin's younger brother Andrew wasn't there, so I was assuming he was downstairs or working.

Allie greeted me with a big smile as soon as I entered the open concept living area. "Hey Blake! Pull up a chair, I'm finally beating Brandon and he can hardly take it!" she said excitedly.

I grabbed a chair and held on to my wine glass as I was scared that it would get knocked over on the overly crowded table. "Where's Andrew?" I asked.

"He's just finishing up at work, he called Sandra about a half hour ago saying he would be here around three," replied Adam.

The game continued and Colin had come to join soon after. He grabbed himself a beer and pulled up a chair to the table. The game was almost done, and as much as Allie was bragging earlier, Brandon had taken the lead in the final round and had won the game.

"Uggghhh! Dang it Brandon! I hate it when you do that! It's like you save up all your resources and then just build the longest road right at the end to get those extra points!" Exclaimed Allie.

"All part of the plan my dear," retorted Brandon.

The rest of the afternoon was filled with board games and drinks, and occasionally Colin's dad Victor would join in on a round or two in between helping Sandra in the kitchen. Andrew got home right around three, he showered, and then joined us in playing board games. I got up to use the washroom and offered my help in the kitchen, but Sandra was adamant I enjoy myself with the others.

Dinner was served around six p.m. and my head was already feeling a bit fuzzy. I had had two glasses of wine, and Allie was insisting we open the rosé that I brought to have with dinner. It seemed as though all of us kids were feeling the same as Mia insisted on having water with dinner as she '"had had enough already'."

I was always so comfortable at Colin's house. His family was extremely welcoming, and it was very clear that they really liked me. Allie would always comment on when our wedding would be. Sandra would always say things like 'Oh, we just love having you here Blake,' and 'We never see Colin smile so much, he's always so serious with school." It always made me feel good to know that I was accepted by my boyfriends' family. I also got along really well with his dad Vic. He had a sort of dry sense of humour that I was able to play in to and I think my blunt personality and quick wit kept him quite entertained.

When supper was over, all of us kids cleaned up the table, the pots and pans from cooking, all the dishes, and then tidied the kitchen and dining room. Sandra and Vic were finally able to relax on the couch with a beer each. Once we finished the cleaning we sat around and chatted, catching up on each others' lives.

Brandon was just starting out as a newly graduated medical doctor. He had just finished his final residency up in Prince George and was now working as a hospitalist in the Victoria hospital. He actually wasn't enjoying the acuity as much as he was thinking he would and was looking forward to saving up enough money so he could open up his own family practice. Mia was adjusting to having just moved back to Victoria (they had only been here for two weeks), and so she was still job searching. She was an early childhood educator, so she was looking for positions in day cares.

Allie and Adam were enjoying the honeymoon stage of their relationship as they had just gotten married this past summer. They were preparing to sell their townhouse as they wanted to purchase a home with their own yard instead.

Andrew was doing well and trying to get into the kinesiology program in either Vancouver or Victoria, but he didn't get in this fall. He was quite bummed so decided to work full time as a server at a fancy restaurant as well as do more science courses on the side so he would be prepared to apply again for next fall.

Then the conversation pointed at Colin and me. His family wanted to know how we were doing, both individually, and us together.

Colin looked at me, and I signaled for him to go first. "Good, I'm good. Busy, obviously, but good. School is already super challenging, and trying to balance the hospital on top of that has been tiring. It's nice when I actually get a day off. And Blake and I are the same. No change. Like good. We're good."

I thought it was sort of weird how he spoke of our relationship, so I wasn't exactly sure how to proceed. "And nothing too new with me. I'm still busy with school, it's nice to be in my 3rd year, as I can finally see the light at the end of the tunnel. And I don't know, for me, Colin and I are doing great. I still like him, so that's a plus," I said with a grin.

Colin's family laughed and we all continued with the small chat, then moved on to playing cards before we all retired to bed.

When we got down to Colin's room, I couldn't help but feel confused at his answer. "The same, no change..." What did he mean by that?

Colin was setting up Netflix when I crawled into the bed and asked, "Hey what did you mean by, 'there's no change with Blake and I, we're the same?'"

Colin paused the show he had chosen before turning to look at me and replied, "What do you mean, what did I mean? I don't like there's nothing new to report. We aren't in a fight, we're not making any life changing decisions, we're the same as we were a couple months ago. I didn't mean it in a bad way."

"Do you think that's bad though? That we've been together a year and you feel like we're just 'the same'" I asked curiously.

"Blake, you're overthinking. I think we're great. I don't think we're in a funk, I think we're comfortable, and for me, I'm happy. I'm just busy a lot of the time."

"Okay, well I'm happy too," I said with a smile.

"Good. Can I hit play now?"

Alec Kohl: Winter, 2014

"I literally don't care. This is the third time you've cancelled at the last minute. I'm going with or without you, and I'm leaving in five minutes," I said impatiently.

"Well, I just don't even feel like Blake, and I will get along," replied Heather.

"Well, you're never going to know if you never come. Blake is great. Her boyfriend Colin is great. The last two times that they have invited us out to join them at McDuffs pub, you have come up with some lame excuse and I've gone by myself. I don't need to keep going by myself to get to know them, because I do know them. Blake and I are friends. Get over it."

I was so tired of Heather giving me a hard time about Blake. It's been about three months since she had moved in, and Heather still wouldn't give her the time of day. I think she's jealous that I have yet another friend who is a girl. All my life I have always connected easier with women. I've always had more girl friends than I have had guy friends, and I think Heather has a problem with it. I kept trying to explain to her, that the sooner she actually takes the time to meet Blake, the sooner she would be fine with my friendship with her.

"K I'll brush my teeth then I'll meet you in the truck. If I don't like her, I'm having my girlfriend pick me up early," Heather said as she stomped up the stairs dramatically.

We walked into the pub, which was a bit dark, which is very with typical sports bar lighting. All the tables were dark wood with matching wooden chairs. No tablecloth, no seat cushions, just wood on wood. They did have some pops of orange throughout, but mostly everything was just wood and beige walls. Nothing fancy, but that allowed for less distractions from the TVs. The bar was shaped as a large U in the center, and then the wooden tables were dispersed around in no particular order, as well as some tables out on the patio. The patio had a large outdoor fireplace and more large flat screen TVs. No matter where you sat at McDuffs, you always had a view of the game. As we entered, I could see Colin sitting at a table at the back, but I couldn't see Blake. Heather and I approached the table.

"Hey. How's it going? Heather, this is Colin," I said politely.

Colin shook Heather's hand before answering, "Hey. I'm Colin, Blake just went to the washroom, but she ordered you guys a beer."

"How sweet," Heather replied before sliding into the booth.

Blake had arrived a few seconds later and immediately lit up. "Hey! Heather it's so nice to finally meet you! I can't believe we live next door and haven't actually met yet! I'm Blake, and I'm assuming you've already met Colin," Blake said reaching out her hand across the table.

Heather shook Blakes hand as she responded, "Oh I know, work's been so busy. Sorry I haven't been able to make it the past couple of times."

"No problem! Trust us, we get it. Colin has been swamped with school and working so we definitely get the lack of having a social life," Blake said.

"Yeah, Colin, how's that going anyway? Where are you located in the hospital?" I asked.

"It's good. I actually rotate throughout the year. I do about six weeks in different specialties, I guess you could say. Right now, I'm on pediatrics."

"That must be nice getting to switch things up, that way you can get a feel for what you like too," I replied.

"Exactly, it's good that way. It definitely helps you to realize what area you actually enjoy practicing in. For example, I thought I was going to like pediatrics, but I actually don't. It's not that I don't like kids, I just like when my patient can communicate back with me, and lately we've been dealing with a lot of babies. It makes it hard to know if they're in pain, or where exactly something hurts, that sort of thing. So, it definitely opens up your eyes. What about you guys? How's your work? Do you guys work together?" Colin asked.

"No, I work general duty. I have a partner that I work with every shift, whereas Alec's partner is a dog," Heather said dryly.

"Seriously?" Colin asked looking in my direction.

"Haha, yeah. I'm sort of part of a specialized unit. I have a drug detection dog, so I patrol the highways looking for drug traffickers. It's really interesting, and it's something different everyday. I don't actually ever see Heather at work. We aren't even in the same detachment."

"That sucks!" Blake chimed in. "Like how shitty that you guys couldn't even see each other in the office and stuff. At least you could try and meet for coffee or something throughout the day. Isn't that what you guys do most of the day anyway? Drink coffee and eat donuts," Blake said laughingly.

"Never heard that one before," Heather said rolling her eyes.

"Good one. We don't actually take too many coffee breaks. Some of the GD guys, sorry, general duty guys take their time at their morning coffee, but I actually like to be on the road. We don't mind it though. It allows us to focus on our work, and then have something to talk about when we come home," I replied, smiling at Heather.

The rest of the evening was so awkward and uncomfortable. I'm not sure if it was for Blake and Colin, but I could tell that Heather did not want to be at that table and could care less for the small talk. I was hoping Blake couldn't sense that because I would feel bad. She was being so polite and trying so hard to include Heather in conversations, but Heather would just answer with one-word responses.

Heather nudged my side and indicated that I look at my phone. At some point she had sent me a text saying that she was uncomfortable and would like to leave after they were done their beer.

The waitress came by and asked if we were up for a second beer. Before anyone could answer, Heather responded to the waitress, "No we're actually good. We'll take the bill please. Sorry guys, I have an early morning tomorrow."

The waitress nodded and asked if Blake and Colin wanted a second beer, but they also agreed to take their bill.

We all squared up and paid our separate bills and then agreed to do this again soon. I personally knew that that would probably never happen again, just based on the way Heather was marching off to the truck as if someone had lit a fire under her ass.

We weren't even in the truck long enough to buckle our seat belts before she started. To be honest I had to tune her out. It seemed as though it was the same fight over and over again. I just nodded my head and focused on the road. The odd time that I would tune back in, she was going on about something like, "And like I told you, how do I even have anything in common with her, she's like seven years younger than me and still a student. Her boyfriend is a student. What am I supposed to talk to them about? Oh, how was your note taking today? Like, I don't care. I'm sorry Alec, I just don't see them as long-term friends. They're so young and immature."

"Okay. Well at least you tried," I answered as we rounded the corner to our street.

"Well, are you still going to be friends with them?" Heather asked anxiously.

"Yeah. I'm not just going to stop being friends with them because you think they're boring students. They're actually nice, and Blake has a good heart. Plus, I like her family, and she's, our neighbour. I can't make it awkward."

"Wow. Okay."

"Okay then. I don't really know what else to say. I'm sorry you don't like them. You have plenty of friends who I don't like, but I don't ask you to stop hanging out with them. They're your friends, I don't have to love them, I just have to show up and be nice when we're at group things, which you couldn't even do tonight," I answered, now starting to get a bit heated.

"Which of my friends do you not like!? Everyone is so nice. And I was nice! How was I not nice?" Heather said defensively.

"You literally were giving Blake one-word responses. Your answers were rude, and you practically ran out of there when it was time to leave. You weren't nice at all. And Brooke drives me nuts. She's a drama queen who loves to gossip, and drinks way too much."

"Seriously!? Now you're going to bash my friends!?" Heather yelled as we pulled into our driveway.

"Okay let's try not to have a domestic in our driveway. You just asked me which of your friends I don't like, and I answered. Sorry you didn't like my response," I said as I stepped out of the truck.

Heather slammed her truck door and made her way to the side door. Once we entered, she took her shoes off, and immediately went upstairs to our room, avoiding all eye contact. I decided to give her a few minutes to cool off, before going upstairs to see how she was doing.

About five minutes later, Heather came down the stairs in a completely different outfit. She had on tight jeans and a tight top. Again, without making eye contact she went back over to the side door and started to put on her tall boots.

"Are you going out?" I asked.

"Yep. Going to meet my gossipy friend Brooke for a drink. Sounds suiting right? Since apparently, she drinks too much. Don't worry, I'll take a cab home if I decide to follow in her footsteps." Heather shut the door and left before I could even respond.

I went to the fridge and grabbed myself a coke, then made my way back to the living room to turn on the Xbox. I kept going back and forth in my head if I should text Heather or not. I felt like she was being super immature, and it drives me nuts that she just walked out because she didn't like something that I said. How were we ever supposed to work through things or learn how to communicate if she always acts like a two-year-old.

I caved and ended up sending her a text.

I get that you were upset, but you didn't have to leave. We should have talked about it, instead of you storming out.

I got caught up playing Rainbow Six before I even realized that Heather had responded to my text.

Nothing to talk about. Just wanted a girl's night. Don't wait up.

Clearly, she's still mad, I thought. Whatever. I'm sure we won't talk about it, and she'll hold her little grudge and this will never be solved. Story of my life.

I ended up playing Xbox until midnight and Heather still wasn't home. I let the dogs out for a quick pee and then made my way up to the bedroom. I turned on Netflix and decided to watch Family Guy for a bit before going to bed, as I had to be up early for work in the morning.

When my alarm went off at six-fifteen, Heather wasn't in bed with me. I quickly checked my phone, and I had no missed calls or texts. Maybe she stayed out all night. I showered and put on my uniform before going downstairs to leave for work. I noticed Heather's boots were by the side door, so she must have come home and slept in the spare room. Heather was petty like that. Anytime we would get into a fight, whether it be a small disagreement, or a long-overdrawn argument, she would always go and sleep in the spare room. I think she thought that it would bother me, or teach me a lesson or something, but if she wants to be immature and sleep in another room, be my guest.

I quickly fed Chip and Guinness their breakfast and loaded them both up in the police cruiser. Hopefully today will be a good day and I can keep my mind occupied rather than dwell about my relationship.

Blake Taylor

Life in general was becoming busier as school was picking up, plus I've been trying to attend hockey on Friday nights, and even work as much as possible, so trying to find time to see Colin has been tough. Today was Sunday, and I had the day off from work, but Colin was stuck at the hospital.

One bonus to this very hectic lifestyle, is that Alec and I have actually started to grow quite a bit closer, and I would even consider him one of my closest friends. We tend to drive together to hockey and even take the dogs out for walks regularly. Alec has been one of those friends who I have been very comfortable with, and I've actually been able to talk to him about school, my family, and even my relationship. He's been such a good listener, and I've been so appreciative of his male perspective, and his great advice.

I decided to send him a quick text to see if he wanted to take the dogs for a walk, as I sort of wanted his advice on Colin. Especially now that he's met and spent time with Colin a few times, it helps when he gives advice, because he actually knows him, and is able to see how we interact and whatnot.

Alec responded that he was just finishing up lunch and that he would meet me out back in fifteen minutes. I made myself a quick sandwich, and then met him by our backyard gates. I threw the ball for Merc as I waited for him to join.

Guinness and Chip ran for the ball after I threw it for the fourth time, and Alec was close behind them as they exited their yard. "Hey," he said, closing his gate.

"Hey. Nice day for November, eh?" I replied.

"Yeah, not bad at all. How was your weekend?"

"Not bad. I have a big project for school due this upcoming week, and then I worked yesterday, but only six hours because I wanted time to work on homework. It's so nice to have today off."

"Yeah, I bet. Sounds pretty busy. How's Colin?" Alec asked, as he threw the ball for a whining Chip.

"Busy. As usual. That's actually why I wanted to go for a walk. I sort of needed some advice, and a male's perspective is always beneficial."

"Go ahead," Alec said encouragingly.

"I just feel like I'm caught between a rock and a hard place. Sometimes I feel guilty for feeling the way I feel, or even like maybe it's all in my head. He's such a great guy, and always treats me so well, and we have such an amazing time together, and I'm constantly trying new things because his hobbies are so different than my own, and I love his friend circle, and I love his family, and his family loves me..." I trailed off.

"Okay...So what's the catch?" Alec replied curiously.

"He's just so, so, so, soooo busy, to the point where I don't feel like a priority. Part of me thinks that I should be proud, and understanding, and I am, and I do. I understand how much work school is, let alone medical school, but I feel like I want this relationship more than he does, and I don't know if it's just a situational thing, like, it'll get better when he's not so busy with school cause he'll have more time, or if he just isn't sure about me."

"Hmm, well if I'm being honest, I don't think he will ever be any less busy. When he's finished with school then he'll be a doctor. I don't know too many doctors, especially ones just starting out, that aren't super busy. I think you need to talk to him and let him know how you're feeling and see what he has to say. Who knows, he could have no idea that you even feel that way. We're not mind readers you know," Alec said with a smirk.

"You got that right. I know that I should talk to him about it, I'm just worried I'll stress him out even more, you know?"

"Yeah, I get that. But it's not worth you being stressed out and think of how much better you'll feel to actually have him understand how you're feeling," Alec replied.

"Yeah, okay you're right. Okay, well thank you. That helped a lot. So, what about you? How's Heather?"

"Heather's her normal self."

"What does that even mean? I barely know the woman, so I don't really know what her normal self is. Plus, you asked me about Colin, so I'm allowed to ask you about Heather," I said quickly. Merc brought me a stick to throw, but as I was about to throw it, Alec threw the ball for Chip and Guinness, and Merc took off after the ball as well, leaving his stick behind.

"I guess so. Heather and I aren't doing so good. We sort of go through these cycles. Maybe it's because we've been together for a while that we become comfortable, and sometimes think that it is just easier to be together, because going through a breakup is hard, but I'm not happy, and I don't think she is either."

"Have you guys broken up before?" I asked. My turn to be curious.

"Yeah. Twice. They didn't last long. Like I said, going through a breakup is hard. I think the longest was six days. We live together, work together, have similar friends, so there's a lot of outside factors than just how we feel about each other, if that makes sense," Alec said, avoiding eye contact.

"That really sucks. I'm sorry you're feeling stuck. Have you ever tried taking your own advice?"

"What do you mean?"

"Exactly what you told me. Maybe you should talk to her and see if she's on the same page. Maybe she's just going through something personal so it's affecting your guys' relationship. Or maybe she feels the same and is sort of looking for a way out but knows how difficult the drawn-out process of a breakup is," I replied throwing the ball for the dogs.

"I see what you mean by it being hard to actually talk to the person. I've tried before, but Heather shuts down. She either leaves, like physically leaves the house, or she just stops talking. It's like talking to a wall, so it discourages me from even wanting to try."

"Well clearly that hasn't been workin' for ya pal. Maybe you need to just lay it out there and see what she thinks. No point in living in this limbo. Plus, a wise guy told me 'think how much better you'd feel to have her understand how you're feeling'," I said, also with a smirk.

"Haha, okay I get it. So, looks like we have some talking to do."

After our dog walk, I made myself a hot chocolate, put on some comfy sweats and set up my laptop on my desk in my little den area. I turned on the desk lamp and started to work on some of the research that I needed to do for my project. Merc had plopped himself down on the floor at my feet. I was just getting in the swing of things when my mom had texted me inviting myself and Colin up for dinner. I responded that I would come up around five-thirty as I was busy studying and that I would invite Colin, but he was at the hospital so doubted he would make it.

The time flew by as I worked on my research project, and to my surprise I actually heard back from Colin.

Dinner sounds good. I'm scheduled to work until six, so if I actually get out on time I'll come by. I'll let you know. Have a good afternoon. Read Colin's text.

I replied with a simple *you too* and continued my work.

At about five-fifteen Merc started to get antsy, signalling that it was time to eat supper and go outside for a quick pee. I got his supper ready and then let him out. It was starting to cool down and I wouldn't be surprised if we actually got a light dusting of snow overnight. Merc finished up, and then he and I made our way upstairs to join the rest of the family.

Dad was sitting on the couch watching football, (it was Sunday after all), Brenna was sitting at the table working on something for school, Audi wasn't home, and mom was in the kitchen working on supper.

"Hey, I brought Merc, hope that's okay," I said as Merc made his presence known by greeting everyone with a happy tail wag and kiss.

"Of course! No problem," replied my mom.

"Is there anything I can help you with?"

"Oh no, I'm almost done, and then it can just simmer, thanks," mom said as she stirred the sauce.

I joined my dad on the couch, and we talked football and school, explaining a bit about my research paper to him. We were given a topic to research, and we had to decide if we were for or against it and why. I was given the topic of medical marijuana use in psychiatric patients to treat depression and anxiety. I decided to write that I was against it, and I sort of explained my reasons to dad and he had agreed. He didn't have much knowledge on the subject, so I think he would have agreed with either argument.

Just then the door swung open and both Colin and Audi had entered. Colin had a pie in his hand.

"Hey! Funny seeing the both of you arrive like that!" I said.

"Yeah, I was just parking on the street when your sister was pulling into the driveway. Hey guys, thanks for having me for dinner," Colin said, signalling to my parents.

I got up and greeted Colin at the door with a quick kiss and said hi to Audi at the same time. We grabbed a seat at the couch to wait for dinner.

In the background I could hear my mom asking Brenna to tidy her things as dinner was almost ready and she would like to set the table. I decided to get up and help. I don't know what it was, but ever since my talk with Alec earlier I was feeling anxious around Colin, it was almost like an elephant in the room, except he didn't know about the elephant, if that makes sense. I knew that I needed to talk to him, but it was a conversation that needed to be had in private, therefore needed to wait until after dinner, so the anxiety and anticipation of this important conversation was killing me, especially because I feel like he would be blindsided. I was happy to get up from the couch, take a breather, and set the table.

Dinner was great, as always, and we all enjoyed the pie that Colin had picked up afterward. We stayed and socialized for about an hour before making our way down to my place.

"Nice that you were able to make it to dinner. I really wasn't expecting you to show up," I said as we kicked our shoes off entering the suite.

"I know hey, I actually got off like twenty minutes early. My last patient was very simple, so I was able to just head out once I was done. Worked out well. How was your day?"

I grabbed two beers from the fridge and joined Colin on the couch before responding, "It was good, I actually got a lot done on my paper, which I was surprised because I've been feeling quite distracted today."

"What do you mean?" Colin asked.

"I've just been doing a lot of thinking lately and feeling like maybe we're on different pages when it comes to our relationship," I take a deep breath before continuing. "I get that you're super busy with school, and work, trust me I get it, and I am proud of you, it takes so much dedication and ambition to even be where you are, and you wouldn't be you, if you didn't give it 110%. I just sometimes feel like I'm at the very bottom of your priority list, and that you sort of see me or make time for me because you have to, not because you want to."

Colin took a minute to digest my words before answering. "Okay, that's fair. I could see how you would feel that way because you're right. School and work *are* my life right now, and it has to be. It sucks that I can't have more of a life outside of this, but I rarely see my friends, my family, I rarely get to do any of the activities that I actually want to do because I'm either busy studying, or busy at the hospital, and so when I do have an afternoon free, I have to choose between you, friends, family, and myself. It's hard to balance it all. I don't really know what else there is for me to do. I think its sort of up to you and what you want. I know that I want to be with you, and this is what our future is going to look like for the next couple years while I'm in med school. It basically comes down to if you can handle that or not. I don't know what else to say, I'm sorry."

"Don't be sorry. I'm glad that you're being honest, and I'm sorry for making you feel bad. Everything you're saying is completely valid, and I'm sure it's so hard for you to have to balance everything," I took a long sip from my beer before continuing. "I want to be with you too. I love our time together, the little that we have, and I'm glad that we're on the same page." I leaned in for a kiss and was pleasantly surprised with the force behind Colin's kiss. He's typically not the affectionate type, we're not the kind of couple to just make out on the couch, but this time I guess he wanted me to feel how serious he was.

"I'll just spend the night here if that's okay," Colin said, as he took off his shirt and walked toward the bedroom.

We woke up early the next morning as we both had class. It's sort of nice to be in school together, but Colin still starts his days earlier than I do. I decided to get up with him to his alarm. We shared a quick shower, and I quickly whipped us up some breakfast sandwiches as Colin finished getting ready in the bathroom. I knew that I would have time to at least put a smidge of makeup on before I would have to leave. Colin took his sandwich to go, gave me a kiss, and made his way to his vehicle.

I fed Merc his breakfast, finished my sandwich, and applied some quick makeup. I let Merc outside to use the bathroom while I changed into my scrubs. I gathered my laptop, stethoscope and quickly made a lunch to bring to school before letting Merc back in and heading out the door.

Class went by slow, and in the afternoon, we were actually given time to work on our papers which was nice. I finished class at three and made my way to Urban Garage to work a very quick shift. I was scheduled from three-thirty to six-thirty so I would be closing up with Abby today.

"Hey Blakey! How ya going?" Abby greeted me as I entered the front door to the store.

"Good, long day. I hate Monday's. I don't know why I do this to myself. Full day of school and then work. Ugh," I replied.

Abby and I chatted for the rest of our shift, assisting the occasional customer. As we were closing up, Abby actually suggested grabbing a quick bite and drink at the new restaurant across the street.

The restaurant was called Stix and it had a sort of Earls vibe to it. The hostesses and waitresses were dressed in all black, and the décor was all black, with gold accents. The bar was very swanky, shaped like a half crescent moon in the center of the restaurant. The bar top itself was glass and gold pendant lighting hung above. All the tables in the restaurant were high top tables with black suede chairs, and the occasional oversized booth, again with black suede and a chandelier hanging above. It was very sleek and classy.

We got seated at one of the high tables in the corner of the restaurant and sat across from each other. We both ordered a glass of their red cinnamon cranberry sangria, which was their November special, to welcome the Christmas spirit. We shared a few appetizers, which were delicious, and spoke about our relationships and some of the gossip at work. We didn't stay long as I was tired, but it was nice to have that bond and friendship with Abby.

As I walked to my car, my phone started to buzz, and I looked down and it was Colin. I quickly answered as I unlocked my car.

The phone call was quick as Colin just wanted to see how my day was as he hadn't heard from me after work. I explained my last-minute dinner with Abby, and he told me his day was busy as well. He was heading down to the public pool to swim some laps, then sauna and hot tub and invited me to join. I explained how tired I was and that I had to get home to feed and let out Merc but invited him to come spend the night after he was done instead. He agreed and said he should be over to my place between nine and ten.

It felt nice to have spoken to Colin, it seemed as though our conversation sparked something in him and that he actually wants to make the effort to see me more.

I drove home and was greeted by a very excited Merc. I fed him supper, let him out, and then changed into some comfy PJs. I put on Netflix as I waited for Colin to arrive.

Alec Kohl

It was another busy day at work, and I couldn't wait to get home and just relax, but I knew that I should probably take Blake's advice and talk to Heather about our relationship. As I drove home at the end of my shift, the driver ahead of me blew a four way stop sign, so I quickly pulled him over, gave him a warning, and then continued home. Because of this, I was a few minutes late getting home in comparison to Heather. We were working the same shift today, and I noticed her vehicle was already parked in the driveway.

I came in through the front door and was immediately greeted by the smell of dinner, and very excited kisses from Guinness and Chip. After taking off my boots I made my way up the stairs to my room to take off my uniform and change into regular clothes. I quickly rinsed my face and brushed my teeth before heading back down.

"Hey, dinner smells great, thanks for cooking," I said as I grabbed a Coke from the fridge.

"Thanks. Did you get held up? One moment we were leaving together and then the next moment you're home a half hour after me," Heather asked.

"Yeah, I had a guy blow a stop sign right in front of me, just around the corner from our house. Can I help you with anything?" I asked.

"If you could actually just set the table that would be good. Supper will be ready in about five minutes, it's just cooling," Heather replied.

As I grabbed the plates and cutlery, I started thinking about Heather being in a surprisingly good mood, which was giving me cold feet in trying to bring up that I was unhappy in our relationship. I honestly had no idea how I was going to approach this.

A few minutes later, I help carry some of the hotdishes over to the table, we sit down, and serve our own plates.

"Thanks, this looks really good," I said as I looked across the table at Heather. Heather had made a roast in the slow cooker that she had turned on before we had left for work this morning.

"Oh, it was easy," She replied, without making eye contact and buttering a dinner roll.

"Look, I just have something I really need to get off my chest. To be honest, I'm a little nervous now, because you were so nice to make such a great meal, but I feel like this shouldn't be avoided for any longer."

Heather takes a bite of her supper before saying hesitantly, "Okay…"

"I think we need to take a break. I know this dinner is nice and we're actually talking and getting along, but this rarely happens." I took a slight pause to see how

Heather was reacting and how I should proceed. Heather sat there looking at me, but emotionless, difficult to read.

As I was about to continue talking, she asked, "Well if that's what you want, then that's what you want. I think it's dumb. Either you break up or you don't. Like a break makes no sense. Can we see other people, or can we not see other people? You own the house so obviously I have to move out, but how long do I have. I don't like breaks. Either we're done or we're not. I need to know if I'm moving on or not."

"Okay…well I just thought maybe if we took some space from each other, we could see what it was like to be apart, grow to miss each other, see if we actually want to be with each other. Right now, we're in such a routine, such a rut even. We work together but we stay professional at work so it's not like we're spending quality time together. I hate your friends; you hate my friends. We don't share any hobbies or interests together, so when we come home from work, we eat a meal and then you go up to the room and I stay in the living room. Just seems like we're more like roommates, and I thought that maybe if we spend some time apart it might make us realize that we do love each other and help us to remember what it was that brought us together in the first place," I replied.

"What brought us together in the first place was a little too much tequila on my behalf," Heather said in a snarky tone.

That pissed me off. Yes, Heather and I were drinking at a staff Christmas party the night where we actually took the time to get to know each other, but nothing happened that night, and she wasn't drunk the couple days later when I asked her to coffee. Believe it or not, we actually used to respect each other and value each other's company, but I guess from her point of view, it was alcohol that convinced her to date me.

"Alright, well on that note, I think we should take some time a part and see where things lead us in a month or something. Who knows, maybe we'll actually miss each other," I said.

"So, are we free to see other people then, or?" Heather asked.

"You seem really adamant on dating other people. I don't plan on seeing anyone. I'm focusing on me and figuring out what I want for my life, and my future, and if I think that future has you in it."

"Gotchya. Okay well I'll stay at Brooke's tonight. I will pack a quick bag then head out. I have tomorrow off, so I'll come by to gather more things and then I'll be out."

"Sounds good. I'm sorry Heather, I know this sucks, especially since we've been together for so long," before I could finish my sentence, Heather interrupted me.

"It's fine, I get it. I just want to go."

Heather stood up from the table leaving her plate behind and made her way up to our bedroom. I had suddenly lost my appetite. I sat at the table looking at the meal that Heather had prepared, and I felt awful. Maybe I should have waited until we were done eating so that we both could have eaten what she had made. I guess the anticipation of the conversation got the best of me.

I grabbed both of our plates and cleared them away slowly tiding up the kitchen as I could hear Heather upstairs. It's hard because I feel like I was way more upset about this breakup then she was. It's almost as if I was doing her a favour and she couldn't get out of here quick enough. Immediately I'm starting to feel a sense of regret, like maybe we shouldn't have just jumped to breaking up, maybe I should have told her how I felt, and we could have worked together on trying to fix our problems.

I decided to walk up to the bedroom and tell her my realization. As I made my way up the stairs, she was already on her way down with a duffel bag of items and clothes spilling out in one hand, and her overstuffed purse in the other.

"I'm sorry. Maybe this isn't the right approach. Maybe we should just try and work things out instead of just jumping straight to a breakup," I said apologetically.

As Heather moved past me down the stairs, she replied, "No, you know what Alec, you're right, we are like roommates and it's about time you start to realize just how amazing of a girlfriend I was to you, and how much I did for you, and how bad you needed me. I'll give you your space and I give it ten days before you'll be missing me and wanting me back, and who knows, I might be over it by then. Bye."

And then she walked out the door.

I made my way to the living room and sat next to Guinness on the couch. He was snoring away with no inclination of what just happened. Must be nice. I turned on the TV to get ready for the Flames game, when suddenly my phone lit up on the coffee table. It was a text message. Maybe it was Heather apologizing and saying she was turning around.

Instead, it was a text from Blake.

Took your advice. Spoke to Colin and it went great! I think things are actually better now. Thanks! What about you?

I didn't even know what to say. I was happy for Blake that it worked out and that she and Colin are okay, so I didn't really want to burst her bubble, but I also didn't want to talk about it, but she likes to be nosy and ask questions. I quickly typed back.

That's great Blake, I'm happy for you guys. Talked to her. We broke up. Don't want to talk about it.

A few minutes went by, and her text response appeared.

Shit. Beers and watch the Flames game at McDuffs?

Meet you there in ten.

I went upstairs and brushed my teeth, put on some deodorant, sprayed a sprit of my cologne, then hopped in the truck. I arrived before Blake, so I grabbed a corner table that had a good view of the TV. The game was about twelve minutes into the first period and the Flames were up by one. The waitress came by and asked for my order, and I asked for two Stella's. Is it weird that I know Blake's beer order? I rationalized my thoughts with the fact that we go out for beers with the guys all the time and I've noticed what she orders. No big deal.

"Hey, good table. I noticed where you were and asked a waitress to bring us over two beers. Figured you'd need it," Blake said.

"Hah. I just ordered us a beer," I replied.

"Well, I guess we better get some wings or something. So, I know you don't want to talk about it, but it's sort of like the elephant in the room, and I just wanted to make sure you were okay," Blake said caringly.

"Yeah, I'm good, hasn't really hit me yet, but she packed a bag and went to her friend Brooke's place so...She said she would be by tomorrow to grab more of her things."

"Dang, that sucks. So, I guess she wasn't on the same page as you?" Blake asked.

The waitress came by and gave us our beers. We quickly ordered some wings before I continued, "Actually, she sort of was. I sort of messed up. Instead of telling her how I feel and just seeing if we could try and work on things, I just immediately jumped to taking a break. And I think because I didn't give her the chance to, like I say, work on things, she got mad and said 'okay' and left. Anyway, like I told her, I'm going to focus on me and my future and see if I think Heather fits in that future and if she does, then I'll try and see if she's willing to work things out. Okay you got your information now let's just eat, drink, and watch the game."

"Ten four, pal. Cheers to you doin' you," Blake said as she reached her glass out for a clink with a big smile.

The rest of the night was exactly what I needed. Laughing and jokes with a good friend, beers, wings, and the Flames game. We stayed until the end of the game, in which the Flames won, so it actually turned out to be a decent night. Blake paid for my wings and two beers. I think she felt bad that Heather and I broke up and was trying to be a good friend. We both made our way out to the parking lot, and I followed her home. It's kind of funny when we both drive home from the same place 'cause we always get home at the same time and walk up our driveway and into our house at the same time. I gave her a quick 'thanks for dinner, goodnight' as I made my way into the house.

I kicked off my shoes and turned on the Xbox. Tonight, actually turned around.

Blake Taylor

A few days had gone by since Alec and Heather broke up, and I hadn't really heard much from him. He really keeps to himself with these sorts of things. He's very private. But I'm starting to crack him, and I find he's actually been opening up to me a lot more, and I'm just glad I can be there for him as a friend, as he's been there for me.

Today was lab day at school, which meant that we were in the classroom for a few hours in the morning, but then after lunch we would go over real-life scenarios on dummy's or on each other. It was the most practical way to learn, other than direct hands-on practice during our clinical rotations. Today we were going over full medical assessments for patients on a medical/surgical floor. The head-to-toe assessment was incredibly in-depth. You had to do mini mental status exams, neurological response exams, gastro exams (listening to the four quadrants of the stomach), respiratory exams, endocrine exams, and that's not even the half of it. Needless to say, my brain will be fried by the end of the day, and I'll be in need of a drink. We should be done here by four thirty, so I asked Audi if she was working this evening and she was, so I told her I would pop by for a drink and some appies.

For the past week, if I haven't been in class or working, I've been busting my butt on my research paper, but I finally finished it, which had felt great, and there was only two more days until the weekend. I work this Saturday, but only until five, and Alec invited Colin and I to a house party Saturday night. I guess one of his girl friends who also plays hockey is having a bunch of people over. The girl actually lives right near McDuffs, so it is super close to our house. I mentioned it to Colin, but he has to do an over night shift at the hospital, but he said he didn't care if I went. I have Sunday off so I told him I would come over to his place and we could hang out once he woke up from his night shift.

Lab day went by extremely quickly, I think because there was so much to cover, and you were either constantly assessing a friend or having them assess you. Teagan Crest and I paired up together. Teagan and I met in our first year of nursing together and instantly became best friends. We're both incredibly hard working, but also laid back and love to have a good time. Teagan is extremely brilliant, because although nursing is the end of the line career wise for me, Teagan wants to specialize in psychology and eventually get her masters. We work really well together, and always split jobs 50/50 so neither of us was working more than the other. By the time four thirty came, I was pleasantly surprised, but rush hour traffic was brutal in downtown

Victoria, so I texted Audi to let her know I might be a few minutes behind.

Twenty-five minutes later I had arrived at Viva. Viva Victoria was *the* most popular bar in Victoria. It was super high end, sleek, and posh. The colour palette was all jewel tones, diamonds, and silver. Everything exuded opulence. The bar itself had a waterfall display of liquor, with bright lights illuminating all the expensive liquor choices. Each bar stool had a low back on it, and they were all velvet. I believe around eleven p.m. or so, the lower level becomes a dancefloor, and a DJ is brought in. It's definitely one of the classy hot spots, so it was no doubt that this was where Audi worked as a bartender. Audi worked at Viva four nights a week and took evening art classes at the university twice a week. She was a busy gal, but it was no doubt exactly how she liked it.

I approached the bar and saw Audi adding muddled mint to a tall skinny glass that I could only assume was a mojito. There was no one sitting at the bar, so I was thinking it must be for a customer somewhere in the restaurant. Viva just opened at four, so it was still very quiet in here. I gave her a quick smile and wave and sat down at the bar. Audi was dressed in a tight black dress with her hair down and in loose waves. She had darker hair than mine, but she's been adding some highlights so right now it's a really pretty dark blonde. I swear she and I didn't come from the same parents because she is extremely thin, like model thin, and absolutely drop dead gorgeous. I'm not being self-deprecating and acting like I'm throwing myself a pity party, but I'm more of an athletic curvy build, and a natural look. Both of which are beautiful, but Audi is the kind of girl where guys see her and stare for an extra second too long, and girls want to look like her.

"Hey! I'll be right there I just have to make another drink quick," Audi said over the swanky upbeat music.

I browsed the cocktail list while she made a drink. I quickly checked my phone and sent Colin a text saying that I just got to Viva, and I'd text him on my way home. Colin had today off, so he had been spending the day rock climbing with a few friends, and then he was going to have dinner with his parents, and then come over this evening.

"What'd you decide on?" Audi asked with a smile.

"I think I'll do the Red Velvet martini, and I'm just going to get the chicken bites and goat cheese balls, please and thank you. How are you? I feel like it's been forever since I've seen you?"

"I know! Well, I'm so busy with work and school, and Trevor, and friends, I never really stop," Audi replied as she entered my order into her computer screen behind the bar.

"Yeah, no kidding. How is school going?" I asked interestedly.

"It's okay. I love the one fashion history art class, but the art history class is sort of boring, because it's all about the famous paintings in the museums, and how they did this brush stroke, and what emotion is conveyed in this colour palette, blah blah blah. I want to be a fashionista, not a museum geek," Audi said as she started preparing my drink.

"Ah, you'll figure it out, plus, it's not like these courses will go to waste, I'm sure you can put them toward your portfolio, which will only help you to get into the Art Institute. How are things with Trevor?" I asked curiously.

"Oh my gosh Blake, don't even get me started."

"That bad?"

"He's just pissing me off lately. He came in here last Friday evening after work with a bunch of guy friends while I was working. They all got drunk, their whole table was loud and obnoxious, and I had to kick them out. But then of course he got mad at me for kicking them out, but I didn't want my boss to see that it was my boyfriend and his friends causing such a scene. It's like, seriously, is there no where else in this city you could go to get drunk? Come on, don't come to my work. So annoying," Audi replied, as she handed me my drink.

"Wow, yeah that is annoying. So, was he still mad the next day?"

"No, he was all sorry and apologetic, and saying it won't happen again. I swear he's a different guy when he's drunk."

"That sucks, I'm sorry. Hopefully, he'll grow up soon," I said encouragingly.

"What are you up to this weekend?" Audi asked.

"Not a whole lot, I work Saturday until five, and then I'm actually going to a party with Alec Saturday night, and then Colin and I are going to do something on Sunday."

"That sounds like fun. Alec seems nice hey. When dad is out of town and mom needs help with stuff outside, she always texts him and he comes over to help her, so I thought that was nice of him. You don't think it's weird though Blake, that just you and Alec are going to a party? Colin or his girlfriend don't want to go?" Audi asked.

"Haha, no I don't think it's weird. Alec is like, I want to say a brother but that's sort of weird, but he's seriously nothing more than a friend. I don't know how to stress how truly platonic we are. He has never once flirted with me, said something inappropriate, nothing. Hee told me to invite Colin, but Colin is working a night shift, and Alec and his girl friend broke up a few days ago," I responded.

"Yeah, I could see that, Alec is so nice that I don't think he would ever be inappropriate. But that sucks for him. Well maybe this party will be good for him."

A few minutes later my food arrived, and I ate and continued to chat with Audi. I didn't stay for too long and gave her a good tip and a hug before leaving.

Once I got home, Merc was excited to see me and needed to be let outside. As I waited for him to finish his business, I texted Colin to let him know that I was going to take Merc for a walk, but if he got here before I was back, then to let himself in.

I put my bag and keys on the kitchen island, grabbed Merc's leash and made my way out the back gate.

Alec Kohl

It was so nice to have the weekend off and I was actually looking forward to Jenn's party tonight. I was looking forward to seeing a bunch of friends, having a few beers, and shooting the shit. I wasn't looking forward to everyone asking me where Heather was though. Heather had come by yesterday to pick up more of her things and that just turned into another argument. She was mad that I was going to Jenn's party tonight because she thought that it was me going out to try and meet girls. She was especially mad that I was going with Blake. I tried to explain that I had invited Colin as well, but he was working and couldn't come. But Heather didn't care, she grabbed two suitcases of things, and before she left, she made a snarky comment about having fun tonight.

I spent the day being productive, cleaning the house, meal prepping for the next few nights, and organizing Heather's things because she left our closet and bathroom in a complete disaster. I took Guinness and Chip to the dog park in the late afternoon, then came home and had a quick shower. I threw on one of my comfiest plaid button-down shirt, a pair of dark jeans, and my black Flames hat.

I went downstairs and texted Blake if she wanted to drive down together, since I knew where Jenn lived. As I waited for her response, I made a quick homemade pizza and tossed it in the oven.

Blake said that worked and asked what time she should come over, and I let her know I would be ready in about a half an hour.

As I was rinsing my plate off in the sink from having finished my meal, Blake walked in from my garage.

"Just figured I'd walk in since I knew you were expecting me," she said, holding a six pack of Stella Artois beer.

"Oh, hey, yeah that's no problem. Did you want anything to eat or drink or anything, or are you ready to go?" I asked.

"I'm good, I just had some spaghetti, but thanks. So, you know Jenn from hockey?" Blake asked.

I grabbed the truck keys from the kitchen island and through a stick of gum in my mouth before responding. "Yeah, she is one the girls who comes out and plays regularly with us. Her boyfriend Chad is a regular too, so I've been playing with both of them for a few years now. You'll like her, she's similar to you, and easy to get along with."

"Sweet, I'm excited to meet everyone. Thanks for inviting me, I just wish Colin could have come."

"Me too. I'm grabbing a small cooler for beer to put on their deck. Did you want to throw yours in too?" I asked Blake as I pointed to the six pack.

"That would be great! Thanks. I probably won't drink all of them, but it's always good to have extra in case someone needs one," Blake replied, handing me her beers.

Blake and I got into the truck and made our way down to Jenn and Chad's place. It was a quick drive, so we just casually chatted about our weekend plans before we arrived.

I parked three doors down as there were no spots right out front. As I pulled the keys from the ignition, I got a sudden wave of nervousness. Suddenly, I cared what people were going to think. Why wasn't Heather here? Why was I bringing some new chick to the party? Who is this new chick? Are we *sure* we're just friends? As my palms began to sweat thinking about the possible questions I'd be getting, Blake shouted at me to hurry up. I quickly put my keys in my pocket and made my way to the driveway.

Jenn and Chad lived in a split-level home, so as soon as you walk in, you immediately have to go up a flight of stairs. Blake and I both took off our shoes, and I lead the way upstairs. The apartment was an open concept with the living room, dining room and kitchen all combined. Some people were in the living room sitting and chatting, while others were in the kitchen mixing drinks, and playing drinking games in the dining room.

Blake and I made our way to the kitchen to start greeting people, and so I could introduce Blake. Everyone was happy to see me, and although I told them I would be bringing my neighbour named Blake, I think they were expecting a guy.

Blake seemed really comfortable, not shy at all, which, if it were me, I think I would be feeling quite shy meeting a group of people that I've never met. She actually offered to put our beers outside on the deck and grabbed one for the both of us.

After saying hello and introducing Blake to everyone in the kitchen and dining room, we made our way to the living room to chill and socialize. It was nice to see all my friends and catch up on everyday life. I could notice Blake listening intently, and I often found myself steering away from the room conversation and starting up my own one on one conversation just between Blake and me.

Blake sat on the end seat of a couch, and I sat on a dining room chair that was next to the couch she was on. There were times when it was hard to hear what she was saying because of the music blasting, so occasionally I would have to lean in closer to hear her. Eventually I had to get up and go to the kitchen to get another beer because every time I would lean in, I would get a whiff of her perfume and it would make my head spin. She smelled like a mix of the salty smell of the beach, but also that delicious smell of suntan lotion. *Why was I paying so much attention to Blake's perfume? It's not like I care what the other girls' perfume smells like.* That's when I decided to get up and grab another beer. I did not want to process my thoughts.

Blake also got up to use the washroom and asked me to grab her a beer. I went out on the deck and some of the guys were out there smoking cigarettes, so I made it quick, because I can't stand the smell of smoke. Before I could get back inside, one of my friends started asking me about Blake.

"So, what's the deal Alec? Where's Heather, and this is your neighbour?" Kyle asked curiously.

Great. I've been here for thirty minutes, and I'm already being questioned. I knew it would happen though. It would make anyone curious to see a guy show up without his girlfriend and bring a different girl. Can't blame Kyle for asking.

"There's no deal. Blake is my neighbour, she moved in at the end of August. We play hockey together sometimes, I'm sure you've seen her out on the ice," I replied nonchalantly.

"So, is she single? And where's Heather?" Kyle questioned.

"She's not single. She's dating a guy named Colin who's going to UVic to be a doctor. He's a cool guy, I like him. I invited him tonight, but he's working at the hospital. Heather and I are taking a break."

"Oh. Sorry dude. I didn't know that about you and Heather. That sucks. So, are you into Blake then?" Kyle asked, getting straight to the point.

"Not at all. Like I said, I invited Colin tonight too, just so happens he couldn't make it. No feelings on my end, she's just new to the area and getting involved with our hockey group, so figured I'd bring her out so she could meet more of the hockey people. Anyway, I'm going back in, I can't stand the smell of the smoke" I said, pulling the patio door open.

When I walked back in, Blake was standing around the kitchen island talking to a few people. I didn't really want to interrupt her and feel like I was smothering her, so I decided to open her beer, hand it to her and walk back into the living room to let her meet new people without the neighbour guy hovering over her all night.

We spent the night socializing with friends and playing drinking games. Kyle didn't seem to take the "No she isn't single" statement too seriously, as he was spending a lot of the night talking to her and asking to be her partner for beer pong. Blake was polite and friendly and entertained the idea of being his partner for one game then insisted she take a break and he play with someone else. She seemed to hold her own, and she seemed to be having a good time.

I did notice myself constantly looking over to see how she was doing throughout the evening, looking for any sign that she may be uncomfortable, but every time she would catch me looking, she would shoot me a quick smile. I don't know if it was the beers that I had consumed, or what, but I swear I could feel electricity jump through the room from Blake to myself when she would give me a grin.

The night passed in a blur, with more beers and more games, and finally around one in the morning we decided to head home. I was in no state to drive, and neither was Blake, so we decided to walk home. As we were saying our goodbyes to everyone, and put on our shoes and jackets, I looked outside to notice the snow falling quite heavily.

"You gonna be okay to walk home in this?" I asked, pointing out the window.

Blake looked in the direction I was pointing before responding, "Look I know I'm sweet like sugar, but I'm not gonna melt. Let's go."

The whole walk home I tried my best not to make eye contact with Blake. I couldn't let myself feel the electricity any more, otherwise I would start questioning my feelings for her. And I couldn't do that. Heather and I were in a sticky situation, but I love Heather, and I want things to workout with her. Plus, Blake has Colin, and she is happy, and she would never be interested in me anyway, so for the majority of the walk home, I just looked down at the road, which was beneficial to avoid snowflakes in my eyes.

The walk took longer than we both anticipated, especially considering some of the walk home was uphill. Blake thanked me for inviting her out, and she stated a few times how nice my friends were, and that she would love to hang out with everyone again.

"Looked like Kyle was really feeling you out hey?" I asked teasingly.

Blake chuckled before responding, "Yeah, he definitely is a little flirt. I think I did a good job making it clear I wasn't interested though…I'm not sure how many times I kept saying 'my boyfriend this, or my boyfriend that.' I've gotten pretty good at handling myself with men."

"Oh yeah?" I asked, prompting her to elaborate.

"Yeah… about a year before I started dating Colin, I had just ended an extremely toxic relationship with a guy named Grant. He wasn't healthy, and I'm definitely a stronger woman now that I'm out of that."

Again, I don't know if it was the beers I had consumed or what, but I was eager to know more about Blake. I wanted to know about her, and her life, and her past. We continued to walk home, and she opened up to me about how Grant was a bad guy and didn't treat her the way any woman should be treated. It was hard to listen to, and it hurt me to know that someone could hurt someone like Blake.

"I've never told anyone about my past with Grant. I don't even know why I just told you that. I must be drunk," Blake said, as she looked at me embarrassingly.

I looked back at her, and could see pain in her eyes, but also comfort. She was clearly hurt in her past, but felt comfortable sharing with me, and that made me feel warm, and it made me feel like I wanted to protect her, and make sure she didn't have to go through something like that again. The snowflakes were falling, and they must have been the size of quarters. It was truly like a scene out of a movie, and I couldn't help myself to feel like I wanted to kiss her. I wanted to stop her in her tracks, tell her she would be okay, and kiss her.

Blake broke our eye contact and continued walking. We were about a three minute walk from home, and I couldn't do it. I couldn't risk ruining our friendship, and I couldn't disrespect her relationship by kissing her.

We got to the ends of our driveways and Blake once again thanked me for taking her out and thanked me for letting her open up about her past. We both made our ways up our respectful driveways when all of a sudden, I heard a screech. I turned around to see Blake flat on her back.

"Are you okay!?" I asked, trying not to laugh.

"Yeah, I'm okay, just slipped on the ice. Ugh, that hurt my ass," Blake responded, laughing at herself.

I joined in on the laughter, and thought it was pretty great that she could laugh at her own self. I told her good night and opened my garage door to be greeted by Chip and Guinness. I pulled out my stool that sits along my kitchen island and began to try and process the night. Holy crap, I actually wanted to kiss Blake tonight. Holy crap, I actually looked into Blake's eyes, and could see more than just hazel iris' looking back at me. Holy crap,

I found myself admiring the way Blake looked, she was beautiful.

I decided right then and there, sitting at the kitchen island, that I would make a promise to myself, to never explore these feelings again. I made a promise to myself to never look at Blake as anything more than a platonic friend. I made a promise to myself that Blake is my friend, and only ever will be my friend. I decided that the feelings from this evening was simply intoxication, and nothing more, and I made a promise that I would never, ever, have those feelings again. Ever.

Blake Taylor

I have to admit, last night was a lot of fun. It was so nice to meet a new group of people, and to have fun and not worry about school. All of Alec's friends were super nice, and it'll be great to be able to socialize with even more people at Friday night hockey. I had no idea that a lot of the people who were at the party last night were mostly hockey people.

I had texted Colin once or twice when I would use the washroom at the party just to check in, but he was super busy with practicum so he couldn't even respond right away. He laughed when I told him that I slipped walking up my driveway and didn't seem to mind that I had walked home with Alec. I think he was just glad that I got home safely. Colin seems to like Alec, he has never said anything to make me believe otherwise, and sometimes, I almost want Colin to be a bit jealous or make a comment like 'wow you spend a lot of time with Alec,' but he never does. It's like he doesn't have a jealous bone in his body.

I'm looking forward to seeing him today, but I'm currently laying on the couch nursing a hangover. Thankfully, it's not a brutal hangover, it's more of the tired kind rather than the sick kind. Colin finished his shift at six a.m. this morning, and I was only able to sleep until eight-thirty. It's weird because sometimes when I drink, I can't sleep in the next day even though my body needs it. Colin said he would text me when he was up so I could go over and spend the afternoon with him.

I decided that I needed a carb loaded breakfast so after downing a large glass of water, and brewing up a coffee, I decided to whip up some pancakes. Sort of over the top for only one person, but it's definitely needed this morning.

Merc was lying next to my kitchen island patiently awaiting any bit of scrap that may fall to the floor. He's my own personal kitchen crumb picker upper. I decided to eat at the kitchen island and turn on the TV and watch some recorded Christmas baking shows. It's one of my guilty pleasures to watch when I need to pass time and there isn't anything else on. I'm always amazed at how these bakers can make such masterpieces out of cookies and cake.

As I'm getting ready to see which baking team will be eliminated, I get a text from Colin that says he didn't sleep well and I'm welcome to come by anytime after noon.

I check the clock and it reads nine-forty-five a.m. I text back and say that I'll be there around twelve-thirty, that I'm going to take Merc for a walk and then work on some things for school then come by.

The rest of the morning passes by quite quickly, so it doesn't leave me much time to shower and get ready before leaving for Colins. Thankfully, he likes the au natural look, so it doesn't take me long.

When I get to Colin's, his mom was in the kitchen busy making lunch.

"Hi Sandra, smells good in here!" I say as I enter their home.

"Oh, hey Blake. Thanks, I'm just making a quick sandwich for lunch, but I have a spaghetti sauce going for dinner tonight, so that must be what you smell."

"Mmmm, yeah it smells great!" I replied.

"Colin mentioned you'd be here for supper so hopefully it tastes as good as it smells! He's downstairs, I think he was just getting in the shower a few minutes ago," Sandra said as she motioned toward the basement stairs.

"Great, I might just make Colin and I a coffee if that's okay, did you want one?" I asked politely.

"No that's okay I just had one," Sandra responded.

As I got the coffee pods for the Keurig, Sandra and I casually chatted about our weekend and what we had planned for the upcoming week. Sandra was so kind, friendly, and warm. She was always so welcoming to me and seemed as though she thoroughly enjoyed my company. I always felt very comfortable in Colin's home and both of his parents always took the time to have conversations with me or go out of their way to ensure I was comfortable and welcome.

As I was adding milk to the coffee's, Colin had entered the kitchen and made his way toward me. He gave me a quick peck on the cheek as he said hello.

"Hey! You must be so tired after working all night. I just finished up a coffee for you," I said as I handed him his freshly brewed java.

"Perfect, thanks. Yeah, I'm definitely feeling sluggish, especially since I didn't sleep as long as I was hoping, but it is what it is. I'll just take it easy today. Smells good mom," Colin said, motioning to the pot of sauce on the stove.

We made our way down to Colin's room to be able to relax and watch a bit of a movie. We spent the afternoon being lazy and chatting about school and practicum.

While laying on the bed with my head against Colin's chest as we watch some murder documentary on Netflix, I started thinking about it being hard because I absolutely love being around Colin. I love talking to him and seeing how his brain works and how he processes information, and his outlook on life. I love his ambition and his drive. I love his personality, and how we can be doing nothing and still seem to have a good time. But the reason I say that it is hard is because I feel like we have hit a plateau. We don't really talk about our future as a couple, it's more about our individual careers. Sometimes I feel like I'm into this relationship way more than he is, but then I tell myself to get out of my own head, because he wouldn't be with me, and be struggling to balance so many things if he didn't want to be with me. And I know that we just had that talk, and it was great to receive the reassurance that he does want to be with me, but it's still hard when it feels like our relationship isn't progressing.

I decided to snap out of it and enjoy the rest of the day, because who knows with Colin's hectic schedule when we would get to hang out again. As we were getting ready to make our way upstairs Colin caught me off guard with a quick question.

"I totally forgot to ask, but how was the party last night?"

"Oh my gosh yeah, I forgot too! It was good, as I mentioned to you, we ended up walking home and it was snowing like crazy. But the party was good, everyone was super nice. A lot of people were asking how I knew Alec and if I was single and stuff. Definitely sucked not having you there. I feel like I'm talking about an imaginary boyfriend sometimes. But yeah, everyone was cool, and a lot of them play on the Friday night ice time, so I'll be able to see them a lot more. Hopefully, you'll get to meet everyone soon.

"There was one guy who was flirting with me a lot, his name was Kyle, and I kept having to say stuff like 'Oh, my boyfriend is in med school,' 'Oh yeah, my boyfriend loves that beer,' or whatever to make it clear that I wasn't interested, but I think he's just a flirty kinda guy."

"Hah, yeah, some guys just like to flirt, or like the idea of someone unavailable. But yeah, wish I could have been there. I'm glad you had a good time. Did Heather go too?" Colin asked.

"What? I thought I told you that they broke up the other day. Maybe I forgot, but no she didn't go, so that was another topic of discussion. Poor Alec was getting grilled by all his friends asking where she was. I think a lot of them found it weird that he showed up with me instead. But whatever, we made it clear that we are just friends and I have you, so," I trailed off.

"Yeah, exactly. Okay let's go eat," Colin said as he opened up the bedroom door for me to walk out.

Dinner was great and Sandra is such a good cook. It was nice to spend the evening with Colin's family and play board games after. I didn't stay too late as Colin was tired, and I had an early morning with school the next day. Colin walked me to the door and gave me sweet, but quick goodbye kiss.

As I walked to my car, I was remembering Colin's face when I told him that people were grilling Alec about not bringing Heather and us showing up together. It was actually one of the first times he looked a bit jealous or uncomfortable. Which is fair enough, I know if the situation was reversed, no matter how platonic the relationship, I wouldn't want Colin showing up to a party with his newly single female friend. Not that I don't trust him, but you never know what the other person is thinking or feeling. But I know Alec, and I know he doesn't think of me as anything more than a best friend. He's always been super respectful, and he's never even said a single flirty thing. He's just a really good friend. I think it would be weird if he said something inappropriate, so I'm glad we can just be friends. It helps that Colin and Alec like each other too. I just don't ever want to do anything to disrespect my relationship or make Colin feel uncomfortable, so hopefully if Colin does have an issue, he would voice it.

I drove home and fed Merc a late supper before winding down for the evening. I still had my Christmas baking show paused from earlier, so I finished that episode, did some light reading, and then went to bed.

Alec Kohl

It's been about a week since Jenn and Chad's party, and I felt a bit awkward with Blake. She wasn't awkward, it was just my own self, trying to process the way I felt the other night, and then continuously reminding myself to forget those feelings, as it wasn't worth jeopardizing our friendship. And, to make things even more confusing, Heather decided we needed to have a talk and so she's actually on her way over.

I just finished having a shower and getting myself ready for the day, when I started to make a couple of coffees, there was a knock at the door. I put the coffee creamer on the kitchen island as I made my way to answer the door.

"Hey, you could have just walked in," I said to Heather as I opened the door.

"Yeah, I wasn't sure what to do so I figured I should knock."

"I was just making some coffee; did you want one?"

"Actually yes, that would be good, thank you" Heather said while placing her purse down on the couch and greeting Chip and Guinness.

As I made Heather's coffee it allowed me a few minutes to collect my thoughts before diving into whatever she was here to talk about. I'm sure I could guess because we've been through this whole break up then get back together cycle before, but as I stood in the kitchen and watched her greet the dogs, I guess I didn't realize how much I had missed her until I came face to face with her.

I walked over to the living room and placed our coffees on the coffee table and grabbed a seat on the couch opposite Heather.

"Thanks for the coffee, how have you been?" Heather asked.

"No worries. I've been good, the same, nothing really changes, just working. You?"

"Yeah same. I miss you though. That's sort of why I'm here. I want to start fresh. Start over. Lay everything out, see what you need and want from this relationship and vice versa, and see if it's something we can both agree to and try to make this work. If you want. I mean, I know initially you said you wanted to have some space to see if we would actually miss each other and see where we are at in a month, but I don't want to wait that long. I do miss you, and I do want to be with you," Heather trailed off, waiting for my response.

I wasn't surprised because I figured she was here to talk about getting back together, but I didn't expect her to just jump right into it. I took a sip of coffee before responding.

"I miss you too. I didn't really realize how much I missed you until now. But I do think we need to figure out what needs to change in order to make it work, because I can't keep breaking up and getting back together all the time."

"I agree, okay well what's important to you? What do you need to change for this relationship to work?" heather asked genuinely.

"Well, I think we need to have time set aside for us to be able to connect. One of my biggest issues is that it felt like we were more like roommates rather than a couple. We got into such a routine of work and then separate lives outside of work, so I think it's important to have a date night maybe like once a week, and I think it's important to start fresh with each other's friends. I need to be more open minded about your friends and you need to be more open minded with mine. We both take our friendships seriously, and I think it's great that we can have friendships outside of our relationship to allow for that space, but I also want to be able to do things as a couple with other people. What do you think?" I asked.

Heather sat listening intently as if she was really trying to absorb everything I was saying. She took a moment before responding.

"I actually completely agree. It's important for me to have time to do my own hobbies, to see my own friends, and to have my me-time, but I realized that I was putting those things above my relationship with you, and I think that's where a lot of our problems stemmed from. I think we should try and link up our work schedules a bit, so we always have a few days off a week together, and then always designate one night to date night. And I will try to make a better effort with your friends…I know I can be a bit of a bitch, but sometimes I just don't like people, I can't help it!" Heather said with a little laugh.

"I think as long as we try and stay open and honest with communication and express when something is bothering us right away instead of letting it bottle up and be passive aggressive toward each other it'll help a lot."

"I think so too. So, can I kiss you now?" Heather said as she made her way over to my couch.

Before I could respond Heather was already making herself comfortable on the couch next to me, with her lips pressed against mine.

We decided to plan something fun and special for the day to celebrate our relationship, so we finished our coffees and packed the dogs in the truck and drove about thirty minutes out of town where they have great snowshoeing trails and took the dogs out for a day hike. It was great because we were able to exercise and spend time in the fresh air, hold hands and chat and the dogs loved trekking through the snow.

We decided to stop at the grocery store on the way home and pick up some items to cook a nice dinner together. We enjoyed some wine and a movie, and even

I'm surprised to say it, but truly enjoyed each other's company.

Waking up next to Heather was nice, familiar, but different at the same time. This is the first time where we decided to get back together and actually talk about what we wanted to see change and what we were both committed to doing in order to make it work. It felt different this time, like we were truly starting fresh.

Blake Taylor: Spring 2015

I swear, the later I go to bed at night, the louder my alarm seems to sound the next morning. Last night I was up late trying to finish a paper for my ethics class, and the pure dullness of the subject matter made concentrating nearly impossible. By the time I closed my laptop it was a little after one in the morning. Thankfully, today is Friday and I have a slow day today, but school has been kicking my ass lately, so being asked by Alec to join him and Heather for some wings tonight, was very much needed. Alec mentioned that hockey was cancelled tonight because the rink manager accidentally double booked us with another group, so suggested wings instead and told me to invite Colin, and surprisingly, Colin was supposed to be off at noon today, so he would be able to come with us.

Today I have an eight-hour clinical shift and then I have a group project I need to work on with a couple girls from school and then I'll be able to relax. Clinical is going well. I'm a hands-on learner, so I do my best to volunteer for every task, ask questions if I'm confused, and treat my patients with respect and empathy. I always get good review from my clinical instructors, and one instructor even said I should consider medical school.

My goodness, I already feel swamped in nursing school, I couldn't even imagine medical school.

Thoughts of medical school made me think of Colin, so I texted him back after he said he could come for wings, to let him know that he could pick me up at my place at seven p.m. and that I was excited to see him.

The taste of weekend freedom was so close, that it made for a dragging type of day. By the time clinical was done, I just wanted to go home, but I had to meet with some classmates in the hospital library for a few hours to work on our power point presentation about psychotherapy on mentally ill patients.

After about two hours of gossip mixed with work, we called it quits and I made m way home. It was five p.m. which meant it was a long day for Merc to be left alone at home. I hate days like that, I always feel bad for him.

As soon as I got home, I was welcomed by major licks and dog tail wags. I quickly set down my bags and grabbed a leash and brought Merc outside. We stepped out the back gate and made our way to Beacon Hill Park for a good walk. Merc is really great off leash, so I let him free and called him over as needed if he got too close to other people walking.

We made our way to the dog park where Merc ran wild socializing with other dogs, and chasing after a ball, while I sat on a bench watching him live his best life. I sat on the bench thinking to myself, I remember Alec telling me something to the effect of, that a dogs' life is so incredibly short, and how you choose to fill their days can be life changing for them. There will be days that you don't want to talk them for a walk because you're just too tired, but you have to think about them, and when they're gone, you don't want to have regrets. They're a man's best friend for a reason. They are there for you 100% of the time, the least you can do is walk them. After about forty-five minutes we made our way back home.

I changed out of my scrubs and put on a bit of makeup when suddenly my apartment door opened. I checked my phone. It said six-thirty, and I hadn't received a text from Colin saying he was on his way, so I was surprised to see him walking toward me.

"Hey! You surprised me, I wasn't expecting you to be early!" I said, greeting Colin.

"Yeah, I wasn't up to much and figured if you were ready, we could head over there and sneak in a beer before Heather and Alec showed up," Colin replied.

"Sounds good, let me brush my teeth then I'll be ready."

Colin sat on the couch scratching Merc behind the ears as he waited for me. I brushed my teeth and grabbed my wallet from my backpack before kissing Merc goodbye.

Colin drove us over to the pub and we got a table in the corner next to the pool table. We both ordered a beer, and I texted Alec to let him know we were here and where we were sitting.

Alec and Heather ended up arriving late, which was typical anytime Heather was with Alec.

"Hey guys. Hi Heather, you look cute," I said with a smile.

"Hey" said Alec.

"Thanks" said Heather.

"Sorry if you guys were waiting long, we had to grab gas quickly," said Alec, looking apologetic.

Weird I thought. Sounded like an excuse because we literally live like a three-minute drive to the pub, so unless he was running on fumes, I thought it was odd. Based on Heather's short answer and body language, it looks to me like they just finished up a decent argument.

"How's school going Colin? Blake says you've been pretty busy at the hospital?" Alec asked Colin.

The guys engaged in small chat while I listened, and Heather sat on her phone. Occasionally I would try to ask Heather things, but she didn't seem that interested. So, I gave up on that and I decided to just chat with the guys.

We had a great time laughing and chatting sports and talking about work and school. I was surprised with how well Alec and Colin got along and that made my heart happy. They were both easy going, so there was never room for silence because someone always had something to say.

At about ten p.m. we all decided to call it a night. We said our goodbyes in the parking lot and Colin drove me back to my place. Alec was following behind but got stuck behind a red light, so we didn't end up all arriving at our driveways at the same time.

Colin decided to spend the night as it was getting late but told me he would have to be up early as he didn't pack a bag and had to be at the hospital in the morning. A while back I had bought Colin a toothbrush for impromptu sleepovers, and tonight it had come in handy. While Colin greeted Merc and changed into a pair of sweatpants he would leave at my place, I quickly made him a lunch for the following day so he wouldn't have to rush and make one in the morning.

We turned the TV on in bed as we settled in for the night.

"Tonight, was fun, Heather didn't seem too talkative, but I had a great time," I said as I pulled the sheets back from the bed and got in.

"Yeah, Alec is a nice guy, I didn't realize how intense his job could be, it was neat learning about that," Colin replied.

"Yeah, sometimes I don't even want to know the shit he deals with, I feel like it would be scary. Anyway, it's nice being able to hang out in a group. Sometimes it's hard balancing all our different friend groups with how busy we both are, so I appreciate you spending your time off with me and my friends. Next time we can do something with your friends," I said cuddling in closer to Colin.

"Yeah, that sounds good."

We didn't watch TV for long as Colin had to be up early. I was tired from a long day, so I had no complaints turning it off and going to sleep.

Blake Taylor: Late Summer, 2015

A few months passed with not a whole heck of a lot changing. I was still busy with school and my part time job. Colin was still busy with his hospital work and school. Alec and I truly developed such an amazing platonic friendship, that I considered him my best friend. We still played hockey together on Friday nights, and I always invited him out with my friends, and vice versa. It seemed as though he and Heather were doing okay, he never really mentioned if their relationship was struggling or not. Colin and I were good. Sort of the same as before. We were in such a routine of school and work that any free time was sacred and had to be planned out to ensure we were giving our relationship the love it needed.

Rib Fest was coming up downtown and Colin and a bunch of our friends were going. He told me to invite Alec and Heather, so I did. I'm sure it'll be fun. Colin told me that he would be late because of the hospital but that he would meet us all there. I'm not much of a rib person, I actually hate ribs, but I love the beer and atmosphere, so I was still looking forward to it.

Alec Kohl

Last night was a long shift and I only got home at three a.m. so sleeping in until noon was very much needed. I woke up to a text from both Heather and Blake. I opened Heather's first, which read that she was going out for lunch with a few girlfriends and would be back in a bit. The text from Blake was her asking if I could still make it to rib fest later today. I looked outside and it was pouring rain, so I asked her if it was still happening. She let me know that her and her friends were going to skip the whole outdoor part and actually just meet at a pub across the street and have appies and drinks. She said that Colin would be late, but everyone was meeting around six p.m. I told her Heather couldn't come because she had to work (which she actually did), and Blake asked if she could get a ride with me, I told her no problem and to meet me at my truck at five-thirty p.m. and we could drive over.

After laying in bed for close to an hour answering e-mails on my phone and exchanging texts with Blake and a few of my guy friends, I decided it was time to get up. I made my way downstairs and let the dogs out the back door as I made myself a coffee.

I turned on Sports Center as I slowly began my day. After watching the Calgary Flames highlights, I turned off the TV and took a shower. I decided to take the dogs for a walk and have a chill afternoon before a busier evening.

Heather arrived home while I was still walking the dogs, and when I get home from my walk, I could hear the water running, so she must have been in the shower. I made my way upstairs to greet her. The door was locked so I knocked and said it was me.

"Hey! Just a sec, I'm almost done, then I'll let you in," Heather shouted over the shower water.

A few minutes later Heather opened the door, and a rush of warm air and steam smacked me in the face.

"I just wanted to say hey and ask you how your lunch went," I said.

Heather slipped on her robe before answering, "Oh it was good. Brooke and I went to that new brunch place downtown, it was so good. Her and Jason broke up, but got back together like forty hours later, he was being such an ass to her, so I'm actually annoyed that they got back together, it's like okay break up or stay together, and then I laughed at myself cause hello, look at us."

I stood there not really knowing what to say. Heather and Brooke love to chit chat and gossip and I always never know what to say cause I'm not into that stuff. I decided on, "Oh yeah, well as long as they're happy I guess that's all that matters."

"I guess so Heather said. So yeah, anyway, I'm getting ready for work, and then what are you up to tonight?" Heather asked.

"Tonight, is that rib fest thing remember? Blake and Colin had invited the both of us."

"Oh. Right. Well, that should be fun. Is Colin going?" Heather asked.

"Yeah, I guess he's working at the hospital a bit late, so he will be meeting us there, so Blake actually asked if I could drive her, I didn't think it would be a big deal, so I said sure. She's gonna meet me at my truck at five-thirty." I responded.

"Right. Cause heaven for bid she drive herself anywhere," Heather said, rolling her eyes.

"If you're not comfortable with it, I could tell her to drive herself or whatever, I just figured it was fine cause we drive to hockey together," I said.

"Yeah, whatever it's fine. If I tell you to tell her that, then she will think I'm a bitch, so whatever."

I get it. I do. I'm sure it's hard for Heather because no one would like their significant other spending so much alone time with someone of the opposite sex, but I guess because I know how I feel about Blake it just seems so minimal. For me, it feels no different than if I were to drive with a guy or something, there's just seriously nothing there for me other than friendship. But I get it from Heathers side too because Blake is a girl and everything. I just wish Heather could be inside my head so she could realise there really is nothing there.

163

"Okay well if you ever change your mind just let me know, but for real Heather, you have nothing to worry about. Blake is like family. You never have to worry about me with anyone for that matter," I said as I hugged Heather from behind.

Heather finished getting ready and then made herself a lunch to bring to work. I wished her a safe and good shift and kissed her on her way out. I told her I would text her when I was home from rib fest.

I just finished feeding the dogs an early supper as Blake texted me saying she was outside my truck and to hurry up because it was raining. I locked up and met her at the driveway.

"Hey, thanks for driving," Blake said as she waited pressed up against the garage trying to stay sheltered by the roof from the rain.

"No problem."

We drove and chatted about hockey and what not, but I was a bit distracted with feelings of guilt knowing Heather was upset by me driving Blake. I tried to ignore it and be present.

We got to Common Grounds, the pub across the street from where rib fest was happening and the rain had actually slowed down, so we met a few of Blake's friends out on the patio.

There were a few empty chairs down at the end of the table and we grabbed two that were next to each other.

"Hey Blakey! Hey Alec! Nice to see you guys. Is Colin not coming? I thought James said he was coming?" Asked Abby.

I like Abby. I've met her a few times every time Blake would invite me out to something, Abby and James would always be there. I don't know if it's their Australian accents, or what, but they've always been so welcoming and treat me like I've been friends with them for years.

"Ya, ya, he's coming. He was working until six p.m. at the hospital, so he said he would meet us here. He wanted to run home and shower quick, then pop over, so I'm assuming he'll be here around seven. He texted me as we were pulling up letting me know he was just finishing up," Blake replied, picking up the menu.

I was sitting across from James and asked, "So did you guys do all the food trucks and try ribs from each one, or did you skip out cause the rain?"

"Nah, we hit a couple. Couldn't let a little rain get in the way of some good ribs!" James said with a laugh. "They were really good actually, you guys missed out."

A waitress came by and asked for our order. Blake and I both ordered a beer. I ordered a cheeseburger and Blake didn't get anything saying she ate before she came.

We all socialized and ate, and it wasn't long before Colin had arrived. He greeted everyone at the table and grabbed a seat across form Blake after greeting her with a quick kiss. I've never really seen them kiss before, they're not a huge PDA type of couple. It was sort of weird to see, like when you see a teacher outside of school or something, and you forget that they have their own personal life.

James and I spoke off an on, and I tried to keep up with the general conversation of the table, but there were so many different conversations happening at once, that I found myself speaking with Blake for the majority of the evening.

I would try to include Colin in our conversations because I never wanted him to feel threatened by me, but Blake told me once that he doesn't seem to have a jealous bone in his body, and I feel like she was right. Colin didn't seem remotely bothered by me monopolizing Blake's attention, but like I said, I really did try to include him as much as I could, so maybe he could notice that and, and that was enough for him.

The night was fun, but I was tired after working all night so I told Blake that I was going to head out and made sure that she would be able to get home okay with Colin. She said of course and I made my way to my truck.

I sent a quick text to Heather before leaving letting her know that I was tired and on my way home. I told her to work safe and that I would see her when she got off work.

When I got home Guinness and Chip jumped up to kiss me right on my face and I let them outside to do their business. I grabbed a Coke from the fridge and turned on the Xbox to play a couple rounds.

Blake Taylor

Summer was coming to an end, which meant the sun was setting a little bit earlier every night, and the breeze started to cool in the evenings.

Although today was Saturday, I still had a busy day ahead. I was working the morning shift at Urban Garage, and then I told Audi I would meet her for coffee after my shift at two.

The morning was going by quickly so far, as most people like to do their shopping on Saturday's, so we had a lot of customers to keep us busy, and because I was working with Abby. I love working with Abby because we can just chat and catch up our whole entire shift and the time flies.

"So, how are things with Colin? I hadn't seen him in a while because he is always so busy, and James mentioned to me that he spoke with Colin at the rib fest thing and said that he was so busy with school and the hospital that he didn't even know how he had time for friends," Abby asked as she re-arranged throw blankets on a living room display.

"Well yeah, that basically sums it up. He's so busy, and I always feel bad for him because he barely has time to do anything. Sometimes I feel guilty for when he has an afternoon or evening free, when he decides to spend it with me, because I know it must be hard for him to balance his own friends, or seeing his family, or even doing any of his own hobbies. Like, I don't even know the last time he rock climbed. But he did say to me the other day that he was planning a day trip with his dad to go climbing so that made me happy for him. But yeah, it's just busy," I replied.

"Oh Blakey, I can't even imagine. But at least you're so understanding and supportive and I'm sure Colin appreciates that," Abby said with a smile.

"Thanks Abbs. Anyway, how are you and James? What are you guys up to this weekend?"

"Oh, not much. I'm here until five today, so I think I'll stop at the store on my way home to pick up some groceries and a wine to cook a nice dinner for James and me. Have a little date night in. He's also been quite busy at work and working six days a week, so I'm sure he will be tired by the time he gets off this evening," Abby said.

"Wow that is busy. Well, I'm sure you guys will have a great time, and give him a big hug and tell him hello for me! I'm just going to grab my bag and keys then I'll be outta here. I'm meeting Audi for coffee," I said, making my way to the back employee room.

"Oh fun! Okay well tell Audi I say hi, I miss her!" Abby said enthusiastically.

"I will!"

I kept my car parked in the employee parking of Urban Garage and walked the three blocks to Discovery Coffee in the heart of downtown. Audi had texted to say that she had a small little table on the outside patio. I had never been here before, but it was so cute, with the bright yellow/lime outdoor seating.

"Hey!" I said to Audi as I approached her with a warm hug. "What do you want? I'm going to run in and order quick!" I asked.

"Oh, I just ordered, someone will bring it out in a few minutes. I'll wait here though while you go in and order," Audi replied.

The cafe interior had a very modern aesthetic. The shop had small white mosaic tile flooring, with a big round counter to order your coffee at, and the entire perimeter of the shop was bordered by black seating. It was really sharp.

I ordered a Mocha and pointed to the table I was sitting at, and the barista said she would bring it out right away.

I sat down across from Audi and placed my phone in my pocket to allow for no distractions. That's one of my pet peeves. I hate meeting with someone and the other person being on the phone. Drives me nuts. So, I always make it a point to put my phone away any time I'm with someone, so they can have my full attention.

"Okay so what's new," I asked Audi as I took a sip of ice water that was already at the table.

"Ummm I actually have some exciting news to tell you, I've been dying to tell you!" Audi said excitedly as the barista brought over our coffees.

"Okay well what! It's killing me!"

"I got in! I got into the Art School! Oh my gosh I'm so excited! Normally applicants fund out in the Spring, and they contacted me a few weeks ago, I went to Vancouver for three days and did a bunch of interviews and what not, and then never heard back. But then two days ago I got a call from them, and they said that I had been accepted but for the January semester," Audi said taking a huge gulp of her Americano.

"What! That's amazing! Congratulations! I'm so happy for you! So now what?"

"Well, I asked work for any and all extra hours, because now I'm wanting to save as much money as I can. I cancelled my two-night classes at UVic that were supposed to start next week because obviously I don't need those any more, and so yeah, I'm just working as much as I can, and I'm casually starting to look at apartments in Vancouver," Audi replied.

"Wow, this is so exciting. So, when does the semester officially start? When do you hope to move? Did you tell Trevor yet?" I asked curiously.

"Yeah, so it starts the first Monday of January, I think it's the 4th, and so I'm thinking of moving in December, that way I'm settled and comfortable and plus I want to get a part time job while I'm in school, so that will give me a month to settle in to a new place, find a part time job and prepare for school."

"Yeah, that's a great idea. I mean obviously it sucks that you're moving, but I know it's your dream, and it's only a boat ride away. Did you tell Trevor?" I asked again.

"Yeah, I told him. He said he's happy for me, but he's obviously bummed about the move too. He can't exactly quit his job, so I'm not sure. I think we might try long distance. I don't even know, I'm trying not to think that far ahead and just enjoy the excitement," Audi said smiling.

"Yeah, that makes sense. Well, I'm so happy for you, and if you need anything before you move let me know!" I exclaimed.

We stayed for about an hour just catching up and talking about work, and school, and Audi's exciting new adventure before heading out. Audi got a ride to the city with a friend earlier in the day, so I offered to drive her home.

When I got home, I got a text from mom inviting me to dinner. I told her I would take Merc for a walk then I would come up.

The evening was already starting to cool down, it was only four-thirty, and I needed a sweater or light jacket to take Merc out. He was so happy to be outside running and chasing his ball that I don't even think he noticed the small chill to the air.

I took Merc with me to mom and dad's seeing as I hadn't seen him all day.

We all sat around the table congratulating Audi on her acceptance and made small talk when mom had brought up Thanksgiving.

"Okay, so I'm just trying to figure out what to cook, and if I should get two Turkeys or not. Blake, have you invited Abby and James again this year? Can Colin make it? Audi, will Trevor be coming? Dad and I are also inviting Rebecca and Paul, so there will be a big enough group of us. Also, Blake, you should invite Alec and his girlfriend. We all like Alec and should probably try to get to know his girlfriend better," Mom said rather quickly.

"Yeah, Trevor's coming. What time again?"

"Well, I was going to serve little finger foods and stuff before hand, so why don't we say three?" Mom answered.

"But yeah, I did invite Abby and James, they said they were going to come. Colin will be coming too, which is nice that he has the day off. He actually has the Monday off too, so we are going to have Thanksgiving again with his family on Monday as well. And sure, I'll mention it to Alec," I responded.

"Great! Just let me know, so that I can plan out the dinner and all the sides and what not. Anyway Audi, what are you most excited about with going to Art school?" Mom asked.

The rest of the evening was spent laughing and talking and supporting Audi on her new journey. I didn't stay too late as I had an early morning walk/jog planned with Abby, so I decided to head home shortly after dinner.

Alec Kohl: Fall 2015

"Heather," I shouted up the stairs. "So, Blake invited you and I to her mom and dad's place for Thanksgiving dinner. I told her we would go since neither of us had plans, that okay?" I asked yelling up the stairs.

Heather walked to the top of the stairs before responding, "I'm trying to get ready for work, could you not yell at me and just come up here if you need to talk to me, I couldn't even hear a word you said."

I repeated myself as I walked up the stairs to follow her into the master bathroom.

"Ummm, I'm not going," Heather said with a bitter tone.

"What do you mean you're not going? We don't have other plans, do we?" I asked genuinely curious.

"No, but I don't even know Blake's parents and I think it's weird. Like our neighbours who my boyfriend is all of a sudden best friend with wants to have us over? I don't get it. I'm pretty sure she's in love with you because why else does she want to hang out all the time, and like, why do her parents want us over. It's weird. I'm not going. You can go, and you can tell them I'm going to my parents for Thanksgiving."

My knee jerk reaction is to be stubborn when someone pisses me off, so that's what happened. "Okay, I'll let them know," I said, and then walked back down the stairs before Heather could reply.

First of all, I thought to myself, I've always been friends with my neighbours because I think it's important to have a good relationship with the people who live near you. Second, Blake and I are just friends, so for Heather to insinuate there was anything more pissed me off. Third, I really liked Dean and Kara. I always take time to chat with them outside if we're all out at the same time and they're just super nice and welcoming. It's hard living in a whole different province from my family, and in a way, Dean and Kara and their family feel like family to me, so of course I want to spend Thanksgiving with them. I was honoured that they invited us so I wouldn't miss it. If Heather doesn't want to come, I'm not gonna force her, it's just annoying. Plus, it's not like it's just going to be me and Blake's family. Blake told me that some family friends as well as Abby and James are going too, so it sounds like it's more of a big dinner party. Maybe I should have made that clearer and then maybe Heather would have been more okay with it. I'll try again.

I walked back upstairs and said, "Just so you know, Kara is inviting some of her family friends, Abby and James are going, Audi's boyfriend will be there, and Colin is going too. They're just being polite and nice and inviting us too. Are you sure you don't want to come?"

"Yeah, I'm sure, I actually texted Brooke while you were downstairs and asked what she was doing for Thanksgiving. She said that she and Jason broke up *again*, so she invited me over for a 'Friendsgiving' so I'm just going to go there. Thanks though," Heather said as she put on her RCMP vest. She quickly fixed her bun that got tasselled as she put the vest over her head then made her way out of the bedroom.

"Okay well if you change your mind, you can always join me," I said as we both walked down the stairs.

Heather grabbed a few things from the fridge, gave me a quick kiss and then left for work.

The next couple of days flew by because my boss was on holidays, so I had to step into his role, and I was swamped with paperwork and basically babysitting the other members. It was exhausting. Poor Chip didn't even get that much action at work because the majority of my shifts were spent in the office working on files. I still took time to do some training and even got outside twice a day to play fetch so he could burn off some of his energy, but it's not the same.

I was relieved to wake up on Thanksgiving morning and not have to work, and to also enjoy a nice meal this evening.

Heather didn't come around on the offer and was adamant on spending Thanksgiving with Brooke, so I didn't push it. I spent the morning relaxing and sat outside in the crisp morning air to drink my coffee on the back deck and Guinness and Chip had an old ball that they kept dropping at my feet to throw.

Dean had stepped out on to his back deck to have a quick smoke, so I stood up and said hey to him over the fence. We can actually see into each others' back yards when we're on our own decks, so it makes conversation really easy.

"Hey what's up Alec, how's it going? Are you and the lady coming over today?" Dean asked.

"Hey, uh, actually it'll just be me. Heather is having Thanksgiving at her parents' place. Is there anything I can bring?" I asked.

"Oh God no, Kara's got everything in there. It's not even noon yet and the kitchen is already a mess. Smells delicious though. Anyway, I should wash up and see if she needs any help. See you in a bit!" Dean said as he went back in the house.

I continued to throw the ball for the boys until I finished my coffee. I made my way back inside and took a shower and got ready for the day. I decided to run out to the store quickly and pick up some wine and a big pie to bring over for dinner tonight. I asked Heather to join me in case there was anything she needed to bring to Brooke's, but she said she would just stop on her way.

I gave her a kiss because I assumed she wouldn't be home by the time I got back from the store and told her to have fun.

She said thanks, but didn't say 'you too,' so I guess she didn't want me to have fun.

Blake Taylor

People were coming over left right and center and I felt like I could barely keep up with all the new faces coming in. But let me back up a smidge.

I decided to come over a bit early to help mom with any meal preparations and any last-minute cleaning. I brought Merc with me and put him out back so he could run around and play with my parents' dog. I had to bring up my bar stools to accommodate the extra seating that was needed. I set the table, and quickly wrote up little name tags to place everyone. I know it seems a bit formal, but it just makes it easier instead of everyone scrambling right at the meal hour trying to be polite and not wanting to sit in the 'wrong' spot.

I just finished placing the cutlery on the table when there was a quick knock at the door, and then Trevor walked in. I came over and greeted Trevor with a hug and told him that Audi was up in her room still getting ready. He had a large cooler on wheels dragging behind him.

"Oh okay, thanks, I think I'll put this cooler out on the back deck and then run up and say hi," Trevor said before making his way to the patio.

"Did you guys want anything over there?" I asked Dad and Brenna as they sat in the living room watching football.

"That's okay Blake, I just grabbed a soda," said Brenna.

"Actually, can you just bring me a few of those crackers and cheese that mom has over on the island?" Dad asked all the while not removing his eyes from the TV screen.

As I was preparing dad's snack, my mom asked me to move the whole platter over to the coffee table. As I was carrying the platter over to the living room, there was another knock at the door. I set up the platter and then answered the door and was happy to see Abby and James.

"Hi there Blakey! Well don't you look pretty," Abby said excitedly as she came in for hug.

"Thanks love, right back at you! Hi James, how are you," I said as I hugged James and then welcomed them both inside.

Abby and James both came inside and made their way into the living room to greet my dad and sister. Abby had a bouquet of flowers in her hand, so she walked over to my mom to hand them to her and give her a hug as well. I followed her into the kitchen while James stayed to chat with dad.

"Hi Kara, so lovely to see you, thank you again for having us. It smells so good I'm practically drooling," Abby said with a laugh.

"Oh wow, these are beautiful, you really didn't have to bring flowers Abby, thank you," Mom replied as she looked for a vase to put them in. "Can I get you anything to drink? I have red or white wine, beer, water, soda, or, no I think that's it."

"Ummm, I'll have a glass of white, I can get it though, is it just in the fridge? I might grab James a beer too. Thank you. Blakey, do you want anything?"

"I think I'll have a beer, and then I might do a glass of red with dinner. Thank you," I said as Abby handed me a bottle of Stella.

"Kara, can we help you with anything?" Abby asked.

"Oh, my goodness no, you girls relax, everything is basically done here now, I just like to putter."

"Is Colin coming or is he stuck at the hospital? Is Audi here?" Abby asked as she pulled up a seat at the island.

"Yes, Colin is coming, he should be here any minute. He texted me like twenty minutes ago saying he was on his way. Audi is here, she's finishing getting ready upstairs, and her boyfriend Trevor is upstairs with her. Then my parents two best friends Paul and Rebecca are coming, they're like my second parents. Oh, and then we invited Alec and his girlfriend, my parents love Alec and invite him to everything, especially since he doesn't have family here," I said as I grabbed a seat next to Abby.

"Oh great! Wow that's a lot of people, I'm excited to meet Alec's girlfriend, I don't think I have yet."

"She's nice, her name is Heather, but she actually won't be coming. I guess she's having Thanksgiving with her dad. I'm actually surprised Alec is coming here instead of going with her. But anyway, none of my business," I said taking a sip of beer.

Abby and I continued to chat casually when Audi and Trevor walked down the stairs, and Audi approached, giving Abby a big hug. Audi has always loved Abby and is always so excited when she and James come over. Trevor also said hello and stepped out onto the back deck to grab a few beers out of the cooler he had brought over. He made his way to the living room to offer dad and James a beer. James had a full one, so he put the extra on the coffee table.

As Abby and I were about to discuss *The Bachelor* finale, Colin had walked through the front door. He struggled to shut the door behind him as he was trying to balance a dessert, a bottle of wine, his keys, and his phone.

I made my way over to him and shut the door behind him. I greeted him with a quick kiss and welcomed him inside. I took the wine and dessert and brought it to the living room so he could say hello to everyone.

Colin greeted everyone in the living room with a quick hug or handshake and as he was saying hello to

Trevor, Trevor indicated that he already grabbed Colin a beer.

"Oh perfect, thanks," Colin replied. He opened the beer and placed it on the coffee table then made his way to the kitchen to say hi to my mom and Abby.

Colin greeted them both with a hug and answered questions about practicum and how busy he's been. I listened appreciatively and I must have been beaming from ear to ear because I've always been so proud of Colin and his hard work.

Colin made his way back to the living room and shortly after there was another knock at the door. Paul and Rebecca were standing at the doorstep with huge smiles on their faces and a large Thanksgiving themed gift basket. I gave them each a big hug and they came in saying hello to everyone. Rebecca joined my mom in the kitchen, Paul helped himself to a drink and then joined everyone else in the living room.

Alec arrived shortly after when the football game had started the half time show. He had knocked on the door and Audi had answered as I was busy chatting and didn't even hear his knock. He had also brought a huge pie and said hello to everyone before joining the crowd in the living room.

"Hey!" I said to Alec, rather enthusiastically. However, in my defence, I hadn't really eaten much today, and I was just finishing up my second beer, so I hate to admit it, but I'm a bit of a light weight and I was definitely feeling good already.

"Hey, how's it going," Alec replied not quite matching my level of enthusiasm and excitement.

"Good, it's so nice having the house filled with so many people, this is why I love Thanksgiving, well and the food of course," I replied.

The rest of the afternoon was spent socializing in the living room, kitchen, and even out on the back deck so we could play with the dogs.

Mom and Rebecca set the kitchen island with all the Thanksgiving trimmings and kept the Turkey on the stove top so everyone could serve themselves in the kitchen to leave space on the table. We had to push the large dining room table together with a fold up table next to it to create one long table to seat all twelve of us. By the time dinner was served, I was definitely quite tipsy. We do a tradition every year on Thanksgiving and as we all started to dig in, Audi started.

"Okay, for those of you who have not had Thanksgiving at our house before, we do a little Thanksgiving tradition every year, where we go around the table one at a time, and we each say something that we're thankful for."

"Oh, I loooooove that!" exclaimed Abby excitedly.

"Good! Okay, I'll go first. This year I'm thankful for being accepted into the Vancouver Art Institute and working toward my future! Of course, I'm also thankful for my family and Trevor, but this is pretty big!" Audi said with the biggest smile on her face.

Everyone at the table congratulated her and were so thrilled for her. We continued around the table until everyone said their gratitude's. We ate our meal, and the dinning room was filled with chatter, laughter, and love.

Maybe it was the alcohol, or maybe it was just my heart, (I'm pretty sure it was the alcohol), but I started to feel this sense of overwhelming gratitude and decided to get up from my seat, and walk around the table and give each guest a kiss on the cheek and thank them for coming.

Everyone seemed very appreciative of my kiss on the cheek, saying things like "'Oh, that's so sweet!'" and "'No, thank you so much for having us!'" but when I got to Alec, he didn't quite respond the same. First of all, Alec and I have never even hugged. We've never actually touched. I don't know why, now that I think of it, because I always greet my friends with a hug when I first see them. But for some reason, Alec and I never have. So, when I get next to him, and it's his turn to receive my kiss on the cheek, what does he do? He wipes off the kiss from his cheek like he's some five-year-old kid in kindergarten who hates girls. Some people notice, some don't but of course my mom had to tease him about it.

"Oh, what Alec, you scared Blake has cooties or something?" Mom said playfully.

"Hah, yeah I guess so," Alec said jokingly back.

The rest of the evening carried on in a similar manner. Everyone enjoyed the food, the dessert, the atmosphere, and each other's company.

Everyone stayed until about nine p.m., but Paul and Rebecca actually stayed after Colin, and I left. Alec decided to leave when Abby and James left, and they all thanked my parents for a wonderful evening.

Colin and I took Merc back to my place shortly after Alec, James and Abby left.

"Well, that was fun hey," I asked Colin as we got into my place.

"Yeah, for sure. It was nice to see Abby and James, it's been a while since I'd seen them," Colin replied as he made his way to the bedroom to change out of his clothes.

I poured us both another glass of red wine and turned on the TV to one of the Netflix shows we were watching. I placed our glasses on the coffee table and then went to the bedroom to change into pyjamas.

"You were awfully friendly tonight, throwing out kisses left right and centre," Colin said jokingly as I entered the bedroom.

'Yeah, well you know me. I always get so lovey dovey after I've had a few drinks. Everyone didn't seem to mind. Except Alec, but he's weird like that."

We made our way back to the living room, enjoyed our wine and our show and then turned in for the evening shortly there after.

Alec Kohl: Winter 2015

The rest of the Fall months seemed to have passed in a blur. Heather and I were doing okay, not great, but not bad. She was still busy with work, as was I, and so it seemed as though we were back in the same rut, we found ourselves in months ago.

Christmas music was playing in every store you walked through, which drives me nuts, to be honest. I don't mind it every once a while, but when it's constant Christmas song, after Christmas song, it get's annoying. It also seems like they only play the same twenty songs and never change it up, so I'm ready for Christmas to be over in the next few days just because of the music alone. Well, partly too because I won't be going home for Christmas this year. I'm scheduled to work Christmas Eve and Boxing Day, and Heather is working Christmas Day, so we were just planning a small Christmas alone together this year. Which is fine, but I hate not seeing my family over Christmas.

Thankfully, Blake's family truly has taken me in like I'm part of their family. They did invite me over to spend Christmas morning with them, and even Christmas dinner, but I told them I would be spending it with Heather, but would pop in. I am going to Blake's

Birthday tonight though, so that should be fun. I guess every year it's been a tradition that on the night before Blake's Birthday, they always go bowling. I have no idea where the tradition came from, but I'm guessing it's because her Birthday is Christmas Eve, nothing is ever open, so she has to celebrate a night early.

I was able to make it home on time to ensure that I would be able to shower and get ready and stop at the store on my way to get her a quick Birthday present. I had no idea what to get her. Do adults even get each other gifts? I was thinking of getting her a gift card to somewhere, but that's sort of lame. I asked Heather what she thought, and she thought it was dumb that I was getting her something to begin with. Clearly, she still has an issue with my friendship with Blake, which was evident in the fact that she is refusing to come with me tonight, on the pretense of having 'previous plans with Brooke.' Whatever.

I decided on chocolate. Chocolate is one of Blake's favourite things, so I got her a huge chocolate bar and called it a day. I've actually never met someone who ate as much chocolate as her, so it was settled.

Dean, Kara, Brenna, Blake, and Colin were already at the bowling alley. They were putting on their shoes, and ordering drinks and food by the time I had arrived.

"Hey, happy Birthday!" I said to Blake as I approached their table, handing her her present.

"Hey! Thanks for coming! Oh my gosh, you really didn't have to get me anything, that was so nice of you!"

189

Blake said as she peeked through the gift bag. "Oh wow! This chocolate bar is huge! Thanks! Do you want a beer? We have a pitcher started on the table here, and a few more people should be here soon," Blake replied.

I poured myself a beer before walking toward Colin.

"Hey, Colin, how's it going?" I said as I shook Colin's hand hello. We had a quick catch up before Dean interrupted asking how I was doing.

Shortly after, a few of Blake and I's mutual friends from hockey showed up, as well as Audi and Trevor. It wasn't long before everyone was bowling, eating, and drinking.

Well, the night was still young, but Blake was sure feeling the beers she was consuming. I wasn't sure if she was flirting with me or not, but it could have just been the alcohol. No, she wasn't flirting because she doesn't look at me that way, plus Colin is here and she's happy with Colin. But it seemed as though she was spending more time with myself than she was with her own boyfriend. That sort of made me feel sad for her. Not like pity or anything, but I felt bad that her own boyfriend didn't seem too engaged and didn't seem too bothered that I was spending more time with Blake than he was. Odd I thought. Not to mention the fact that she pulled a prank on me by hiding my boots from the entry way and putting them under one of the decorative Christmas trees. I noticed them when I walked to the bathroom and then asked her about it. All she could do was laugh, so I knew it was her.

I spent the night bowling but kept my beer intake to a minimum because I had to drive later. Bowling was fun, even though I sucked. People got a kick out of my over dramatic bowling approach. I felt like I needed to kill the pins, so I typically bowled a little too aggressively. I wasn't on Blake's team, but I was in the lane next to her, so sometimes we would be up bowling at the same time. We would take turns trying to spook the other to throw off their bowl, and then laugh when the other would get a gutter ball.

By the time the bowling alley was getting ready to close I was ready to go. I finished my last bowl, said goodbye to Kara and Dean and then wished Blake a quick Happy Birthday before making my exit.

Heather wasn't home yet by the time I got home. I sent her a quick text to see how long she would be, but I didn't get a reply. Guinness and Chip were happy to see me, and I let them outside quickly while I changed into some sweats.

I turned on Sports Centre and shortly after Heather had come in through the garage door.

"Hey, how was your night with Brooke?" I asked as Heather put her purse on the kitchen island.

"It was good. She and Jason are on the rocks again, so she needed a girl's night. She's debating staying with him and settling because she doesn't want to be alone for Christmas and she already bought him his gifts."

I walked toward Heather and greeted her with a kiss hello.

"Sound like those two are always on the rocks. Hopefully, they can sort it out," I replied.

"How was your night?" Heather asked.

"It was good, I just got home like ten minutes ago. The neighbours were there and Colin too. Oh, and a quite a few people from hockey. A lot of people were asking where you were. I told everyone that you have previous plans with a girl friend, but they all say hello. I think everyone misses you and was hoping to see you. I missed you," I said, looking at Heather and giving her another kiss.

"Aww, that's sweet. I missed you too. Maybe next time I'll be able to go. It would be nice to see everyone again. I'm going to go put some PJs on and get ready for bed. Do you want to come up?" Heather asked.

Strange. Heather was being so nice, and she never invited me to come up with her, I definitely had to take advantage. Without saying a word, I turned off the TV and followed her into the bedroom.

Blake Taylor

The Christmas holidays passed in a blur. The holidays are always so busy. Colin and I spent Christmas Eve with his family and had a nice dinner. It was so nice because all of his siblings and their partners were there, and then of course both his parents too, so it was a nice group of us. After dinner we all played board games, and at about midnight I made my way home because I wanted to wake up for Christmas morning with my family.

Colin had to work a shift at the hospital on Christmas, so that's also why we celebrated on Christmas Eve, but unfortunately, he wasn't able to make it to my house on Christmas to celebrate with my family.

Because we're all older, we didn't get up and start opening presents until about nine, which is so nice considering I didn't fall asleep until a little after one a.m.

"Morning, Merry Christmas!" I said to my family as Merc, and I came into the house on Christmas morning. I was smacked in the face by the most amazing smell, the smell of Christmas. When you think of Christmas, there's always a smell that to mind. I think everyone has a different answer as to what they think Christmas smells like, because it depends on your Christmas Day traditions. But as I walk through the door, I get hit with rich smells of cinnamon (my mom keeps cinnamon sticks over a pot on the stove to keep that smell present), Christmas homemade baking, coffee, fresh pine (from the Christmas tree), and a warm cooked meal, all wrapped in one. It's the best smell ever.

"Morning! Merry Christmas Blake," Mom said.

I had a stack of presents in my arms and had to leave some on the front step and make a couple trips because there were too many to carry all at once. I organized all my presents for my family under the tree and put a few stocking stuffers in everyone's stocking. It took everything out of me to try not to look for any presents with my name on it. Brenna was sitting on the couch anxiously awaiting everyone to arrive so she could start opening presents.

I made my way to the kitchen to make a coffee and mom had a really cute coffee and hot chocolate bar all set up, so I decided to add some crushed candy cane and marshmallows to my coffee. Dad was outside having a quick smoke, Audi was on her way down the stairs, and mom was just coming out of her room all at the same time.

"I hope you don't mind, but I invited Alec to join us this morning. When we were all bowling, he mentioned that he wasn't going home for Christmas and that Heather was working so he was going to be alone, so I invited him. I'm not sure if he will even show up, but I told him to wear his PJs," Mom said as I took a sip of my coffee.

"I don't care at all, that was really nice of you. No one should be alone on Christmas."

I made my way over to the living room and turned on some Christmas music. I always love hearing a mix of the classic Christmas songs, as well as the new up and coming artists who re-do the classics and make them a little more hip-hoppy, but then I also love hearing brand new Christmas songs. I'm the type of person who would totally listen to Christmas music all year round, I could never get sick of it.

I sat on the couch next to Brenna and found the movie "A Christmas Vacation" and put it on the TV to have playing in the background. It's one of our family favourite Christmas movies, and even though we know every single line from the movie, we still laugh at every joke, every single time. It's one of our Christmas traditions to watch it on Christmas day. Brenna and I chatted about all things Christmas while mom, dad, and Audi got themselves a drink and could join us. When they all finally made their way to the living room, Brenna jumped up in excitement and offered to begin handing out everyone's stocking.

Everyone enjoyed opening up our stockings and then we eventually began handing each other gifts that we had gotten for each other. I always found the best part of Christmas was watching everyone else open up their presents, and the excitement on their faces to have received something that they really wanted. I got spoiled this year and felt very grateful and lucky for all my beautiful gifts. I got some amazing décor pieces for my apartment, some nice smelling candles, a few stationary items for my small home desk to help with studying, and of course some new clothes. I always like to pile my gifts in a small pile on the floor or on the couch so that it's easy to take back to my room, or in this case, my suite afterward.

After about an hour we had finished opening all our gifts from each other, when there was a quick knock on the door and Alec had entered. As expected, he was wearing a pair of Calgary Flames pajama bottoms, and a plain black hoodie. He even had Calgary Flames slippers on. Dork. He did, however, have a nicely wrapped present in his hand and greeted us all with a smile and a hello.

"Hey! So glad you could come and join us, too bad you had to wear pajamas that you found in a dumpster somewhere," I said mockingly as Alec entered the living room.

"Okay, just for that comment, this gift was supposed to be for the entire family, but now it's just for everyone except you," Alec said jokingly as he handed the gift to Brenna to open.

Brenna didn't hesitate as she took the gift and opened it within a few seconds. It was actually a really cool board game that I heard had great reviews, so that was really nice.

"Thanks!" Brenna said. We all chimed in after her, also thanking Alec for the thoughtful gift.

My mom had something small for Alec and Heather and Alec decided to open his present quickly. My mom got him a Calgary Flames tee shirt and said it was from the family. Alec looked like he loved it and thanked us all too. He kept the small present, which I believe was a candle for Heather, wrapped, so that she could open it later.

Alec sat next to Audi on the couch, and we all talked about some of our favourite Christmas traditions, or Christmas baking, or Christmas meals while the movie played in the background. Alec joined in on the conversation, but he seemed a little off. I felt bad for him that he couldn't be with his family during the holidays.

When the movie was over, he thanked us all for having him and said that he was going to head home to start preparing some dishes for his supper and phone his parents and siblings.

I decided to bring my gifts back to my apartment and take a shower and change into one of my new outfits. We then spent the afternoon playing board games, including the one that Alec got us all and laughing and reminiscing on the year we just had.

Dinner was great, and Trevor was actually able to join us for dinner, so that made Audi happy. Mom did a great job preparing the turkey and she made two different types of stuffings. She made one that was her mother's recipe, and one that was my dad's moms' recipe. I had some of each. I have to say, stuffing is my favourite Christmas side dish. As enjoyable as dinner was, I had dessert in the back of my mind, and ensured that I left enough room for some chocolate cheesecake, which of course was delicious.

I made my way down to my apartment around ten p.m. and sent Colin a text to see how his shift was going. I heard form him about an hour later saying he was quite busy but was heading home soon. I wished him a Merry Christmas and turned on a cheesy Christmas movie before falling asleep.

Alec Kohl

Christmas morning at the Taylor house was nice, obviously not the same as what I'm used to, and it actually only made me my miss my family even more, but it was so kind of them to invite me over. I had made a small dinner for Heather and myself, which again was nice, but not what I'm used to. I'm used to a home filled with family and kids. I have three siblings and they all have kids so it's usually a pretty busy day when we are all there. I love being an uncle and spending time with my nieces and nephew, and so it was really a bummer that I couldn't be with everyone this year.

I was able to FaceTime my parents and speak to everyone on Christmas, but it still isn't the same. I sort of made a promise to myself that moving forward, I'll do my best to get home for Christmas every year, because it's too hard missing out.

It's been about three weeks since Christmas and I actually haven't seen Blake all that much as she has been busy with school since starting a new semester. I did receive a text this morning though saying that she needed to talk and was hoping I could meet her for a dog walk or beers this evening. I asked if everything was okay and all she said was "yup" but didn't really get into it. I agreed to meet her for a dog walk after dinner.

Heather was at work for an afternoon shift, and today was my third day off (out of four), so we spent the morning being lazy and then I did some errands and groceries in the afternoon. By the time dinner had come around, I was starting to feel anxious about what Blake needed to talk about. Normally she's so open and just tells it like it is, so for her to not really elaborate over text makes me think that something is wrong.

I made my way to the back gate with Guinness and Chip and texted Blake to let her know I was out back, and shortly after, she arrived with Merc.

"Hey, what's up," I said as Blake approached.

As Blake drew nearer, I could see that she looked upset. She wasn't wearing any makeup, her eyes were bloodshot, and the end of her nose was red. She looked as though she'd been crying all day. Uh oh, I thought.

"Oh, you know. Not much."

"Cut the crap, I know something's up, you look like you've been crying. What's going on, are you okay?" I asked.

"Colin broke up with me this morning, so it's been a pretty shitty day to be honest. Just came out of nowhere. Took me by surprise. I'm completely devastated," Blake responded looking at the ground. She couldn't even make eye contact with me. She looked pathetically sad. I felt bad for her.

"Damn. That sucks. I'm sorry. What happened? Like what did he say?"

Blake grabbed the ball to throw for the dogs before answering. "Well, I slept over at his place last night and everything was fine, normal, I couldn't even sense that something was off. We hung out and did our usual thing, and then when we woke up this morning, he just randomly said we needed to talk, and that things weren't working. He explained that he was having a hard time getting to the next level of our relationship with me, and that he was too focused on school and felt that I deserved better. He said that I should be with someone who can give me the time, energy, and attention that I deserve and need. I explained to him that I was okay with his busy schedule, and I knew from the beginning that he would be busy, and I didn't mind being independent. He just wasn't even really open to hearing my side much. It's like he had it in his mind when he woke up, he was breaking up with me and wasn't going to waver from that. He just reiterated that he didn't think his feelings were as strong for me, as mine were for him, and that it wasn't fair to me. And that hurt."

"What an ass hole," I said out loud, but wishing I had said it in my head.

"What?" Blake asked.

"Well, I just mean what an ass for leading you on for so long. I never liked the guy to be honest. I always felt like he was never into you. Any time we would be out as a group he didn't really pay that much attention to you. I always felt bad."

"Wow, thanks. That makes me feel so much better," Blake said as she walked toward Merc and away from me.

"No, I'm sorry, I didn't mean to upset you. I'm sorry. I know its hard now, but you're better off. You deserve better. And he is right that you do deserve someone who can give you the time of day. It super sucks right now but it'll get easier. It really is his loss," I said sympathetically.

"I guess. It just sucks because I really was fine with our relationship and being second priority to his schooling. I knew how important that was and then once he was done school, we could focus on us. I was willing to wait, and I also just love his family so much. That's the other thing that sucks, is I'm so close to his mom and sister that it'll suck not being around them any more," Blake said.

"You just said it yourself though. That you're fine with being second priority. That's not right. And when he's done school do you think it'll be any better? It won't. Then he'll be a doctor and working crazy hours. You thought he was busy now, imagine how busy he will be when he is working. Look I'm sorry. I know I'm being a bit blunt and harsh. Sometimes you need that friend that will tell you how it is. I'm not trying to piss you off."

"I know," Blake replied. "That's why I texted you. I knew you wouldn't sugar coat it," she said as she threw the ball again for the dogs.

"In all seriousness, that really does suck, and I'm sorry for you. You'll be okay though. You have a lot going on and a great family and good friends," I said encouragingly.

"Yeah, you're right. Thanks."

We walked the dogs on our normal route and just talked about normal things and didn't really mention Colin again. The dogs played and sometimes even wrestled for the ball when it would bounce between them. After about forty minutes, we were back home at our back gates. I told Blake goodnight and told her to feel better. She smiled and made her way into her suite.

I got back inside and thought about texting Blake something else encouraging, but it's a fine line of not wanting to be annoying, or too pushy and just wanting to give her space. I decided to give her space and play Xbox instead. I did feel bad though. Although I personally felt as though Blake was better off without Colin, and come to think of it, I actually do completely agree with Colin in thinking that Blake deserves better, I still know how hard a breakup is, and that whole adjustment period. I do feel for her, but I know she'll be okay. Maybe I was a little bit hard on him in calling him an ass hole, and in hindsight it was selfless of him to break up with her instead of leading her on, but still, I don't like when anyone hurts someone I care about. Too bad he couldn't have come to that conclusion sooner, rather than after a year's relationship when she was so invested in him. Anyway, enough of that.

I texted Heather to ask how work was going but hadn't heard back so I was assuming she was busy. I hung out with the dogs on the couch while I played my game and then made my way to bed shortly after midnight. Heather should be home soon I thought as I watched YouTube videos on my phone in bed.

I fell asleep still having not heard from Heather. When I woke up in the morning Heather wasn't in bed, and as I made my way down the stairs, I noticed the spare room door slightly cracked. I peeked my head in and saw her sleeping in there.

When Heather woke up, I asked her why she slept in the spare room, and she said that she got in super late and didn't want to wake me. I tried to tell her that I didn't mind her coming in to bed, but she insisted that she wanted to be able to watch a show before bed and not wake me. I didn't really think anything of it.

For about a week, this kept happening consecutively, and I was wondering why she kept working so late, and why she kept sleeping in the spare room. I finally confronted her about it, and she said that nothing was going on, she has just been swamped at work, but she will make a better effort at leaving at a decent time and coming home to join me in bed. When Heather was on days off, she came to bed on time, which was nice, who doesn't want to share a bed with their girlfriend. But then about two weeks after the first time she slept in the spare room, she got back into that habit again.

Heather had been working late, again, and I tried texting her before bed, but she didn't respond. When I woke up in the morning, she wasn't in bed with me. At this point I was a bit worried considering there was still no text from her, and she wasn't home. I tried phoning but she didn't pick up. Once again, I quietly opened the spare room door and saw her sleeping in the bed. I was relieved that she was home safely, but why did she decide to sleep in the spare room, again, especially after we had spoken about it. Odd.

I greeted the dog's good morning and made a cup of coffee. Heather's phone was charging next to the fridge and as I was grabbing coffee creamer, her phone dinged, to signal a new message. I saw a text come in from another police member named Parker, so I quickly browsed to see what it said. I actually had to blink and rub my eyes to make sure that I was reading it correctly. The text message said *Tonight was fun. Same thing tomorrow night?* What does that even mean? Why would a cop be texting my girlfriend about having fun? Obviously, my brain jumped to worst case scenario. Obviously, this means she's cheating on me. Obviously, this means she's having an affair with one of our co-workers. Obviously, this means that I'm an idiot and have been missing the signs lately.

I had a few options. Option one, storm into the spare room, angry, with an assumption in hand and ask what the hell was going on. Option two, wait until she wakes up, and ask her about the text. Or option three, text him back.

Option three was enticing, but I couldn't do it. I just couldn't pretend to be her, but I did stoop low enough to read through their phone conversation. And there it was. In black and white, exactly what my gut instinct was telling me. They were hooking up. They were hooking up after work and have been for quite some time now. My blood began to boil, and quite honestly, I didn't really know what to do with myself. I needed some air.

I grabbed the dog leashes and signalled for Guinness and Chip to come outside with me, and we began walking on the trails behind the house. I needed some time to think, and I needed a distraction. I just wanted to be outside and throw the ball for the dogs. But my mind was racing, I couldn't help it. I was shocked. Well sort of shocked. Okay I wasn't all that shocked because of how distant Heather has become and how many problems we have been having, and how we just truly haven't been happy together. But I was shocked that she has been cheating. And not with just anybody, but with Parker. Ugh, Parker. I hate him. I hate her. How could they do this to me? Did they think that I wouldn't find out? We work together for crying out loud. I mean not exactly together, considering I'm in a different office than them, but still. I wonder if other members in their office know. And how stupid was she to leave her phone plugged in next to the fridge. And to have your messages come right up on the screen like that? You're a cop for crying out loud, don't you know the importance of privacy. Dumb. It's almost as if she was wanting me to find out.

I needed to bring my blood pressure back down to an appropriate level before returning home and confronting Heather. I tossed the ball and tried to change my mindset and enjoy the company of my dogs and just being outside. After about forty minutes, I made my way back home.

Heather was sitting on the couch with her back to me watching TV, with her phone in her hand. I could only assume that she had read the text from Parker, so I was curious to see if she would say anything. I'll give her the benefit of the doubt, maybe it was a one off, and maybe she will take it upon herself to come clean.

"Hey," I said, entering the house from the patio door. No response.

"Hey," I repeated as I approached a very distracted Heather.

"Oh hi, I didn't even hear you come in," Heather replied.

"Well, I did say "hey" twice. How was work last night?" I asked.

"It was good, the usual. Got caught up with paperwork so I got in late. I know you said not to sleep in the spare room, it's just easier because it always takes me a while to wind down after work."

That was her chance, right? That was her chance to come clean. She's been sitting on this text for how long, she should have just come out and said it right? I'll give her one more chance.

"Right. Well like I said, I would rather be woken briefly then have you sleep in the spare room. You seem distracted on your phone, who are you talking to?"

Heather looked at me quickly before responding, "What? Oh nothing, it's just work emails."

Okay, that's it. Two chances. I gave her two chances to come clean, to avoid me having to make an accusation and she didn't do it. Now I'm pissed because she is also intentionally lying to me.

"Don't lie to me Heather," I began, as I approached her sitting on the couch. Heather looked startled, and genuinely confused. "Before I took the dogs for a walk, your phone was charging next to the fridge. A text message came in as I was standing right there. You don't have your messages set as private, which is surprising, especially when someone is being sneaky. So, unfortunately for you, I saw the text." Heather continued to look at me with a startled expression, almost like a deer in headlights. But I still wanted to make sure there were no miscommunications here, so I ended my thought with, "The text I saw was from Parker. Care to explain?"

Small tears started to form in the lower lids of Heather's eyes. The type of tears where she is one blink away from them streaming down her face. And to be honest, I'm glad those tears were there, she should feel bad. She knows she betrayed me, now it's time to fess up.

"Alec, I'm sorry. I'm so sorry. Parker and I, I don't know how it happened. I don't even know what to say, I'm sorry. I'm so sorry" Heather answered, with the tears now streaming down her cheeks.

"Was it just one time?" I asked. I knew the answer to this, because I saw their text conversation when I went through it. Their texting about meeting up had dated back to about four months ago. Even though I knew the answer, I wanted to see if she would at least be honest or continue to lie.

Heather took a moment before responding as if contemplating how to respond. "No, it's been a couple of months. I don't even know how it started. It happened one night and then we swore to never let it happen again, and then it just sort of did. I'm sorry."

"Heather, you're just sorry because you got caught. If I hadn't asked you about it today, you would have met up with him again tonight. Right?" I asked, laying on the anger in my voice pretty thick.

Heather stared at me blankly. Not moving. Barely breathing. Not saying a word. Seeing her unable to respond meant that I was right, she would have seen him tonight. At this point I could feel my blood start to boil again, and without being able to control it, I yelled at her, "Am I right!?"

Between the anger in my voice, and the sheer volume of my question, it is no doubt that I startled Heather. Quietly, without making eye contact, with her head looking down, like a dog with it's tail between their legs, the small three letter word, "yes" escaped her lips.

"We're done. Grab your shit. Get out. I'm not doing this back-and-forth bull shit this time either. You take your shit, and you don't come back. Don't look at me at work. Don't talk to me at work. Don't anything," I said with disgust reeking from my pores.

Heather sat quietly for a moment wiping her tears away and then slowly made her way up the stairs to start packing her things.

I needed to get away from Heather, I couldn't even stand to look at her, but at the same time, I wanted to make sure she actually left, so once she was upstairs, I sat at the table and waited for her to be finished, fuming with my own thoughts. Surprisingly, she was quite quick. Maybe its because she has done this before, I don't know. But she left out the front door and I refused to get up from my seat to say goodbye.

I went upstairs to see if she purposefully left anything as an excuse to come back for her belongings, but she didn't. Toiletries, gone. Clothes in closet, gone. Junk on her side table, gone. Cell phone charger, gone. It was all gone, and I was a ball of emotions.

Blake Taylor

Something was off with Alec. He wasn't his usual self when he was texting me. He was short with his responses, and I hadn't seen Heather's vehicle in his driveway for a few days. Something was up.

So, I texted him straight up, asking what was going on, and I stated that I hadn't seen Heather's vehicle in a few days. He responded back, once again pretty short stating *At work. We broke up. Dog walk at six tonight and I'll explain?*

I quickly typed back, *See you then* and hit send.

Well good riddance, it's about time they break up. I shouldn't say that. I should be supportive of my friend, and I'm sure he is having a hard time, but I'm not the biggest fan of Heather, and it's hard for me to ignore the fact that I think Alec can do better.

My mind ran scenarios trying to figure out why they could have broken up, I hate that I'm so curious and invested, but I can't help it. After spit balling ideas, I came to the conclusion that they got into some sort of big fight, they both did some yelling, and just decided to take a break. I wouldn't be surprised if they were back together in a week, solely based on their history.

I made myself a quick dinner, one of my favourite go to meals, chicken Greek pita wraps. I did a quick tidy, fed Merc, and then made my way for the back gate at five to six. No sign of Alec yet. His car is in the driveway though, so I'm sure he will be out any moment. As I finished that thought, his back door opened, and his two happy dogs came running toward his back gate.

Alec steps out of his house and a wave of butterflies erupt in my tummy. I don't know why. Don't ask me why. Maybe it's because I'm anxious to hear what's going on with him and Heather. Yeah, lets go with that. I mean, it's not like I'm crushing on Alec, that would be weird. I'm just curious, that's it, that's all.

"Hey Alec," I say as he approaches. So formal. Why am I being so formal, I never say his name.

"Hey," he replies as he closes his gate and begins to walk along the path heading toward Beacon Hill Park. Alec brought along his green chuck it dog toy for the dogs and threw the ball for the boys before asking me how my day was.

"It was good, I didn't get up too much. I had class and then I was actually off early which was nice. What about you?" I asked, not making eye contact. I feel like I'm in my head now. I typically have no problem looking at Alec, maintaining eye contact, talking like a normal human being. But since having that rush of gastric flutters, I'm trying to figure out where that came from rather than be present with my friend. I snap back to reality as Alec continues with his response.

"Oh, you know. Yeah, sorry I haven't texted much lately, I've just been trying to sort things out. I didn't really know what to say over text and wasn't fully ready to talk about it in person yet."

I picked up the ball that Merc dropped at my feet and handed it to Alec so he could toss it with the chuck it. The dogs took off in a heart beet kicking back loose gravel toward us.

"I get that. Are you ready to talk about it now? I'm assuming you are, otherwise, you wouldn't have suggested a walk. So…what happened?" I asked genuinely curious.

"Heather cheated on me with another member from the downtown office. Parker. Her phone was plugged in in the kitchen and a text popped up from Parker. I read it. I asked her about it. They had been seeing each other for a few months. I kicked her out."

The look on my face must have been a sight to see. I'm sure I was a mix between a kid seeing Santa Claus for the first time and someone getting dental surgery, so their mouth needs to be opened as wide as possible. After I picked my jaw up off the floor, I was able to formulate a sentence.

"Wow." Okay, maybe not a whole sentence. But it was something. I took a breath and then continued. "Wow. I don't even know what to say. I'm so sorry. I was not expecting that at all. Have you heard from her?"

"Yeah. It's been a few days and she has texted me a few times each day saying how sorry she is. That she wants to talk. That she will never see or talk to Parker again. She said she will go to couples' therapy. She even offered to transfer out of his unit, so she doesn't have to work near him. I don't really know what to do," he answered.

Without filtering my thoughts, I replied, "Well you can't take her back! Alec, she cheated on you. With someone you know. For months. She lied to your face every single day. How will you ever be able to trust her again?"

"I don't know. But her willingness to fix the situation must mean something. I don't know Blake. I don't know what to think. That's also why I didn't want to tell you right away. You're always so blunt and honest, which is great, but I wasn't ready for it. No offence"

"None taken."

We walked in silence for a few minutes throwing the ball for the dogs, checking out our surroundings, listening to the conversations around us. Every once and a while I would look up at Alec, but I couldn't get a read on his face. He didn't look overly sad, he didn't look mad, he obviously didn't look happy, (but the odd time that the dogs would do something doggish, he would let a small smile leave his lips). He just looked blank. Empty. And this broke my heart. I hate to see him hurting. I could kill Heather. I better not tell him that though, wouldn't want him to think I'm a total nut job. Plus, he is a cop after all. Who knows if he has to report that sort of thing. I'll just continue my approach of being a supportive friend.

"Is there anything I can do?" I asked him as we took the loop path that returns us back to our homes.

"No, it just felt good to get it off my chest. I'm all good. Thanks though," He replied.

I always knew Alec was the quiet type, so I'm sure even just telling me all of this was a lot for him. I've always appreciated that about our friendship. No bullshit. Respect. Friendship. Honesty. Openness.

We make our way back to our back gates and as the dogs' wrestle and tug of war for the ball, I have a moment where I want to give Alec a hug. Not a romantic hug. Just a friendly comforting hug. I feel like he could use one, but I don't even know how he would feel about that. In all our time spent as friends, we aren't affectionate. I mean, maybe the odd high five at hockey, but that's with gloves on. We have just never been the type of friends to welcome each other with a hug. He would probably think it's weird if I went in for a hug right now. That's just not what we do. Instead, I settle with a classic lighthearted comment to alleviate some of the heaviness, but to also let him know that I'm here.

"Anyway, thanks for the walk. I'm sorry for everything you're going through. You deserve better. Heather's an idiot. Try not to beat yourself up over it too much. It's truly her loss. I know you kept it together here today on our walk but try not to bawl your eyes out too loud tonight, I really don't need to hear that," I say with a smirk and a bit of a wink.

Alec grins before replying, "Yeah, I'll try my best. Thanks, have a good night."

"You too."

I make my way inside and change into some PJ's before sitting on the couch with Merc. I grab my kindle and continue where I left off in reading *Harry Potter and the Half Blood Prince*, but I find my mind wandering. After reading about ten pages, I realize that I haven't absorbed a single thing, and that my mind keeps wandering to Alec and just hoping that he's okay.

Alec Kohl

The one bonus that comes from going through a breakup is that I put all my energy into work. All I want to do is work to keep my mind off Heather. It's four a.m. and I just pulled someone over who had a bunch of drugs on them, so being on my 11th hour of work, I still have quite a few hours ahead of me, so this will make for a long night. It's fine though, hauling this many drugs looks great on my resume, and obviously, being able to get any number of drugs off the street is a win.

After having another officer come and take my guy to the station, I was able to cease the drugs, have his vehicle towed and now, three hours later, I'm on my way to the office to secure the drugs.

I'm just arriving at the downtown office (because this is the only office in town that can hold drugs of this quantity) right at shift change as all the officers are starting their day shifts. I'm down in the processing room when I hear a knock at the door. I look up and see Heather in the doorway. Her hair is still wet and tied back in a slick bun, so it looks as though she is about to start her shift.

"I saw you pull up as I was coming in, I figured you'd be down here. I just wanted to check in. I know you asked me not to contact you at work, or at all, but this is killing me, Alec. Today is my last day in this office. I've asked for a transfer to the West detachment. I meant it when I said I was sorry. That I made a mistake. I meant it when I said I would never see or talk to Parker again. I'm leaving this office to be away from him. Please, Alec, can we please talk? I'm so sorry. I love you. I know I've been difficult to be around, over the past few months, and I take accountability for that. I'm so sorry. I miss you. I love you. I miss the dogs. I miss our life." Heather looks as though she's on the edge of a full-blown breakdown. I can't believe she's saying all this at work. I don't know if it's the lack of sleep but for some reason, I sort of feel bad for her. And seeing her creates a whole wave of emotions and memories start to flood me. I honestly don't know what to say. I don't know what she wants.

"I don't know what to say." That's all I can come up with.

"Can I come over later, so we can talk? I have so much to say to you. I owe you some explanation and a true apology. Please Alec. I'll leave work early. Any time that works for you," Heather replies with desperation in her voice.

Damnit, she caught me at the worst time ever. Being this tired is affecting my thought process. I'm curious to hear what she has to say, so I agree.

"You can come by at four, I'm working again tonight, so it can't be for long," I say, and before she can respond I quickly busy myself with processing the items. I don't look up; I don't make eye contact. I just continue working.

I quietly hear a 'thank you' before Heather makes her way out of the processing room.

Fuck.

No idea why I agreed to that. I need to go home and sleep.

After about an hour of processing, I'm finally able to make my way home. As I get through the garage door, Guinness and Chip are doing their happy dance to see me, but I'm sure they're also needing to get outside and are ready for their breakfast. I let them outside, make my way upstairs to change, and then come down to feed them and make myself a quick breakfast wrap.

I hop in bed and do my best not to let my mind wander to the conversation I had with Heather this morning. Instead, I turn on some mindless TV show, and after about an hour I fall asleep.

My alarm goes off at three p.m. and I slowly make my way into the shower and get myself presentable for work tonight. I make my way down to the kitchen and make some coffee and turn on Sports Center.

As soon as the clock strikes four, I hear a knock at the door. Heather. Deep breath. I got this.

I open the door, and Heather walks in, and the dogs immediately greet her.

"Guinness! Chip! Oh, I've missed you!" Heather says as she crouches down to receive their sloppy kisses, and give them scratches and pats.

"We can just sit at the table," I say. More formal. Less intimate than the couch. "Do you want a drink?"

"Water's fine," Heather replies, as she grabs a seat at the table.

I return with two waters and sit across from her. I want to be able to look at her. Read her face. See if there's any genuineness to her, or if what she has to say is an act.

"Thanks for letting me come over. I know you have to work, so I'm just going to get right to it. I miss you, Alec. Not just that, I love you. I made a mistake. There's no excusing my behaviour. When Parker and I first…got together, I was seeking out attention in all the wrong places. I'm sorry for that. Instead of turning in, turning to you, I stepped out. That was wrong. That is wrong. I will do anything to earn your trust back. Like I said before, I've moved out of the downtown office. I've told Parker to not contact me and that I don't want anything to do with him, that I'm in love with you. I've blocked his number and removed and blocked him from all social media. I'm open and willing to do couples therapy with you. I know I messed up, and it was so wrong of me. I miss how we were. I want to be us again."

Looking at Heather, either she's a really good actress, or she is being genuine. I suppose either could be possible. I don't really know what to say. I know that I've been missing her too. But I don't know if it's *her* that I miss, or just being in a relationship and having that companionship and partner. Seeing her across from me, doesn't make it easier though. It makes me miss her more. I wish I hadn't suggested that she come over.

"I still don't really know what to say. Of course, I miss us being together, but I can't get over what you did. I don't know if I'll ever be able to trust you again," I reply.

"Well then let's take it slow. I promise you; I'll never see or speak to him again. It'll be as if he doesn't exist. We can take things slow, see a therapist, and through my actions, I can prove to you how sorry I am, and slowly earn your trust back," Heather says with hope in her eyes.

"Yeah maybe."

"So, you're willing to give us a chance again? Take things slow? Everyone makes mistakes Alec. I'm not perfect. But I want to grow. I want to learn from my mistakes. To be a better person. Let's just take it one day at a time," Heather explains, somewhat desperately.

"Alright." Before I could even finish saying the word, Heather had already squealed and made her way to my side of the table planting a kiss on my cheek. And as much as I hate to admit it, it does feel nice. What can I say, I'm a serial monogamist, and I want to believe Heather. Hopefully, I don't regret giving her a second chance.

"Okay well I won't keep you, I know you have to get to work. Why don't we do coffee or lunch on your days off?" Heather asks.

"Yeah, we could do that. I'm off tomorrow morning."

"Okay I'll text you tomorrow and see what works. Have a good shift babe," Heather replied as she made her way out the front door.

I have no idea what I just got myself into. I never pictured myself to be the type of person to just get back together with an ex. But I guess we aren't actually technically back together, we're just taking things slow, seeing if we could re-build that trust. Seeing if the spark is still there. Who knows what will happen. Time will tell, I guess.

As I finished my coffee, I grabbed my phone and made my way upstairs to brush my teeth and finish getting ready for work. As I placed my phone on the bathroom counter, I noticed I had a text from Blake that read *Just wanted to check in. Hope you're doing okay.* Okay well that was nice of her. Man is she ever going to be blindsided when I tell her what just happened. It was literally just a few days ago that we had walked the dogs together and I told her that Heather and I broke up. Now I'm supposed to say, 'hey, so about the other day, yeah I decided to try and work on things with Heather.' Why do I get the feeling Blake will be pissed?

Blake Taylor

"You've gotta be fucking kidding me," I mumble under my breath. I would have said that a lot louder, but considering the fact that I'm at work, I probably shouldn't swear very loud.

"What!" Abby yells from the cash counter. I guess she still heard me. Damnit, I don't really want to explain the fact that I just received a text from Alec that he and Heather are trying to work on things. Because to be honest, I don't really want to analyze my own feelings as to why I care so much. So, as bad as it is, I decide to tell a little white lie.

"Oh nothing, I mixed up a due date for one of my assignments."

"Oh, okay, it sounded more serious than that! Anyway, what are you up to this weekend? We are going over to Chris and Talia's tonight if you want to come," Abby suggested.

"Yeah, that would be fun! Would be nice to not think about school and have a few beers with friends, thanks. What time are you James heading over there?" I ask.

"Probably around eight. I'll finish up here, go home and have a quick bite then head over. Do you just want to come with me? Just follow me in your car, but you're welcome to come over for a quick supper and then we can go over the three of us."

"Actually yeah, that would work well. I'll just text my mom to ask her to feed Merc and let him out, but I know that won't be a problem. We should probably stop at the beer store too since I won't be stopping at home to grab any," I suggest.

"Yeah, good idea. I'll text James now to let him know you're coming and that way he can have dinner ready, and then we can go to the liquor store with him. Yay! This will be fun!" Abby exclaims with a little hand clap.

After closing up the store with Abby, I hop in my car and tail behind her. Traffic is always heavy around this time as most commuters are also finishing up their day and trying to get home as quickly as possible. Thankfully, Abby and James live close by, so even with the traffic, we arrive in about fifteen minutes.

"Oh my gosh, smells great James!" I say as I walk in the front door. James greets me with a hug and friendly kiss on the cheek. This is something that Abby and James have always done. Every time I see them, they always greet with a hug and kiss on the cheek. I wish more people did that, it's so nice.

"Thanks Blakey, so happy to have you here. How was work girls?" James asks as he continues to work away in the kitchen.

"Good! We actually sold a fancy dining room set, so that's good. Otherwise, we just chatted and organized stock. It was a pretty easy shift," Abby answered. "What are you making anyways there Jimmy?" Abby asked. She often times will call her husband Jimmy instead of James.

"Beef stroganoff. I'm putting in those noodles you like too," James replied.

It wasn't long before we were serving ourselves in the kitchen and then sitting at the table to eat together.

"Oh my gosh James, this is so good. So, so, good. I'll have to get the recipe off ya later," I say as my mouth practically waters.

"Thanks Blakey," James replies with a bit of a chuckle.

After dinner, Abby and I touch up our makeup and then we pile into their pickup truck, the three of us sitting shoulder to shoulder in the front seat. We make a quick stop at the liquor store and then head over to Chris and Talia's.

Chris and Talia are friends who I met through Abby James, and Colin. Although Colin and I have since broken up, I have built very strong friendships with a lot of his friends, and I've remained close with most of them. Chris and Talia organize the slow pitch baseball team every year, and one night Abby and James asked me to come out as a substitute since they were short a girl. I ended up loving it and joined the team permanently.

We parked on the street a few doors down and made our way up to the house, trying not to slip on the snowy sidewalk. Although it was a short walk it was still a relief once we made it in the house, out of the cold. We could hear people talking and laughing, and we could hear music. The house was a split house, where you walk into a landing with stairs going up and stairs going down, so we couldn't see who was upstairs at the party, but we could hear them. After taking off our boots, we made our way up to join everyone.

People were playing beer pong at the dining room table, some people were outside on the patio having a smoke, (I'm not sure how people can bear to stand outside in the middle of winter just to have a cigarette, but anyhow), and then there were people socializing in the kitchen and living room. I recognized everyone here, and shit, Colin is here too. I haven't seen him since we broke up.

I quickly put my beers out on the deck to keep them cold and grab one for myself. I wave a quick hello to the boys on the patio and make my way back inside greeting the rest of our friends. Abby was already off hugging the girls in the living room. I noticed that Colin was standing chatting with Jed, one of our guy friends in the corner of the living room, so I decide to head for the kitchen.

I'm welcomed with lots of hello's big hugs, and warm smiles. I'm such a social person that being around so many great friends and feeding off their energy fills my cup. It doesn't take very long before Talia comes up and gives me a hug from behind and demands that I be her beer pong partner in the next game.

As soon as the game is done, Talia and I set up our cups and as luck would have it, we're at the end of the dining room table that is closest to the living room, which in turn is closest to where Colin is still talking with Jed. It's only a matter of time now that he notices that I'm here if he hasn't already.

Talia and I make small talk as we play, and obviously, we win the match. New players start filling their cups and start setting up, so I make my way back to the patio to grab another beer since I finished mine with the game.

As I make my way inside, Colin is standing close by and makes his way over to me as I re-enter the house.

"Hey Blake," he says somewhat nonchalantly.

"Oh, hey Colin. I noticed you earlier but didn't want to interrupt you and Jed, how are you?"

"Good, I've just been busy which is typical for me. You look good tonight," he comments as he sips his drink. It looks like an old fashioned. Before we broke up, he was loving those drinks and having fun experimenting with recipes and what not. I guess he's still into them.

"Uh, thanks," I say awkwardly. Isn't that like, something you're not supposed to do, is complement the girl you just broke up with. Maybe not, maybe he's just being friendly. What the hell do I know.

We spend about ten minutes talking, chatting, catching up. Talking about his family, talking about my family. Telling him funny stories about Merc. Explaining one of my latest research papers I've had to work on that I knew he would find interesting. And it's nice. This conversation, the way it's so easily, and naturally comfortable. The way we just slip back into our old ways of laughing and connecting. It's so easy.

As we continue to chat, and I realize how easy this is, and how happy I am to see him, and how great it is to hear about his life, in contrast, I also find myself getting upset, annoyed, angry even. Because when he broke up with me, it was so incredibly difficult. It was not at all what I wanted. I would have followed him through his medical journey. I would have prioritized his career as well. And I was mad that we seemed so great together, but he just didn't feel it the way I did. So now, standing here, looking at him, these feelings start to come to the surface.

As I'm about to excuse myself (I figured I should probably make the excuse that I have to use the washroom before I start hashing out our dirty laundry in front of everyone), Colin surprises me by asking, "Did you want to grab coffee next week? It's been so nice catching up."

Okay, I know I'm only on my second beer, so I can't blame the alcohol on my extremely delayed response, but I'm just so confused. He breaks up with me. He sees me. We chat as though nothing has happened, and now he wants to ask me to coffee. Am I the only one confused by this?

"Uh, what? I'm sorry but you want to go for coffee?" I ask. I guess I need him to spell it out for me, because this just isn't computing.

"Yeah. It's been nice chatting. I guess I've missed it. You."

Yeah, I can't do this. I can't let my heart get broken, then as I'm trying to repair it, trying to heal, trying to move on, have him ask me for coffee. For what? For me to go for coffee and sit across from him at a table, for us to shoot the shit, for me to have old feelings start to re-surface. For all my hard work at trying to move on go right out the window. No, I can't do that. I want to, don't get me wrong. There's a reason I was in love with him. Because I enjoy his company, because he's easy on the eyes, because I enjoy who he is as a person and blah blah blah, but I *know* that if I go to that coffee shop and meet him, that I will want to get back together with him. I know my worth. I know that I deserve someone who will put me first and prioritize me. So as enticing as being able to spend alone time with Colin is, I have to say no. I have to continue down the path of healing.

Wow, that was a lot of thought processing before I am even able to give him a response. I'm sure he must think I can't speak or something. After what seems like an eternity of silence, I finally say, "I'm sorry, I can't. You're right, it has been nice catching up, but I can't keep going back and forth with you. You broke up with me, and I've been working really hard at moving on, and I just can't go backwards. I'm sorry."

A flicker of disappointment flashes across Colin's face before responding, "It's okay, I get it. That makes sense."

"On that note, I do actually have to use the restroom," I say as I awkwardly cheers his fancy cocktail and walk past him toward the hallway that leads to the bedrooms and bathroom. No idea why I cheersed him. No idea.

The rest of the evening I did my best to have fun and socialize and be present with my friends. But you know that feeling where it seems as though someone is looking at you? It seemed as though no matter where I was, I could feel Colin's eyes on me. I did my best to avoid looking at him. I didn't want him to get the wrong idea like I was searching for him too.

A little after midnight, James, Abby and myself all took a cab back to their place as we weren't in a state to drive. I crashed in their spare room and after eating some breakfast in the morning, I drove James back to his truck and then made my way home.

Merc was so happy to see me as I walked into my suite, and I immediately brought him out the back gate for a walk. I was feeling guilty for not coming home to sleep with him last night, so I'll be sure to take him for an extra long walk.

Alec Kohl

"So, you said you want to come and watch me play hockey tonight? Did I hear that right?" I ask Heather as she enters the kitchen.

"Yeah, I don't have any plans after dinner with Brooke tonight, and I never see you play so I can just meet you there and sit in the stands and watch. Unless you don't want me to."

"No, no that's fine. I was just surprised to hear you say you'd want to come that's all," I replied as I mixed my stir fry on the stovetop.

"That smells really good. I'm so hungry, I don't know why Brooke chose six for dinner."

"Do you want some?" I ask Heather.

"No, that's okay, I'm going to be leaving here in a few minutes. Thank you though. I'll see you at the rink in a few hours," Heather replied as she gave me a quick kiss before heading out the door.

The Offspring is blaring as loud as possible in my truck as I drive myself to the rink, but I can't help the fact that instead of enjoying the music, my mind is elsewhere. I'm not sure what to think of Heather coming to watch me play. I guess I should be grateful that she's making an effort.

As I make my way into the dressing room, I notice Blake has already arrived and so I grab my seat next to her. It's funny how in hockey dressing rooms, people always have their 'spot,' who knows if its superstition or habit, but it's nice to have that consistency, and you never know, maybe that's a normal thing for most sports teams.

Sometimes people would bug me about playing hockey and having girls in the dressing room and try to make innuendos that are non-existent, but the truth is, it's not half as scandalous as people like to think. I've yet to meet a girl who plays with us and gets ready with us to fully strip down naked, I've yet to see a girl take a shower after the game, most girls get ready in a tee shirt or tank top, and if anything, they're just like one of the guys. Most of the guys are respectful and conscious of where a lady might be sitting to avoid any unwanted flashing of the genitals, and the girls typically sit away from the shower so we can shower off quickly with privacy. I can see why though, for anyone who has never been in a co-ed dressing room, that they would think it's sexier than what it actually is. Plus, no one looks good after hockey with their sweaty helmet hair and stinky body odour, no one.

As I grab my seat next to Blake, she cracks a Budweiser and hands it over to me. "Hey, thanks," I say as I cheers her.

"No problem, I think you got me beers last game, so I owe you anyway. Why are you so late? Now you're going to have to down that can."

"Heather came by, we had a chat. We're 'working on things.' She's actually going to come and watch tonight for a bit," I say hesitantly. It's not that I'm ashamed or embarrassed, but Blake really doesn't hide her feelings, and I know she's not the biggest fan of Heather's, (fair enough), so I'm proceeding with caution as I tell her this. I'm actually glad we're in the dressing room surrounded by so many people so she can't go off on me.

"Well, I'll be damned. Didn't see that one coming. Is this what you want? Are you happy? Cause I'll always support you; you know that I just can't help but have reservations," Blake says as she is bent over tying her skates.

"I don't know yet. That's sort of why we're working on things. Starting over. Taking it slow. Seeing where things lead. No labels. Time will tell I guess."

"Okay...Well, I mean, I guess it's a good thing that she's coming to watch tonight, right? Shows she's making an effort?" Blake asks.

"Yeah, exactly. Especially since I know she will be bored, and cold, so it is nice of her. Anyway, I'm not the only one re-kindling with an old flame. You said you saw Colin last weekend but never elaborated. How was that?"

Blake lets out a small laugh and says, "Ummm no, not re-kindling an old flame at all, way to jump to conclusions. Colin wanted to re-kindle. I didn't know he was going to be at this house party, and there was no way I could avoid him, so we made small talk, and then he said he missed me and wanted to go for coffee. But I told him I couldn't."

"Oh, really? Why not?" I ask curiously.

Blake puts on the last of her hockey equipment as the Zamboni just finishes up and it's our turn to get out on the ice. As she is clipping her helmet straps, she replies, "Because I told him I've worked too hard to move on and I can't go backward. It was hard, not gonna lie. It would have been nice to catch up and have it be like old times, but that wouldn't be healthy, or fair. He texted me again this week though asking again if I'd go for coffee. I haven't responded yet. I want to say something firm, so he gets the point and knows it's a no. Okay, hurry up, you're taking forever. I'll meet you out there."

As soon as I'm ready I grab my water bottle and my stick that's by the door and make my way onto the ice. I drop off my water bottle on the bench and skate a quick lap. I like to do a hard skate, then a light skate, then get a feel for the puck. Maybe I am superstitious because I always do the same warm up. I take a glance at the stands, but no sign of Heather yet.

It doesn't take long before I have a decent sweat going. I'm the type of player who doesn't let a teammate hanging. Although I play right wing, I'm always known to back check and help out our defencemen. If we're really short on players, I'll even offer to play D (defence), and that's where I'm at tonight. Blake also plays right wing, but hates to play D, but we are often out on the ice together because we only have two sets of D.

After about ten minutes, I'm resting on the bench and chatting with Blake, when I hear a tap on the glass behind me. Blake and I both turn to look and see that it's Heather on the other side of the glass waving and smiling. She must have changed her outfit before going out with Brooke because she is done up to the nines. She has a face full of makeup, her hair is all done up (whereas it was just in a ponytail at my place earlier), and she even has heels on. Heels. In a hockey rink. It's like she's pissing all over the place claiming her territory.

I give a quick wave, and Blake does too actually, which was nice. Before I can even process her being here, it's my turn to head back out on the ice. You know, it doesn't seem to really matter what is going on in my personal life, because as soon as I get on the ice, it all goes away. There's something about the sound of skates digging into the ice making that sweet crunching sound, along with the smell, and even taste of the hockey arena air, and not to mention the feel of the breeze that runs through you when you're skating quickly. Can you tell that this is my happy place?

After seventy-five minutes the Zamboni comes out to clean the ice and then close up for the night. We play on the latest ice time on Friday nights, from nine-fifteen to ten-thirty p.m. I notice Heather still sitting in the stands as I make my way to the dressing room. I'm debating texting her and inviting her to the room, but I don't know.

I guess it doesn't matter, as soon as I get to my spot on the bench, I check my phone and see that I have a passive aggressive text from Heather that said: *I'm so glad I came and watched and got a front row seat to the Alec and Blake show. I'm gonna head home, I'm tired.* So that answers that question, she will not be coming in the dressing room. I forgot how annoying her jealousy was.

I get undressed, have a shower, have another beer, and chat with the guys and Blake before heading out. As I pull into my driveway, I see Heather's car parked on the street. This can't be good. I get out of my truck and make my way to the box of my truck to grab my equipment, and simultaneously, Heather gets out of her car and approaches me.

"Hey. I just wanted to come and say sorry for my text. I overreacted. I guess I forgot that Blake played too, and I didn't realize how much you guys talked when you played, and it made me jealous. I figured coming to say sorry would be more effective than me texting again."

Huh. Interesting. This is not like Heather. She very rarely takes accountability for her actions, and I didn't think she even knew how to give a proper apology. Maybe she really is trying and wants this to work. That, or there were ulterior motives, like she wanted to come to my place to see if I were to come home with Blake or something. She can be crazy like that. "Thanks. Yeah, I was surprised to see your text. I'm over it now, but thanks for the apology," I reply as I grab my hockey bag from the truck box. And now this is awkward. I'm tired and just want to go and play Xbox and she's just standing in my driveway looking at me. Am I supposed to invite her in? I don't even want her to come in. I'm tired.

Almost as if Heather is reading my mind, she slowly makes her way back down the driveway toward her car as she says, "Anyway, I'm going to head home, I'm pretty tired. Have a good night."

"Yeah, you too," I say as I breathe a sigh of relief. *Phew. Dodged that bullet.* Okay wait, is that how I'm supposed to be feeling when I'm trying to 'work on things?'

Blake Taylor

Hockey was fun. Heather was annoying. Who comes to a hockey rink dressed like they're about to hit a fashion runway? Ridiculous. Anyway, the only crappy thing about Friday night hockey is how late it is. By the time I get home, shower, and get ready for bed, I don't fall asleep until about twelve-thirty, which is late for this ol' gal.

I still had to get up at a decent time because I have to work on some assignments and then work a quick shift at Urban Garage this afternoon.

After pouring myself some coffee and waking up a little, I decide I really should text Colin back, and ensure that my message is clear, so that there is no more of him asking me for coffee, and so that we can truly have closure to move on.

Hey. Thanks for the offer, but I meant it when I said that I truly am just wanting to go forward, not backward. I can't go for coffee with you Colin, and I need you to stop asking me. Please respect this boundary and allow me to move on. You broke up with me, now please let me go. I'll always have love and respect for you, but I think we need some time and space from one another. Have a great weekend Col.

There. I think that was pretty straight forward. No room for miscommunications. It was still polite, yet firm. I'm glad I sent that because if I'm being honest, like really deep down, don't tell anyone this, honest, I think I'm starting to crush on Alec. I know, I know, eww, he's like ten years older, and we're such good friends, and he probably looks at me like his annoying little sister or something, plus he's 'working on things' with Heather, so I know there's literally no point in me even having a crush, but I can't help it. When he walked into the dressing room last night and looked at me and then made his way to sit next to me, I got that same wave of butterflies I felt when we went out to walk the dogs. Then when he mentioned working on things with Heather, I immediately thought 'yuck.' I know that I wouldn't have that sort of reaction for any of my platonic male friendships, so why was that my immediate gut reaction this time? Then I started to analyze myself, and I tried to convince myself that the 'yuck' was not a me thing, but a Heather thing. It's because I know what Heather has done to Alec, and I know that he deserves better. That's why I thought the initial 'yuck,', not cause I'm developing feelings.

But then, just to add another curve ball to my overly confusing feelings, when Heather knocked on the glass behind us, waving and almost like, claiming Alec, I felt a sense of protection over him, and annoyance over Heather. Which, again, could be because I just don't like Heather, but then I kept over-analyzing some more, and wondering, okay do I not like Heather because of what she has done to him, or do I not like Heather because she's trying to get back together with the guy I like?

See, see, how messy this is? I just caught myself thinking 'the guy I like.' I haven't even admitted that to myself until right now. This is why, ladies and gentlemen, you don't have deep thinking moments before you even finish your first cup of coffee. You end up mind fucked.

Anyway, let's table these thoughts because I have some serious writing I need to do for my therapeutic communications paper, and I can't be distracted. I need to focus.

Thankfully, I'm actually really good at prioritizing and focusing on school, that I was able to finish my paper before making my way to work. Admittedly, I can't say the same about turning my brain off when I'm working, especially considering the store was surprisingly slow for a Saturday afternoon. To top it off, the girl I was working with is extremely quiet, and is actually studying to become a lawyer, so she was just reading through her books behind the counter the whole shift, which meant I was left with my thoughts, and the store's crummy background music.

Do I have a crush on Alec, or do I just think that he deserves better than Heather? The answer is… I have no idea. I've literally never, ever, looked at him that way. I've always looked at him as a best friend who is so much older. Like family even. So, does that make me gross for now liking someone who I looked at as family? Yes. Yes, it does, so end the thoughts here and now. No more thoughts of crushing on Alec you sicko.

Wow, I really need to work on more positive self-talk.

Almost a week has passed since Friday night's hockey, the night of the butterflies that should not even be acknowledged, and I've done a pretty good job at pushing Alec from my brain. He asked me to join him and Riley for beer and wings last night, but I said I couldn't because I needed to study. But I didn't need to study. Instead, I had dinner with my parents and tried to ignore the thoughts of wishing I was at beer and wings.

Anyway, today's a new day, the sun is shining, and we have an early class day because we have labs in the morning and then we get the afternoon off, so Beacon Hill Dog Park is calling Merc and I's names this afternoon.

Today, we were doing med-surg labs and had to do some hands-on practical skills. We had to learn how to insert catheters in male and females. Thankfully, we had dummies to practice on and didn't actually have to practice on each other. How weird would that be.

Once we mastered that practical, we then had to pair up and do medical head to toe assessments. As always, Teagan and I pair up and get right to it. I love working with Teagan because we just click and get each other's sense of humors, we also have the same work ethic and work style in which we want to fully understand something before moving forward, and we don't like bullshit. No time wasting, get in and get out. Once we practiced on each other a few times, we had to each perform a medical head to toe assessment on each other in front of our clinical teacher, and if we did it properly, then we were free to leave. Because Teagan and I paid attention during the demonstration and practiced thoroughly, we aced our test, and we were the first pair to leave.

"I seriously love days like this. Nursing school is stressful enough, so it's nice when we get early days where we can just go home and relax or whatever," Teagan says as we make our way to the parking lot.

"I know! Even though it's Winter and not the warmest, having a sunny day like this is perfect for being off early. Are you going home? Or what are you up to today?"

"Yeah, I'm heading home, I told my mom I would go for a hike with her, because like you said, you can't beat a sunny day like this. You?"

"I'm heading home to take Merc for a walk, then I think I might legitimately take the rest of the day off from school. I feel like every single day I'm working on some sort of assignment or report or whatever. I think I want to do nothing today," I say as I open my car door to throw my backpack inside.

"Yeah, good plan. K well have a great rest of your day!" Teagan exclaims as she gets into her white Volkswagen Jetta.

I crank up the country radio and relish in the idea of a stress-free afternoon. It's so nice having nothing planned.

As I make my way into my apartment, Merc is super excited to see me, which is obvious by the speed of his tail wags. I quickly place my bag down on the kitchen island, fill up my water bottle, grab my sunglasses and phone, and we make our way out the back gate.

Gosh what a perfect day. This truly couldn't have been a better dog walking weather day than today. Do you ever have those moments, where you're doing something, and it could be something that you do regularly, but all of a sudden, you're hit with a wave of gratitude? That's me right now. To be out of school early. To be walking my dog on such a beautiful day. To even be a dog owner. To have great friendships. To have a loving family. Pretty darn grateful.

Merc is loving life, walking ahead of me and sniffing other people and dogs, then coming back to me to let me know he's still with me, then off again to sniff some flowers and gosh knows what else on the ground. Every so often he looks back to make sure I'm still following him, which is so cute, because it's like he wants his independence, but still wants to know I'm with him.

As we approach the dog park, I notice that it's quite busy, which isn't surprising considering this beautiful sunny day. Merc immediately runs in and joins a pack of dogs that are all taking turns sniffing each other. I close the dog park gate behind me and stand off on the side. I quickly call Merc over, so he knows where I am and then allow him to return to his shenanigans.

Shortly after, I notice Merc doesn't waste any time in joining in the group fetch. One of the dog owners has a chuck it and is throwing an orange ball for a pack of dogs. I love watching Merc play, and run, and chase and just be a dog. About fifteen minutes goes by before I see Merc and five other dogs chase after the ball and all trip into one huge doggy pile up. Within seconds I hear a yelp. I hold my breath hoping it's not Merc. As the dogs clear, I see poor Merc limping over toward me. I immediately feel hot and panicked. What happened? Is he okay? He's walking, so I don't think anything is broken. Oh my gosh is that blood?

I run to Merc and quickly crouch down to see where the blood is coming from. His pad on the inside of his paw is completely torn up and very raw. I feel so bad for him he makes me want to cry. But Merc shows no signs of pain, if anything, he seems annoyed at me that I'm putting him on his leash and leading him away from the fetch game. If it were up to him, I'm sure he would continue playing, chewed up pad and all.

I've never actually dealt with a torn pad to this degree, so I'm not one hundred percent sure how I should care for it. As we walk home (which is slower than usual as Merc is favouring his front paw and limping a little), I decide to text Alec and see what he has to say. I haven't really spoken to him since I've been secretly avoiding him and my feelings that should not be named, so texting him is sort of going against the little rules I made for myself. But this is for Merc. Not for me.

A few minutes later, he responds saying that he is just finishing at the store and then can pop by so he can see for himself. Perfect. I'm such a worry wart. I never want anything bad to happen to my dog, so I'm grateful that Alec can come over and check on him. I can only imagine the type of worry wart I'll be one day when I have kids.

Wait. He's coming to my apartment. Alone. A shrill of goosebumps spreads from my head to my toes and I don't know if it's from excitement, anxiousness, nervousness, or all of the above. Alec has been to my place before, so what's the big deal. Wait, no he hasn't. He's been to my parents place numerous times, but he's never actually been inside my apartment. Alone. With me. Alec and me alone in my apartment. More goosebumps. It's for Merc. Not for me. Get a grip.

We get home and I fill Merc's drinking bowl with fresh water. When he's done, I fill a smaller bowl with lukewarm water and a splash of Dawn dish soap. I submerge his paw in the water and let the soap do its job. Merc shows no sign of pain, but you can tell he's not particularly loving this. I gently clean his paw and the area around his center pad. Once I'm satisfied, I dry it off with paper towel and let him rest on the floor.

Thankfully, the bleeding had stopped shortly before arriving home, so it wasn't a difficult clean.

Moments later, there's a knock at the door. I rise to my feet and quickly sniff under my armpits and check my breath. I don't think I've ever done that in my life, but I guess having Alec into my apartment calls for a body odour check. I'm good by the way.

"Hey," Alec says as he walks in, in his police uniform. Really? You had to come over in uniform. Do you not know how hot a guy is in uniform? Especially a cop's uniform, with handcuffs and everything…What the fuck is wrong with me? I've seen him in uniform before, it really shouldn't be any different. Why am I all of a sudden looking at him like he's the sexiest man to walk this Earth? "Were you gonna say hi back or were you just gonna stand there?" Alec then says, breaking my inappropriate thoughts.

"Yeah, sorry. I thought you said you were coming from the store; I didn't know you were working," I say somewhat flushing.

"I'm just finishing up work but needed to grab a few things for supper. We're still human you know, we still need to buy groceries," Alec says with a smirk. The sexiest smirk ever. Stop it. Get a grip Blake, you're pathetic.

"Right. Okay well thanks for coming to look. We were at the dog park, and he was playing fetch with some other dogs, they all got into a doggy pile up of sorts, and then he yelped and limped over to me and

246

that's when I noticed the bleeding and his pad was really torn up," I explain as I motion to Merc's front paw.

"Oh yeah, poor guy. This is pretty common but to avoid infection you should put poly on it and wrap it. Do you have any vet tape?" Alec asks.

"Ummmm, considering I'm in school to take care of humans, not animals, no I do not have any vet tape." I reply somewhat sarcastically. "Can I just get some from the store?"

"I have some at my place, I'll go grab it." Alec gives Merc a pat and then rises to the door and closes it gently behind him.

I grab Merc a small milk bone while we wait for Alec to return, which is probably only one minute later. He walks in without knocking.

Alec has an oversized red First Aid bag in his hand that he places on the floor next to Merc. I look at the bag, then at him.

"You must get hurt pretty often to require a bag that size," I say jokingly.

"This is just my vet kit. I have everything in here to First Aid a dog. You can never be too prepared. It's good to have when your partner is a dog. What if something happened to him when we're working, at least I could help him right away, smart ass," Alec replies with a grin as he flips through his First Aid bag.

I get Merc in a laying position and sit next to him and comfort him. Alec sits on the other side of Merc, closest to his injured paw.

"Can you hold his paw up for me so I can look at the wound," Alec asks, all professional like.

I do as I'm told, admiring his care, attention to detail, patience, and compassion. I notice myself drawing closer, wanting to observe what he's doing, and also, maybe just to get closer to him. Because the wound is surrounded by hair, Alec needs to trim some of the hair around the pad.

"K, try to hold his paw still so I can trim this hair here," he asks, concentrating on his little vet scissors.

I trust him, but I'm also worried for Merc. I can't help but lean in even closer to be a back seat driver if you will, and inspect his cutting job, ensuring he goes nowhere near the wound by accident. As he finishes cutting, he looks up at me, and we're merely inches apart. I don't think I've ever been this close to Alec. Ever. My breathing slows. My head feels hot. I never realized just how green Alec's eyes were. They're the same colour as freshly mowed grass, in the beginning of spring, after ample amounts of rain, when grass is the greenest. Stunning. I see Alec's lips moving, but I can't hear anything.

"What? Sorry, I missed that," I say, sounding a bit winded. Which makes no sense, considering I'm sitting down, and not doing cardio. But I guess I was actually holding my breath and didn't even realize it.

"I said to just continue holding his paw like that because now I need to apply the Polysporin, and I don't want his paw to touch the floor and get the wound dirty."

Again, I do as I'm told and admire the way he works, and the way he is so gentle with my dog. The way he carefully applies the poly, the way he talks Merc through what he is doing. The way he occasionally looks at me, which seriously sends shockwaves through my system.

Once he's finished with the poly, he reaches into his First Aid kit and pulls out some 2x2 gauze pads as well as green vet tape.

"Okay, now I need you to hold the gauze in place over the wound while I wrap over it to secure it in place," Alec directs me. We're even closer now, as we both need to concentrate at the task at hand. We're so close I can feel his breath on my skin. I can smell his aftershave. Concentrate.

As he finishes up the wrap, we both look up at each other, less than one inch apart from each other, our noses almost touching. We make eye contact. Sparks literally fly. Jolts of electricity shoot through me. I'm feeding off his energy. And its as if in this moment, the electricity between us comes together, forming a circuit.

Breaking our silence Alec quietly says, "That should do it," and stands up, breaking our eye contact, disconnecting the circuit.

"Yeah, thank you. I appreciate it."

"I should get home and start making dinner. Let me know if it gets worse," Alec says as he grabs his First Aid kit and walks out the door.

Well smack my ass and call me Betty, that was one hell of a moment. I've never felt sparks like that. Did he feel them too? Is that why he left so quickly? He must have felt them. I couldn't be the only one to feel the heat between us.

I slowly get up off the floor patting Merc and giving him hugs and kisses. Merc tries to walk around, adjusting to his lack of range of motion in his injured paw, but adapts rather quickly.

I make my way to the fridge grabbing a bottle of water and resting it on the back of my neck trying to cool the heat pouring out of my pores.

What just happened.

Great. This is just great. Seems to me like I've got a crush on the neighbour.

Alec Kohl

I could not get out of Blake's apartment quick enough. I don't know what she was doing, but when we made eye contact, I thought I felt something. I had to quickly break the eye contact, break the moment, because I can't possibly feel something for her. She's, my friend. My neighbour. She's like ten years younger than me, she probably thinks I'm the creepy older neighbour next door. Plus, I'm sort of friends with her parents. That wouldn't be cool. Oh, and I guess I'm technically working on things with Heather too. Yeah, this is not a time for me to start feeling things for Blake. I need to put that to the back of my brain, and never, ever, remember that moment.

The only thing that is going to make this a little more difficult than I was anticipating is the fact that Jenn invited both Blake and I to the co-ed hockey tournament in Duncan next weekend. And stupidly, I agreed to share a hotel room with Blake. Not just Blake and I, another friend of ours, Dan is supposed to share the room too, but still. How am I supposed to share a room with her? In my defence, I did agree to splitting a room with Dan and Blake back when Heather and I were broken up, so it didn't seem like a big deal, but now that she and I are working on things, I don't think she would like it very much if she knew Blake would be sleeping in my hotel room. Obviously, I wouldn't share a bed with her. She could share with Dan. Hell; I could share with Dan if it meant keeping Blake out of my bed. Maybe I'm getting ahead of myself, she probably feels the same way and doesn't want to share a bed with me either. I don't even know how to approach this, but I guess I should start with telling Heather and inviting her to come, that way she can be in the room with us and there will be no room for her not trusting me.

I'll start by telling Heather, but first, I'm supposed to meet up with Riley tonight for wing night. Normally I would invite Blake, it's sort of our weekly group thing, but I need to cool off from Blake a little bit, so tonight will just be a boy's night.

Guinness and Chip are practically begging me to take them out, so after making a coffee to go, I grab their leashes and clip them around myself, (my dogs are well trained and don't need to be on leash, but I always bring the leashes with me, in case someone else's dog isn't well trained, or if kids are afraid of my big dogs or whatever). After grabbing their favourite ball and putting on my shoes, out the door we go.

I put on my favourite *Spittin' Chicklets* podcast and throw the ball for the dogs every time they drop it at my feet. We take our time and spend about forty minutes out walking and playing fetch.

As I make my way to our back gate, I notice Dean out on his back deck puttering around with what looks to be a smoker. I let the dogs in the yard and close the gate behind me.

"That's quite the machine you got there, Dean," I say as I poke my head over the fence.

"Yeah, not bad, eh? Can you actually help me move it over there?" Dean asks as he points to the far side of the deck.

"Yeah, for sure," I say as I make my way over to his yard.

His new smoker is extremely heavy. There's two wheels on one end, but it still takes the two of us to maneuver it around to the far end of the deck. That was good timing for me to come home when I did, because I have no idea how Dean would have moved that himself.

"Okay well thank you, this is much better over here. I wanted it to be out from underneath the pergola because I don't want all the smoke to get entrapped, and that way the pergola can be for sitting and be a good space to stay out of the sun. Plus, not going to lie, with a house full of women, sometimes its nice to have a few minutes away from them so having the smoker over here on its own gives me a little solitude," Dean says with a wink.

"I can't even begin to imagine what it would be like to live in a house full of women. It makes sense why you're out here all the time. Or in the garage," I say with a chuckle.

"Yeah, buddy that's right. I'll be cooking up a bunch of things on this bad boy all week, so feel free to pop over if you smell something good."

"Yeah, okay thanks. Anyway, I should shower and get myself put together. Tell Kara and the girls I say hello. Have a good one!"

I make my way back to my house and jump in the shower to get myself ready to go and see Riley. After getting ready, brushing my teeth, and feeding the dogs, I drive the short distance over to McDuffs Pub.

I notice Riley in the back corner at a table over by the TVs, he already has a beer ordered for him and myself. I make my way over toward him, dodging servers with balanced trays in their hands.

"Hey, hope you weren't waiting long," I state, pulling out the chair to sit down.

"No, not at all, just long enough to order us both a beer. How's it going" Riley asks, gently cheersing my Shock Top beer.

"Oh, not much, just working a lot, as always. Hanging out with the dogs. That sort of thing. What about you?"

"Yeah, same. I've just been busy with work. Boss has me leading a project just outside of town, this bazillionaire wants a mansion, so I've been there every single day pretty much" Riley explains.

Riley is a carpenter and always seems to be pretty busy with his work, which is good for him.

"That's awesome. Are you still trying to renovate your basement too?" I ask.

Before Riley can respond, our waitress comes by to ask if we would like anything to eat. We both order a double order of honey teriyaki wings.

"Sort of. When I can. I'm working so much on this big house, that by the time the weekend comes, I'm usually pretty tired, especially with how late hockey is on Friday nights. Speaking of, I saw you had a lovely visitor drop by the rink. I didn't know Heather was back in the picture" Riley questions with a smirk.

"I knew that would come up. Yeah, I don't know man. We're not back together, and we're not broken up. We are trying to work on things to see if we actually want to be together. It's sort of confusing. I don't even really know what I want" I admit.

"Fair enough. Well hopefully by trying to work on things it'll give you some answers."

The evening passes with small chat as Riley and I catch up on work, relationships, and hockey. Riley is also playing in the upcoming tournament that Jenn is putting together but has to miss the first game on Friday because of work, so he will be driving up and meeting up with us afterward.

After about two hours, our waitress comes by and drops off our bills. We quickly pay and make our way out of the pub. As I'm getting in my truck to leave, I feel my phone vibrate with a text message. I glance down and see that it's from Heather, asking if I want to take the dogs for a hike in the morning. I reply sure, and that I'll meet her at the Lookout trail at ten a.m. This will be a good opportunity for me to tell her about the hockey tournament.

Morning comes quickly, and I told the dogs we're going for a hike, and honestly, I really do think that they can comprehend some words, because they are highly excited.

I park in the parking lot at Henna Park, which is basically just an area with a bunch of hiking, biking, and walking trails, and make my way over to the Lookout trail entrance. Heather arrives shortly after and greets me with a hug.

"Hey! Thanks for coming, I sort of missed these guys...and maybe you too" she says with a flirty smile.

"Yeah, it's a perfect day for it, and I know the boys are excited" I say making my way along the trail.

We chat about everyday things, work, friends, and I can't help but feel a bit distracted knowing that I should be telling her about the hockey tournament but feeling nervous. Which, I don't even know why I'm nervous. It's not like Blake and I are going together as a couple or something. We booked the room as friends, and with another friend going too. Plus, I'm asking Heather to join, so that she can see that there really is nothing to be concerned about. I guess I just know

Heather and I know how jealous she can get. I decide to just jump into it during a moment of silence.

"So, I have that hockey tournament in Duncan coming up," I say nonchalantly.

"Oh yeah, that will be fun. When is it again?"

"Next weekend. Also, I just wanted to let you know that I booked a hotel room with a few friends. There's only three of us, so you're welcome to join if you want."

"What friends?" Heather asks directly.

"Dan and Blake. I think they're driving up together. Riley is coming too, but he has to miss the first game, so he is just going to meet up with us there."

"Blake like, your neighbour Blake? Girls are in this tournament. And you're sharing a room with her?"

"Yeah, it's co-ed, but not just her, like I said Dan is sharing the room too," I respond defensively.

"Figures as much you'd be sharing a room with Blake. She's totally into you and I wouldn't be surprised if you like her too," Heather says, as she increases her walking pace.

"If I liked her Heather then I wouldn't even be telling you about this hotel room situation, and I wouldn't be inviting you to join. I would be secretive and keep it from you and go anyway. Something I'm sure you know a lot about."

Low blow. Even for me, but I'm tired of her jealousy. I'm trying to be upfront and honest, and I'm still met with this.

Heather stares at me blankly, unsure of what to say next.

"Well, that was uncalled for."

"Yeah. Sorry. I just hate how jealous you get sometimes, and I'm trying to be honest with you. I'm trying to invite you so you can be apart of the weekend and see for yourself that there is nothing to be concerned about. Blake and I are just friends. So do you want to come or not. I'm leaving Friday around three p.m." I ask somewhat impatiently.

"Okay. Yeah, I'll come."

Great. I know I should be excited that Heather is coming, but anytime something good happens, Heather always seems to find a way to ruin it. Hopefully, it will be different this time. Hopefully, we can just get along, and she can see firsthand that there is nothing going on between Blake and I and we can all just have a fun weekend.

Hopefully.

Blake Taylor

Dan agreed to drive to Duncan for the tournament and said he would be picking me up around three so that we could stop at the liquor store on the way. I put my hockey bag, overnight bag, and hockey stick at the top of the driveway, and I quickly bring Merc up to my parents' house as he will be staying with them for the weekend while I'm away. As I'm making my way back down to my suite, Dan's black jeep pulls into the driveway.

Dan gets out and makes his way over to my hockey bag, swings it over his shoulder as if the bag weighs two pounds and brings it to his trunk. Dan played competitive baseball, so he's quite athletic and muscular, which is evident in the way he plays hockey, and all sports really.

"Thanks!" I shout, as I approach him with my overnight bag and hockey stick. I throw these in the trunk and hop in the front seat.

"You're really dressed for the part aren't ya?" Dan asks jokingly.

"What do you mean?"

"I'm just bugging, you just totally look like a hockey player right now," he replies.

I guess he's right. I have loose fitting jeans with holes in the knees, Vans sneakers, a plain white V neck tee shirt with an unbuttoned black plaid over top and a black hat on backward. In my defence, this is what I would be wearing even if I wasn't playing a hockey tournament. What can I say, I'm a tom-boy.

"What did you expect me to wear? A dress? Just cause I'm a girl doesn't mean I have to dress like one all the time," I reply jokingly.

"I know, I know, I'm kidding Blake. K we headed to the liquor store first, right?"

"Yeah, that would be good, I didn't have time to pick up beer."

"Okay sounds good. What time is our game again? We basically have to head right to the rink, right?" Dan asks.

How do men get through life without ever knowing plans and how to make a time schedule?

"I have no idea, I thought you knew," I reply, looking at Dan worriedly.

"Seriously? You don't know? Well, I don't either. I don't even know what rink to go to, or what time we're playing. Shit. Do you want to text someone on the team to ask?" Dan replies, slightly panicked.

"I'm kidding, ya dork. Of course, I know. I know all the details because I actually read the texts that Jenn sends out with all the information," I laugh. "Yes, we are driving right to the Duncan Civic Center to play our game which starts at six. It's about an hour drive, so we have plenty of time to get beer and arrive, even with time allotted for traffic. I have no idea how you get through life and make it to anything on time, Dan. What would you do without me," I joke once again.

"Thanks, smart ass."

People seem to think that Dan has the hots for me. I actually met Dan through Colin. Dan is good friends with Chris and Talia, which then led him to becoming friends with Colin, as it's a pretty tight knit group. He joined our beer league baseball team for a tournament when we were short, he ended up loving it, (of course, considering he used to play semi-pro), and joined the team permanently. I've never looked at Dan in any type of way other than a good friend, especially because he was a friend of Colins. Now that I'm single, that still doesn't change. Some would say that my banter with the guys is flirting, but that's honestly just my personality. I treat girls the exact same. I like to joke around, poke fun, make jokes and even joke about my own self. I don't think Dan has the hots for me, but I've also been told that I'm oblivious to those types of things.

"Earth to Blake are you in there?" Dan asks. I guess I was zoned out in thought.

"Yeah what, sorry I was thinking."

"I asked if you knew who else was coming this weekend."

"Sorry, okay well Jenn of course, Riley is coming but he will be late, so that sucks considering he's our goalie, so I think someone has to jump in nets for today's game, Alec is coming, obviously, which you know cause we're sharing a room with him, and I think a few other people from beer league and tournaments we've played in before. It should be a good group." I reply.

I'm wondering if Dan noticed my speech accelerate as I mentioned Alec sharing a room with us. I felt as though my throat was closing, like it was difficult for me to even get that sentence out. I can't believe I'm going to be sleeping in the same room as Alec. I wonder how this is going to work. One girl, two guys. Will they just share a bed together and let me sleep alone? Am I meant to just choose who's bed I want to sleep in? Will one of them just sleep on the floor so we can all sleep alone? I don't know why I'm so stressed about this. I'm just so excited to think that there could be a possibility that I could share a bed with Alec. And that's absolutely thrilling.

After grabbing our beer, I text Alec to see if he's left yet, but I don't hear back from him. By the time we arrive at the rink, it's four-forty-five because traffic was a bit heavier than normal. We decide to pop the trunk and tailgate a quick beer as we wait for teammates to arrive. Tailgate parking lot beers are tradition with hockey tournaments.

Slowly but surely, most of the players arrive, and by five-twenty-five, there's still no sign of Alec. Dan and I decide to make our way into the arena and start getting dressed. We get into our dressing room and take a seat.

"Who said they were bringing the speaker for music again?" Jenn asks the team.

"Alec is bringing it," I reply.

This sucks, getting dressed without music just isn't the same. I text Alec again asking where he is and if he has the speaker.

Still no reply.

By five-forty-five I'm assuming he isn't coming and as I am hunched over lacing up my skates, when the door flies open, and Alec comes rushing in.

"Sorry. I know I'm late, but I've got the speaker, and I'll be dressed in time," he shouts to the room full of players. Do you remember what I was thinking earlier about how do men get through life with no time management skills? Point proven.

Alec grabs a seat next to me and hooks up the speaker and quickly starts getting dressed. I hope he didn't notice my eyes light up as he entered the dressing room and then grabbed his seat next to me. I try not to look at him. I don't know why, but looking at him is sending electric jolts through my body all the way to my toes. It's actually a bit annoying to be honest. I miss the days I could look at my best friend and not feel like a plugged-in toaster that was dropped into a bathtub.

I steady my breath, clasp my hands together to keep them from lightly shaking, before looking toward Alec.

"I'm surprised you made it," I say to him. "What took you so long?"

"Heather and I got in a fight, so we ended up leaving late."

Heather? Alec and Heather got in a fight? He said *we* ended up leaving late. Does that mean Heather is here too? What the hell. Why would she be here, she doesn't even play hockey. Ugh. Well, there goes the shock currents.

"Heather's here too?" I ask, not really hiding the annoyance in my voice.

"Uh, yeah. I thought I told you that. I wanted her to feel comfortable with all of us sharing a room," Alec replied, scrambling to get his hockey equipment on.

She'll be comfortable all right, there's no way in hell I'm staying in the room now, that will practically be a double date, and if Dan does have the hots for me, I don't want to give him any wrong ideas. I'll wait until after the game to tell them I'm out.

The moment I step on the ice, my annoyance dissipates. I'm in my happy place. I place my water bottle on the forward end of the bench and then skate a few laps, grab a puck and take a couple shots on net before making my way to the boards to do a few stretches. Jenn comes up beside me and joins in on the stretches.

"We have such a good turnout of players, there's no way we don't win this tournament!" she says excitedly.

"I know right, I'm so happy there's such a good group of us."

"Hey, don't forget the female rule. Because this tournament is co-ed, there must be one female on the ice per team at all times. So, you and Bailey are each on a separate line and then I'm back on defence, so just make sure we always have one of us out there," Jenn reminds me.

"Right, okay yeah. Are we doing fixed lines or just running wing partners and rotating centres?"

"We are just gonna rotate two centres and have wing partners," Jenn says as she switches into a pigeon stretch. "I have you wing partnered with Alec for the tournament cause you guys play well together. Even though you're both right-handed, he prefers to play left. Weird I know."

Before I can respond she's back up and making her way to the bench to talk to some of the other players.

I finish up my stretch and join the other players in warming up the goalie and taking shots at his pads. Shortly after, the ref blows the whistle, and that's our cue to clean up the pucks and get ready.

The game flies by and I have an absolute blast. Jenn was right, Alec and I do play well together. We both always seem to know where the other will be, so our pass rate is typically 90%. We end up winning the game three to two, and Alec even got a goal.

Back in the dressing room, I put my ballcap back on to try to somewhat tame my sweaty hockey helmet hair as we all debrief about the game, share a beer and get undressed.

I'm sitting in the corner of the dressing and Dan is on my left, and then on the other side of the corner is Alec. Although we are next to each other, because we are right in the corner, it's actually as though we are adjacent to each other, across even. If I'm not careful with how I get changed, Alec will have a front row seat to a peep show.

I have learned over the years of playing co-ed hockey, that it's impossible to try and get in the shower and have any ounce of privacy. There is no curtain or door on dressing room showers, it's literally wide open. So, I have also learned to sit away from the shower, so I don't get any front row tickets to shower peep shows either.

With that being said, sometimes some arenas will have a ref's changeroom that they allow the women to shower in, but this arena doesn't have that option. Thankfully for me, I thought ahead and packed a bikini. Typically, I don't shower after hockey because I'm always going straight home, but with tournaments, we always go out for food or whatever afterward, so it's ten times better for myself, (and those around me) if I show up showered.

I grab my bikini and flip flops and sneak into the toilet stall to change into my bathing suit. I put my clothes back over by my bag, grab my shampoo, brush, and a fresh towel to wrap around me. After about two minutes of waiting, the shower is free, and I jump up to claim it. I'm sure some of the guys are sneaking peaks, but I just try to get in and out as quickly as possible.

Let me tell you. Trying to shower in a bikini and make sure every part of you is getting clean without revealing anything is tougher than you think. And then, trying to change back into your clothes isn't any easier.

While I'm getting my clothes back on, Alec and Dan had made their way to the shower, which works out perfectly because it gives me a little wiggle room to get my clothes on while wrapped in the towel.

When they're finished, they make their way back to their appropriate spots and I do everything I can to keep from staring (and maybe drooling) at Alec as he returns in nothing but a towel low around his waist. How could this even be allowed? Co-ed tournaments. This should not be a thing. Don't they realise that people of the opposite sex have hormones? This is worse than one of those Thunder From Down Under shows.

And then, to top it off, he takes his sweet-ass time getting dressed. He just sits there. Naked. With only a towel. He's just chatting it up with everyone, drinking a beer. Laughing, talking about the game, his goal, a hit he made. His smile is so...mesmerizing. I feel myself getting hot and realize that I've been sitting here staring at him, not actually participating in the conversation. I'm such a creep.

But honestly, does he even realize that where the towel adjoins, the slit runs up the side of his leg to his hip. One sudden movement and I'll definitely be seeing more than I signed up for. Finally, he grabs his underwear and slips them on under his towel. As he stands up to pull them up all the way, his towel does come slightly loose, exposing his deep V by his hip. I panic. I don't see anything, but I basically go into shock. I literally panic as if I've never seen the male body before, as if I'm not currently in school to be a nurse. I panic and quickly close my eyes and turn my head. I'm sure for anyone who may be looking at me from afar would wonder what the hell I'm doing with my eyes closed and why my head whipped from one direction to the other. It's a blessing I didn't give myself whiplash. All that to say, these changerooms are no joke.

By the time everyone is showered up and dressed we all make our way out to the parking lot to discuss the evening's plans. Everyone is staying over in the hotel tonight, but I don't want to stay in the double date room. I quickly pull Dan to the side.

"Are you cool if we drive back tonight? My stomach is pretty upset, and I think I would be more comfortable in my own bed. I'll pay for the gas for the drive back and then our return tomorrow. I'm sorry I feel really bad." I know I shouldn't have lied. But I guess it's not a complete lie. My stomach is in knots especially after seeing Alec almost fully naked.

"Sure, yeah that's no problem and don't even worry about it. Our game tomorrow is at noon, so we will still have plenty of time to get back here tomorrow. Were you wanting to leave now?" Dan asks sincerely.

"Yeah, if that's okay, I'll just say bye to everyone first."

Our team is all in a circle around one of the players trucks. I notice Heather standing next to Alec gripping him at the elbow as if he might suddenly take off. I let the group know that we are heading back because I'm not feeling well, and that we would see them in the morning. Everyone is sad to see us go but understands. I notice Alec shoot me a confused look, but I just wave and make my way to the jeep with Dan.

"Thanks again for driving Dan, I owe you one," I say, looking out the window. It's funny how one little detail can make such a difference. Originally, this was supposed to be the night that possibly Alec and I could sleep under the same roof. I was so excited to just get to spend that extra time with him. And now, here I am, sitting in a jeep, driving an hour back to my house, pouting.

Alec Kohl

That seemed sort of sudden. Blake and Dan just up and leaving. I wonder if they're becoming an item or something and decided they wanted their own privacy. You can tell by the way Dan looks at Blake he's practically in love with her. Well, that sucks, I was looking forward to hanging out with them tonight. I guess it'll just be Heather and I in the room tonight, which makes taking things slow a bit difficult. Maybe I'll fake a stomach issue too and then I don't even have to worry about anything more than sleeping.

After Blake and Dan leave, we all decide to head to the local pub for some dinner and drinks. Some of the other players bring along their girl friends, so it's nice to see that I'm not the only one who brought somebody. Heather looks a bit uncomfortable, as this isn't the type of crowd, she typically surrounds herself with, but it's nice that she's making the effort.

We call it a night around eleven and make our way back to the hotel.

"Thanks for coming out tonight," I say to Heather as I grab my toiletry bag and begin brushing my teeth.

"Yeah, it was good."

We brush our teeth in silence, and I can't help but feel awkward. I don't know what this means for Heather and me. We haven't spent a night together since agreeing to work on things. We haven't really spoken about where we are at in our relationship. I don't know what she is expecting or wanting. I just don't even know. And I can't help but wish that Blake, and I guess Dan too, were also here, to help alleviate some of this awkwardness.

I climb into bed and send a quick text to my friend Jackie who is looking after my dogs to make sure that they're doing okay. She texts back saying that they're doing great and that they enjoyed their hour long hike this afternoon. Spoiled dogs.

Heather makes her way into the bed next to me, and she also appears a bit shy, or awkward.

"Look, I'm just gonna cut right to it. I don't really know what this means for us. I don't want to rush anything. Obviously, we don't need to sleep in separate beds, but I don't want anything happening between us. I'm not there yet," I say to Heather as she pulls the blankets up to her waist. I know that's not typically what a guy would say. Most guys would be gung-ho about having a girl in their bed, but I'm still not over the betrayal from Heather, and I just can't look at her that way yet. Call me crazy, but that's how I feel.

"I totally understand," Heather says with a tiny smile.

We lay in bed watching cable TV for about an hour before finally going to sleep. Sleeping in until nine a.m. feels so refreshing. I'm not sure the last time I had an uninterrupted sleep like that. Normally at home I'm sharing the bed with the dogs, so I always get woken by them repositioning themselves, or occasionally needing to be let out. But last night I crashed, and I'm waking up feeling great.

Heather is already awake, and I can hear the shower running. I decide to turn on Sports Centre and check my phone for any NHL updates. There's a Starbucks Coffee next door that is also calling my name. After waking up a little bit I decide to walk next door and grab us a coffee and breakfast.

Our first game is at noon, so I only have to be at the rink for about eleven-fifteen. It doesn't take me very long to get my equipment on, but I like to take my time and chat with everyone. We leave the hotel at eleven and Heather asks if we can stop at a gas station so she can grab a few magazines so she can read them while she waits for our game to start.

I get into the dressing room and grab my normal seat next to Blake. Dan is also on her other side. I can't help but feel his eyes on me as I sit next to her.

"Hey, sucks you guys didn't stay out last night, would have been nice to hang out at the pub afterward and what not," I say as I place my bag on the floor and sit down.

Blake is opening up her hockey bag and sorting through her equipment. She pauses and looks up before saying "Yeah, I know, I just really wasn't feeling well. Must have been something I ate earlier that day. I'm glad you guys had a good time. Is Heather here watching again?"

"Yeah, she's out in the stands reading a magazine until we hit the ice. Which is fair. That must be boring when you don't even know who's playing. I told her she could come in the dressing room, but she didn't want to," I reply.

We catch up and small chat while slowly getting our equipment on, and then at ten to twelve, we get on the ice and warm up a little bit.

Jenn has Blake and I as wing partners again for this game, which makes sense, because we really do play well together. I don't know what it is, but we seem to be able to know where the other person is, making setting up plays really easy.

After about five minutes into the first period, I'm livid. The referee is completely biased, and favouring the home team, which is completely unfair. We have already had three penalties, for things that shouldn't have even been called in the first place. I can tell already this is going to be a frustrating game. I also have a hard time keeping my cool in regard to things that are blatantly unfair.

Well, eleven minutes in, and I'm in the penalty box. Kyle got a penalty for "tripping" a player on the other team, when he didn't trip him at all, his stick didn't even touch the other player, that guy totally just fell on his own. So, I told the ref to get a pair of glasses as I skated by, and he gave me a penalty for unsportsmanlike.

By the time, the third period comes around we have had around twelve penalties, and we have been turning that rage into points, because we're actually up by one, with the score being four to three. I just did a quick double shift to try and help kill off a penalty, so I'm the first one from my line to get off the ice, while Blake and Kyle are still on.

It's as if it happens in slow motion. Down in our end, Blake gets hit by a 250 pound 6'3 man. He does happen to be on our team, they both just had a weird collision of sorts, but it doesn't excuse the fact that he just flattened her, and she's down, and she's not moving. Heat roars through my body. My hands and toes start to go numb. I go into panic mode as I see her lying on the ice. I can't help myself; it hurts me to see her hurt like that. I don't even realize what I'm doing until I'm already half-way over to her. The whistle blows and I've already left the bench skating as quickly as I can to get to her. By the time I reach her, she's managed to get herself onto her knees and hands. She's gasping for air, dry heaving, actually. It looks as though the wind was completely knocked out of her. I try to lighten the mood.

"Blake, it's me, Alec. Look at me."

Blake is still on all fours, gasping for air. Her eyes look as though they're about to pop out of her head. She actually looks like a cartoon character, but I still can't help but worry about her. She looks scared.

"Blake, just think about the cheeseburgers we can eat when the game is done," I say to her. I don't know why I say that. I'm trying to distract her from the pain, and who doesn't like food? I guess it was poor timing on my part, because she lets out a grunt and gag as it seems as though that probably wasn't the best comment to make on my behalf, especially to someone who is dry heaving. Noted.

After another thirty seconds, Blake stops hyperventilating, and I help her up to her feet. I hold on to her elbow and escort her back to our bench. I sit down next to her and hand her water bottle. She takes a few small sips, finally regaining her breath.

"Thanks. Fuck, that knocked the wind out of me. I thought my lung collapsed, I literally couldn't breathe," She explains.

"Blake! Oh my God, I'm so sorry. I wasn't looking, that was totally my fault. I didn't mean to flatten you like that. Are you okay? I feel terrible!" Dallas says from the other end of the bench, as he shouts over the other players to apologise for hitting Blake.

"Yeah, I'm good Dallas, I know it was an accident!"

Blake skips her next shift as she mentioned that her chest was hurting a bit, which makes sense considering

Dallas is twice her size and he hit her square in the chest. I'm sure a few of her ribs are bruised. Before stepping out for my shift, I look up at the stands, and I don't see Heather.

We finish the game, and although we had a record number of penalties, we still pulled out the win. We get back to the dressing room and because there are games right after us, we have to be quick and be out of the room within a half hour.

"Guys! I know we need to be out of here quick, but the girls are claiming the shower first because we don't want to share with you. So, we are jumping in now super fast and as soon as we are done, you're free to have it!" Blake shouts to the room. She's already in her bathing suit and in the shower before I've even taken my skates off. Jenn and Bailey are quick behind her.

Not gonna lie, last night when Blake got in the shower in the dressing room, she was wearing a peach-coloured bikini, which was similar to her skin tone, and I totally thought she was showering naked. It shocked me. I couldn't believe she was actually naked in a room full of men. I refused to look up from where I was sitting. I did not want to invade in her privacy and accidentally see her naked, so I just didn't look up at all. When she returned to her seat next to me on the bench, I quickly stood up to claim my turn in the shower as I didn't want to be close to her naked body. I don't know why. Don't ask me why. It wasn't until I returned from my shower that I saw her bikini hanging from the hooks behind her that I put two and two together that she wasn't actually naked in the shower.

So today, I may have sneaked a peak as she stepped into the shower, knowing this time that she was wearing a bathing suit. I regret looking. Instant heat filled my body. A dull burning sensation grumbled through me and that's when I knew I had to look away. I focused on taking off my equipment and pushing Blake out of my mind. I'm able to slip my towel over my waist and remove my underwear from underneath and sit on the bench waiting for my turn in the shower. As I hear the water turn off, I start to rise and make my way over to the shower.

Blake, Jenn, and Bailey all start walking back to their respective seats. In the center of the dressing room, Blake and I cross paths. I secure a hand over the fold in my towel to help secure it, to ensure it doesn't fall mid-walk.

I pass by Blake, making eye contact, doing my best not to let my eyes slip downward. Thankfully with peripheral vision, I'm still able to catch a glimpse of –

SMACK! I wince in pain as my ass is suddenly on fire. I turn around to see a howling Blake and all the guys in the dressing room are howling with laughter too. As Blake and I passed each other, she quickly removed her towel, rolled it up and snapped it on my ass. Well played. Well played. Burns like no other, she got a good snap out of it.

"Well played Blake. That one really stung. But the joke's on you, because in your hurry to towel snap me, your top came undone," I laugh pointing at her.

Blake's face flushes with mortification as she quickly grabs her chest looking down. She instantly realizes that I was joking as she can clearly see that her bikini top is still perfectly secured. But I couldn't resist a chance to prank her back.

The dressing room is still laughing by the time I step into the shower. Now I realize that I'm the vulnerable one. I'm the one who is in here showering naked. Hopefully, she doesn't decide to continue this prank war.

I'm able to shower in peace and we all decide that we're going to go to Boston Pizza across the road for lunch before our next game at five. I make my way to the arena lobby with Dan and Blake looking for Heather. She's standing by the canteen looking upset. Uh oh.

"Hey, Heather, I'm not sure if you've met Dan or not, and you already know Blake," I say politely gesturing to Dan.

"Hi Dan," Heather says quickly, avoiding eye contact with Blake.

"Okay, we'll meet you guys at BP's," I say to Blake and Dan as Heather, and I make our way to my truck. I load up my gear into the box of the truck, removing some of the equipment to let it air out before the next game. There's nothing like putting on wet, sweaty equipment. "What did you think of the game?"

"It was fine. You sure couldn't have rushed over to Blake any quicker though," Heather replies with a snarky tone.

Ah, there it is. That's why she looked upset in the lobby. She's mad that I went to Blake when Blake was hurt. Classic jealous Heather.

"She was hurt Heather. I was checking to make sure she was okay."

"Whatever."

We pull up to Boston Pizza and most of the team is already there. The waitress has us along the back wall, where one side is booth bench seating, and the other side of the table is chairs. We have about four tables pushed up together to form one long table. Heather and I climb into the booth side sitting next to Blake. Dan is sitting across from Blake, and I decide to sit next to Blake, with Heather on my other side.

We spend the lunch socializing and chatting, talking about hockey, and laughing and sharing stories. Heather is particularly quiet, and barely touches her lunch. She gets up to use the bathroom and while she is away from the table, I get a text from her saying that she's pissed that all I'm doing is talking to Blake and practically ignoring her. Brooke is on her way to pick her up and would be here in a half hour and that she is leaving. She said she picked up a shift tonight, so she is going home to get ready and then out to work. I stare at my phone blankly. She's out of her mind. I don't reply. As I put my phone back in my pocket, I can't help but notice that my body is positioned toward Blake, and my back is slightly turned to Heather. I guess I didn't realize how much Blake and I were talking. But it wasn't just Blake and me. I was talking a lot to Dan and Kyle was sitting on the other side of Blake, so I was talking to him a lot too. I guess I was talking to everyone and not to Heather all that much. Shit. Guess I can't blame her.

Heather returns to the table and sits next to me, and completely ignores me and the rest of the table and scrolls Instagram on her phone. As everyone is getting ready to pay their bills, Heather hands me a twenty-dollar bill for her meal and excuses herself from the table. Without saying goodbye to anyone, she makes her way out of the restaurant. I don't get up to say goodbye. I just sit there, frozen. A sense of relief consumes me. I didn't realize how stressful it is to always be thinking about Heather, and if she's uncomfortable about something, or if she is having fun, or if she is enjoying herself, or if she is mad at me for something. That when she leaves, I'm able to take a full deep breath.

"Did she just leave?" Blake quietly asks me.

"Yeah, she said she picked up a shift at work, so her friend came to get her."

The rest of the day is a blast. We finish up at Boston Pizza and we all head over to the rink to play our next game. Which we win again. We all have so much fun, and this time there is no dressing room pranks.

I decide to skip out on the hotel tonight too, since Blake and Dan are heading back, and Heather is gone, I'm not going to stay by myself. We all drive back home after the game. We make it to the finals for the tournament in which the final game is tomorrow at eleven a.m. I text Jackie to let her know that I'm actually on my way home and don't need her to house sit tonight and that I will be able to feed and let the dogs out tomorrow morning so not to worry.

By the time I get home, there's still no word from Heather. I texted her before driving home that I was heading back and not staying in the hotel. I told her our game was at eleven tomorrow if she wanted to join, but no answer. I do feel a bit bad. Maybe she had a point. I didn't realize how my body was practically angled away from her. That was not intentional at all.

I'm greeted by slobbery kisses and jumping dogs and I wouldn't want it any other way. I take Guinness and Chip out for a quick evening walk and turn on the Xbox to drown out my wandering thoughts.

Blake Taylor

"So how was the tournament, Blake?" Audi asks as I fill my plate with tortellini and Caesar salad. I got home from Duncan at around three and when I came up to my parents' house to grab Merc, they invited me to stay for dinner.

"It was so much fun! I also loved that I was able to come home and sleep with Merc every night, and I'm glad he was able to spend the days here, so he wasn't lonely. But the tournament was fun. We won every single game. My chest really hurts though. I'm pretty sure I bruised a few ribs. One of my own teammates, who is a giant by the way, accidentally hit me and knocked the wind right out of me. It was brutal. But all in all, it was super fun. I even towel whipped Alec on the ass and the whole dressing room thought it was hilarious," I say grinning.

"Oh my God Blake! You smacked a police officer's bare ass?" Audi shouts.

"What? No! He was getting ready to hop into the shower, and he had his own towel on, so it wasn't directly on his skin. And that's true, I always forget he's a cop. Whatever, it was funny."

"Oh, that is pretty funny actually."

We all sit around the table enjoying our meal and making small chat, and I can't help but notice that my mom has a small twinkle in her eye ever since I mentioned the whole towel whipping situation. I'll have to ask her why she looks so love struck later when we have a moment alone.

"So now that you're into a new semester, what courses are you taking Brenna?" I ask, genuinely curious.

"Political science, pre-calc, English lit, and theatre. It's been a great semester so far. Oh, and you were right about visual arts. Do you remember how last semester I was having a hard time deciding between electives? Well, the visual arts teacher has no problem with me using the classroom after school or during the lunch break, so I did that all last semester, and I'm doing that again for this semester. Miss A is pretty awesome."

"Dang, that is awesome, so nice to hear that teachers are so encouraging, accepting and flexible like that. What are you working on?"

Brenna finishes chewing before replying, "I'm doing this really cool multi canvas painting of the New York City skyline. I was babysitting those two little boys next door, and they made me watch The Secret Life of Pets, and it's based in New York, and there was a few shots of the city, and Central Park and I thought it was so pretty that I wanted to paint it," Brenna says excitedly.

"Wow. That is so cool. I don't have an artistic bone in my body," I reply.

"Yeah Bren, really cool, I can't wait to see it when it's done," Dad says.

"Are you bringing it home when it's done Brenna?" Mom asks.

"I don't think so. It's pretty big, and the geography teacher actually came into the class as he heard I was painting it and loved it, and said that if I wasn't bringing it home, he would love it for his class. I thought that was pretty cool, so I might do that. Miss A also said I should consider selling some of my paintings at that art café downtown. A lot of local artists sell their things there. Miss A said I have to try and build up my portfolio a little bit, take pictures of everything that I'm doing, and then show my portfolio to the café owner to show them what I can do, and then they basically offer you a spot if they feel like your things will sell. Miss A said she would come with me when I present my portfolio. I told you she's awesome."

"Oh my gosh! I know that café, I bought the cutest little hand made clay earrings from there! That would be so, so, cool Brenna if you got your things in there!" Audi says enthusiastically.

We finish our meal and I offer to tidy up as a thanks for cooking and having me over. I'm rinsing off the dishes when I wave my mom over to come see me.

I dry my hands on the dish towel and then turn to look at my mom as she approaches. "What was with you at supper, you had this look on your face like you were trying to keep a happy secret or something?" I ask.

"Oh, it's nothing!" mom replies modestly.

"Bull. Spill it."

"It's honestly nothing, and it's probably something I shouldn't even really say. Because it's none of my business. And possibly inappropriate."

"Okay now I need to know!" I say impatiently, as I give my mom my full attention.

Mom looks around, as if to ensure everyone else is distracted, to ensure that what she will say will only be between the two of us, thereby increasing my anticipation. "Well, it's just, I know he's older or whatever, but hear me out, have you ever thought that on paper, you and Alec would be perfect for each other? I could totally see you two married one day."

Did I just hear her right? She said Alec, right? Like my older neighbour Alec? My best friend, the guy who comes over for dinners and holidays. That Alec? The same Alec that I am currently crushing hard on. She's talking about him, right? I'm sure my cheeks are redder than a tomato before I'm able to formulate a sentence. "Yes, I have." That's it. That's all I can manage.

"Really, you have!" Mom exclaims excitedly.

"Yes, and I'm actually in the middle of a pretty serious crush on Alec at the moment, but nothing can even happen because, well first of all, he's sort of working on things with Heather, and second of all, I'm sure he just looks at me like family, especially given our age difference, and the way he's welcomed into our home, as if he is family."

"Ahhh, I had a feeling, you might have a crush. It makes total sense. You guys really are perfect for each other. You get along so well, and who cares about your age really. When you click, you click. I understand you not being able to act on it because he might be working on things with Heather, but if it's something that you feel really might be worth pursuing, maybe it wouldn't hurt to let him know. I know that's a hard thing to navigate, considering things with Heather, you would never want to be disrespectful of their relationship. But maybe feel it out, see where his head is. Maybe they're not actually back together, and maybe he is looking for a sign, and maybe you're the sign he's waiting for," Mom says with a smirk.

See, this is why I love my mom. She gives the best advice. She knows me better than anyone else. I haven't told a soul about my crush on Alec, and here she is, having known basically this whole time, and encouraging me to pursue it, all the while still being respective of his possible relationship. If that's not a good mom, I don't know what is.

"Yeah… I don't know. It's still nerve racking. Like, we have never, and I mean never looked at each other that way. We have never even flirted or touched! I've never even hugged him. So, it's intimidating, going out on a limb, and expressing myself, with the very possible outcome of him completely rejecting me, and then our friendship is weird. We have always been so platonic. I also don't want to ruin that. He truly is my best friend. What if he says he doesn't like me like that?"

"What if he does?" Mom says as she walks away, leaving me with my thoughts, full well knowing that she just dropped a major thought bomb on me.

I stare at the dishes on the counter blankly, having trouble connecting my brain to my limbs, as I consider her statement, *what if he does.* Hmm, what if he does? Wouldn't that be something. I never actually considered that option, I always just told myself not to act on my crush, that it will go away, that it will never happen between us. But maybe this time I've been wrong. I will never know how he feels if I never tell him how I feel. Maybe mom is right. Maybe it's worth feeling him out, seeing where his head is at with the whole Heather situation and go from there about confessing my feelings for him.

"Are you going to stare at those dishes all night Blake, or can I help you load them into the dishwasher there, pal?" Dad says jokingly, as he points to the pile of dishes still waiting to be rinsed.

"Right, yeah sorry, I was distracted. It's okay dad, I got it. You enjoy your evening and I'll come join you on the deck when I'm all done. I won't be long now that I've got my head in the game again."

I load up the dishwasher and then join my parents on the back deck, for a February evening, it's actually quite mild and with the little heaters turned on, it's quite comfortable. Audi went over to Trevor's and Brenna is in her room, so it's just the three of us and the dogs. I try to stay as present in the conversations with my parents as possible, but sometimes my mind wanders to the neighbour next door. I try to snap out of it, and engage, talking to dad about his new smoker, and sports, and playoffs, and the upcoming Formula 1 season. I also try to engage with my mom, talking about her work, and some of the cute new boutiques downtown, and how school is going, but I can't seem to turn my brain off from Alec.

As if the universe is wanting to play some cruel joke on me, speaking of the devil himself, Alec appears out on his back deck with his two dogs, and makes his way to the back gate. It looks as though he's going out for a walk. I'm flooded with nerves. I don't know if it's because I actually acknowledged my feelings, and verbally said them out loud to another human being, making them feel more real, or what, but I can barely look up and over toward him, without feeling as though I might melt.

"Hey Alec, nice night eh buddy, you're welcome to join us," Dad shouts. What a traitor. Can't he see me writhing in my chair trying to avoid Alec seeing me. Mom and I exchange looks. My eyes must read panic. Mom's eyes read excitement. She even does a little eyebrow wiggle. They're both traitors!

"I'm just taking the dogs out, if you're still out when I get back, I'll pop over," Alec replies as he makes his way out the back gate. I'm pretty sure he didn't see me at all, so that's good. Normally, he would invite me to go with him, so I'm assuming he doesn't know I'm here.

I wait a few minutes until I know the coast is clear and then I tell my mom and dad I should be heading back to work on some homework. I thank them for dinner and skedaddle myself and Merc back to my suite. I'm sure my mom knows why I'm jetting off so quickly, but that's neither here nor there.

Alec Kohl: Spring 2016

Well, it's been almost two weeks since the hockey tournament and I'm pretty sure Blake and Heather are both avoiding me. I can understand why Heather is, but I have no idea what I did to upset Blake. I've asked her to come out for a few dog walks, but each time I've asked, she has some sort of excuse as to why she can't make it. She didn't even come to hockey on Friday.

Heather, on the other hand has made it quite clear that she doesn't like this in between limbo stuff. She either wants to be back together or broken up. She admits that she has a jealous side, and that her jealousy got the best of her at the hockey tournament. I tried to explain that it's her jealousy that pushes her away from me, and I'm trying to gain her trust back again. So, I really have no idea where we even stand to be honest.

Riley and I are going for wing Wednesday in about an hour, and I'm inviting Blake, and hopefully she will want to come. This is sort of our weekly thing, so if she doesn't come, then I'll know something really is up, and I'll have to ask her what's going on. Women's brains I tell ya.

As I'm hating the inner workings of the female brain, my phone alerts me of a text message from Blake saying that she will meet us there. Okay, I take back those thoughts. But in my defence, women really are confusing.

Guinness, Chip, and I are on our way back from our dog walk and they're having a blast chasing after the ball and saying hello to other dogs and people walking by. It's wild how much love you can have for animals. I seriously love these dogs so much. Dogs are so loyal, loving, trusting. They would do anything to please you and make you happy and proud. They continuously show you unwavering love, and they're always so happy. I don't know what I would do without them.

I get back to the house and change my clothes and brush my teeth then make my way to McDuffs. I'm the first one here, so as always, I grab a table in the back corner where we always try to sit. It's sort of become tradition that whoever arrives first will always order a beer right away for whoever is joining. The waitress approaches me shortly after I grab a seat, and I order three Shock Top beers. They're not my top choice in beers, but they're the wing Wednesday special so you really can't go wrong.

A few minutes later, Riley and Blake both arrive at the same time, and they join me at the table.

"Hey, sorry we kept you waiting, the parking lot was full, and I saw Blake pull in as I was parking, but there were no spots, so she had to park on the street, and I just waited for her. Thanks for the beer," Riley says, pulling his chair out to sit. Blake pulls out the chair next to him and sits down, as that's where the waitress put the beer.

"Yes, thanks for the beer!" Blake adds.

"I feel like I haven't seen you guys in forever," I say, sipping on my beer.

"What do you mean? I just saw you at hockey on Friday," Riley says.

"Yeah, that's true, I guess I meant more Blake. Where have you been? I haven't seen you since the tournament."

"I know! I've been so busy with school, and then Friday I had already committed to other plans. What can I say, I'm a hot commodity," Blake replies as she stares me directly in the eye, with a sort of air about her. Is she flirting with me?

The night passes rather quickly, as we're having a great time watching hockey, eating orders after orders of wings, and equally, beer after beer. It isn't until I stand up to use the washroom that I notice myself feeling a bit buzzed. I'm going to have to switch to Coke's otherwise I'll be taking a cab home tonight.

I return from the washroom and notice Blake is also appearing a bit buzzed. Maybe she will follow my lead in switching to Coke when I do. Riley seems fine, but he skipped out on some of the rounds. As the third period of the Flames game finishes, Riley gets up also to use the washroom.

"I gotta say something now that we're in private. And please know, if it weren't for the amount of beer

I've had tonight, I wouldn't be saying this at all. But it's been eating at me Alec. Literally eating at me. Do you know what that's like? To have a thought just literally eat at you?" Blake says.

"Um, no I've never had something literally eat at me."

"Ugh. You know what I mean. I've been fighting this for months now, and I gotta get this off my chest because it's" –

"Let me guess, literally eating at you?" I interrupt.

"Yes! Exactly! See, you do get it."

"Okay, get to it Blake, what's up?" I ask.

"Well, you're not gonna believe it. But my mom and I were talking right after the tournament and she pulled me aside and said that on paper, you and I would be perfect for each other, and she could see us married one day."

Wow. I was not expecting that. Kara said that. Kara said that to her own daughter. About me? Does she realize that I'm almost ten years older than Blake? Wait, Kara said that to Blake? I literally don't even know what to say right now, so I take another drink of my beer. I look at Blake over the lip of my beer glass and suddenly she looks different. It's like I've been wearing fogged up glasses, and Blake's confession completely cleared them up, and I can see her clearly now. Her eyes are twinkling. Her eyes are big and doe like. She almost seems giddy. She's beautiful.

My thoughts are interrupted as Blake continues. "I know. Wild hey. I can't believe my own mom said that to me. But mothers know best I suppose." Blake looks at me with this type of smirk that I haven't really seen before. It's a flirty, excited, and confident look all wrapped up in one. She's making eye contact with me, and it's making me nervous. I've never really been nervous around Blake, and suddenly I'm feeling myself get hot. It doesn't take much, but just looking into Blake's eyes are creating embers. I'm sure onlookers would be able to see the sparks flying all around us. "Anyway, Riley will be back to the table any moment, and I would prefer if we kept this between us, so I'll be changing the subject now, and ordering some water, I'm feeling the beers a little bit."

If I wasn't sipping on my beer, I'm sure my jaw would be hanging open. What does this even mean. Okay, her mom thinks we would be perfect for each other, but Blake didn't say what she thought of it. That was so completely out of the blue and she said it so nonchalantly like she was telling me that she bought a new pair of hockey skates or something. I don't even know what to think right now, and to top it off, Riley is back at the table, and I'm supposed to just act normal.

"Dude, you, okay? You look like you're in shock or something?" Riley asks as he grabs his seat.

"Yeah, sorry. I was lost in thought there for a moment. I'm actually going to follow your lead and use the washroom," I say as I start standing from the table.

Blake shoots me another confident smirk, and suddenly my head is swirling. Has she always smiled like that, and I've just been blind to it? Is this some sort of new smile that she is sporting? Why, all of a sudden does it feel like the room is closing in, and the air is thickening when I look at Blake? I was not expecting that at all, and I'm dying to know what she even thinks, and now I don't even have the chance to ask her because Riley is back. Is it possible she was telling me that because she was hoping I would read between the lines and assume that she feels the same way too? I never even thought in a million years that she would look at me in any type of romantic way at all. I remember when we were walking home from Jenn's house and I was feeling as though maybe I was starting to like Blake and I had to put a kibosh to it because I didn't think there would ever be a chance, and now here she is, telling me that she her mom thinks we're perfect for each other. What parallel universe is this?

I get to the washroom, and I don't actually need to use the washroom, I just needed a moment to collect myself and process what just happened. Between Blakes declaration on behalf of her mother, and my inability to even look at her without my head popping off, I don't know how I'm supposed to return to the table and play it cool. I wash my hands just out of habit of being in a public washroom and return to the table. Blake and Riley are chatting as though the world didn't just fall off it's axis as it had for me moments ago. Waters have been ordered for the table and Blake is already on her second glass.

"A rule of thumb when drinking Riley, is always go to bed sober. So, if you're going to indulge and have a few drinks, in order to beat the hangover, and in order to somewhat take care of your body, always hydrate so that you're not going to bed feeling crappy," Blake says now downing her second glass of water.

"Yeah, that makes sense and all, but water is so boring, I rarely drink it just for kicks. I'm more of a Gatorade or flavoured water kinda guy," Riley responds.

"You sound like the water princess. Just drink it, it's good for you. Add some extra ice then if you want, no one likes room temperature. What about you Alec, how are you feeling? We got you some water," Blake says smiling at me.

It's like she's taunting me. '*How are you feeling*' was that some sort of insider question, meaning she wasn't actually asking how I was feeling drinks wise, but more so how I was feeling about the information she just shared with me. Now she's got me all up in my head and I don't even know what to think. "I'm good, I'll take the water though, thanks."

We sit around for a little while longer, chatting casually, sipping on water and coke, making spontaneous eye contact with Blake that sends a shiver down my spine. We finally decide to get our bills and because we all took separate cars, we all split up in the parking lot. Which is good because I need a few moments to cool off on my own anyhow. The only crappy part is that Blake and I live next door, so the chances of us getting home at the same time and having the awkward walk up the driveway next to each other is quite high.

I decide to make a detour and stop at the gas station on my way home. I fill up the truck, taking my time before driving the rest of the way home. As I pull up my driveway, I notice Blake's car is already parked in her parking spot, and her door light is on, so I'm assuming she made her way inside already.

I get home and I'm immediately greeted by Guinness and Chip, and I let them outside for a quick pee. Through the chaos of the night, I never even had time to check my phone. I notice that I had received a text from Heather earlier asking how my night was. Oh man, what am I going to do. I don't know if I have feelings for Blake. I don't know what I want with Heather. But I do know that hearing Blake's confession made me feel good and sparked something in me. I do know that it made me curious. I do know that it wouldn't be fair of me to continue to try and make something work with Heather if I somewhat have one foot out the door.

The dogs come back inside, and we all collapse on the couch and they both lay on top of me soaking in all the pets, cuddles, and kisses.

"Oh boys, looks like I have some thinking to do, and some decisions to make," I say rhetorically to my four-legged besties.

Blake Taylor

Oh my gosh, what did I do last night. This is all mom's fault. I was doing just fine, living in my own world, silently crushing on Alec, not harming anyone, and then mom has to go ahead and insert her two cents, therefore preoccupying my mind with the "what if" scenario, therefore giving me some sort of beer induced confidence superpower, therefore having me spill my mom's revelation (which is highly embarrassing), to no one other than said crush.

Idiot. What was I thinking? What happens now? What is he thinking? Who knows.

He said nothing. Nothing! So now, my biggest fear may just in fact come true. For all I know he already has my number blocked from his phone, he already is removing me from Facebook. He probably has already told Heather and now she hates my guts. They probably think the neighbours next door are absolute Looney Tunes, where mother's try to pimp out their daughters to the older cop man. I wouldn't even be surprised if I saw a For Sale sign up next door by the end of the day. I most likely just ruined our perfectly perfect platonic friendship. For what? For silence, that's what. Because that's all I'm getting now. Good one Kara. No, that's not fair. She may have been the catalyst, but I'm the one who dropped the truth bomb.

There's part of me that wants to text him and say I'm sorry that I shared my mom's thoughts and that I don't want that to affect our friendship, let's pretend it didn't happen and let's go back to how things were. But then the other part of me, the more authentic part of me, thinks, to just leave it and let the cards fall where they may. One thing I pride myself on is being truthful, blunt, and authentic. Although I didn't come right out and confess that I actually have feelings for Alec, who knows, maybe this will spark some inner thoughts with him, and maybe open his mind to the possibility of seeing me as more than just a friend. Besides, it would be a far bigger pain in my ass to have to fake my feelings around Alec to cater to his feelings.

If he thinks all of this over and thinks both my mom and I are nuts and in turn doesn't want to pursue anything with me, then I will have to slowly distance myself, and get over my crush, before I can continue our friendship as we were. Alec and I were really close, and spent a lot of time together, it would be really hard for me to try and get over my feelings for him if we continued to hangout the way we always do. So that'll suck if that's what happens, but I would rather cool the jets on our friendship for a short duration to try and move on, to then be able to continue our friendship long term. I just can't imagine my life without him, even if that means just being his friend. And I mean, I suppose the other option is that maybe he does like me too. Gosh. The butterflies that erupt just thinking that! Could you imagine? What would my family think? Alec used to be the friend who would come over for dinners, and even holidays, to then my *boyfriend* who comes over for dinners and holidays. Yeah, I can barely even finish the thought without practically dying. Not to be dramatic.

So now, I just have to be patient and wait. I want to give him some space and give him some time to process what I said. I'm sure that was a lot all at once, and then also, I do not have the best timing because Riley returned almost immediately after, so the poor guy couldn't even say anything in return, or even ask me what I think of my mother's opinion.

Thankfully, I have a busy day ahead. I told Audi I would meet her at Viva for a little appy lunch. Sometimes it's hard to see each other and hang out because we're both so busy, so often times I make plans to see her when she is working, but I like to go when it's not busy, so I can sit at the bar and actually chat and catch up with her. And then after I have lunch at Viva, I'm supposed to meet up with Teagan to work on a group project. We are meeting at this really cool indoor-outdoor café called *Working to the Bone,* but most people just call it *The Bone* for short. It's just around the corner from U of Vic and it's dog friendly. So, as long as your dog is on leash, you can bring them to study with you! So, I'll be bringing Merc of course.

I shower and get dressed in my typical Blake attire, Vans shoes, ripped jeans, black V neck tee shirt and because it's a bit chillier out, I added a flannel on top. I blow dry my hair and add on a splash of makeup, and when I say a splash, that really is all it is. I quickly darken my eyebrows and give them a slight shape. Throw on some mascara and a touch of bronzer on my cheekbones. I don't wear foundation or anything because it usually makes me breakout, so with my shower and routine being so fast, I can get out the door fairly quickly.

I quickly pop my head in at mom and dads and notice that Brenna is home. I ask her if she would be willing to let Merc outside for a pee in an hour, and I let her know that I'll be back in a bit to pick him up. She agrees no problem.

I am able to grab a parking spot just around the corner from Viva and I can see that it's pretty quiet in here which is perfect. Audi is polishing glasses as I walk in and greet her. "Hey sista, where should I sit?"

"Hey, hey! Ummm, just sit at the far end over there," Audi points at the end of the bar closest to the tap beer. "Yeah, that's perfect. I like it here because then I don't have to walk very far away from you when I'm behind the bar because everything is so close to this spot."

"Yeah, this works perfect."

"I'll grab you a water and did you want to order right away or wait a few minutes?"

"It's like you read my mind. I'll actually order right away because I missed breakfast this morning. I'll do the steak bites, goat cheese balls, and a coke please," I say. I eat here a lot, so I don't even need a menu any more.

Audi fills up a coke and places it next to my water and continues to polish glasses as she asks me what's new. Oh gosh, do I tell her? Do I tell her what sort of ass I made of myself last night? Yeah, I should. It would be good to get her perspective on it.

I fill her in on the conversation I had with mom after dinner the other night, and then I explain to her that I've actually been crushing on Alec for a little while now, but that I haven't wanted to say anything out of fear of rejection, as well as messing with our friendship. Throughout my little monologue, Audi has completely stopped polishing the glasses, stands completely still listening, and her eyes are wide as if this is the juiciest gossip, she's heard all week. I then proceed to tell her about last night, and that's when her jaw hits the floor.

"Blake! No way! You didn't!" Audi practically shouts.

"Uhh, yeah."

"Oh my gosh! So, what did he say! You know, I can totally see it. At first when you were just telling me all of this, I was like, what Alec? Really? He's literally like family. But the more that I think about it, mom is so right. You two are totally perfect for each other. Oh my gosh! This is so exciting! What did he say!" Audi loves gossip. Perhaps this isn't exactly gossip, but it's juicy information, and she's always all for it. She's over the top enthusiastic because that's just the way she is. It definitely makes me feel good to know that if something were to happen between Alec and I, it seems as though mom and Audi are on board.

"He said nothing," I say with a bit of an awkward chuckle. "I mean, he couldn't really. Riley literally came back to the table seconds after I told him what mom thinks, and I also told him that I want to keep it between us, so not to say anything with Riley at the table. So, he didn't. He seemed, I don't know if uncomfortable is the right word, but it was as if the wheels couldn't stop turning in his head after I said that to him. We didn't stay much longer and then we all went home. And I haven't heard from him."

Before Audi has the chance to respond a little bell 'bings' in the background and she makes her way over to the kitchen to grab my lunch. She places it on the bar in front of me and hands me some silverware and a napkin. "Okay, well that's fair. I mean that would have been super awkward to begin with, but then to add the fact of Riley being there shortly after doesn't help. Oh my gosh, okay well I'm so excited, you have to tell me when you hear from him! Because obviously, I'm totally team Blac."

"Team black?" I ask.

"Not like the colour, like b-l-a-c. It's a combination of your names. It's your relationship name. Team Blac!" Audi says excitedly.

"Oh my. You're way too invested. He might totally turn me down."

"Blake, the only way he's turning you down is if he doesn't have a penis. No man would turn you down," Audi says matter-of-factly.

I laugh at that and take the, what I assume is meant to be a compliment, and change subjects asking Audi about school. I stay for a little over an hour chatting and laughing and then I make my way back home to pick up Merc.

Teagan text me that she will be at The Bone in half an hour. I let her know that I'll meet her there. I get home and can't help but notice Alec's truck in his driveway, and his police cruiser is parked on the street where he always parks it. I wonder what he's doing.

I get home to greet Merc and as I'm about to bring him outside for a pee, I see that Alec is just returning to his backyard from his back gate. It looks like he's just getting home from a dog walk with Guinness and Chip. I panic and quickly shut the door and tell Merc we will go out in a minute. Embarrassment and anxiety swarm as I am not ready to face the music with Alec. A few minutes later I peek out my door and see no sign of him, so I figure the coast is clear to step outside with Merc. Thankfully, I was right.

I throw the ball for Merc for a few minutes and then run inside to grab my laptop and my psychotherapy textbook and toss them in my bag before making my way to the car. Merc follows behind me and he sits comfortably in the shotgun seat. I put his leash and bag in the back and we're off.

Teagan has already found a seat on the patio in the corner, which is perfect. I forgot to tell her I was bringing Merc, but I think she just assumed because this table is great for him. He loves being on the patio so he can look at all the people walking by. He's such a good boy and doesn't bark. He just sits or lays next to me, and he's just the goodest boy.

"Hey girl! I ordered you an iced tea, I hope that's okay. Hi Merc!" Teagan says as she gives Merc some love.

"Yes, that's perfect thank you. Ugh, I hate these stupid group project things. I mean, obviously I love working on them with you, but they're always so boring."

"Oh, I know. But I think we could probably bang it out in one sitting if we just buckle down," Teagan replies.

I set up my laptop and open up PowerPoint as well as the project outline. "Okay, so we need to make a PowerPoint presentation on how we would conduct a psychotherapy group session on any mental illness of our choice. It needs to be a minimum of fifteen slides.

Okay that's easy enough. I think anxiety or PTSD would be easy, what do you think?"

"Yeah, let's do anxiety, it's so broad that we can branch out to specific forms of anxiety too," Teagan adds.

After about an hour of working we order a pizza to share, and I also ask for a little bowl of water for Merc, in which the waitress was happy to provide, and even placed it down for Merc herself. She gave him a few pats before returning to her normal duties.

Teagan and I manage to finish our presentation after about three hours, which seems like a long time, but we would constantly break off into conversation and get easily distracted by catching up on our personal lives. I decided not to tell her about Alec, only because I don't even know what's happening with that right now, and so until I know what's going on, I'm not going to share.

When I get home, I get Merc's dinner ready, and I get changed into comfy lounge wear and relax on the couch with a book. It isn't long before I allow my mind to wander, thinking about Alec and what he's up to. I think about what it would be like to be his girlfriend. To sit on the couch and actually cuddle with him. Would kissing him be weird, would it be like kissing my brother? No, God wouldn't do that to me.

Alec Kohl

After about forty-five minutes, I feel as though I searched my house thoroughly enough to feel confident that I haven't missed any of Heather's belongings. She really didn't have much considering the number of times we have broken up and the fact that she truly moved out after our last break up, so I only conjured up one grocery bag full of her belongings.

It's been about a week since Blake told me what Kara thinks about her and me, and it has thrown me for a loop. It has overly consumed my day-to-day thoughts, and the hardest part is that I don't even know what Blake thinks! Maybe she was just relaying the information as like, locker room talk, you know like 'oh my gosh you would never believe what my mom said to me... crazy right?' For all I know, she might think it's a complete joke and not remotely agree with her mom.

But truthfully, I'm glad Blake told me. I really needed to shit or get off the pot when it came to Heather, and part of me never truly wanted to break up completely because things were comfortable and I'm such a believer in relationships, I'm a serial monogamist, and I just wanted to make it work, and to not fail at something. But I would be lying if I said that

I haven't always wondered about Blake ever since the night at Jenn's. And then to have Blake tell me her mom thinks we're perfect for each other on paper, and that she could see us married one day, it really made me pause and evaluate where I am in life, who I want to be with, and who I can picture myself actually marrying one day.

I mean, to be realistic, it's not like I'm thinking, 'Oh, Kara thinks I should marry Blake, then okay, I'm going to do that!' Not at all, but it has opened my eyes to other possibilities and allow me to really try and examine what I want, and after days and days of self-reflection, I've come to the conclusion that Heather isn't what I want. Even if I don't pursue things with Blake, this reflection time has allowed me to realize that I'm not actually happy with Heather, and I've lost so much respect and trust, and that the biggest reason why I haven't completely ended things, is because I didn't want a failed relationship. But I need to do what is best for me, and what brings me happiness, and it's not fair for either of us if I'm in this relationship not fully satisfied.

Some may say this is really poor timing on my behalf, or some may say it's actually genius, but tonight, myself, Heather, Riley, and one of Heather's friends were all supposed to go to the *Walk Off the Earth* concert together, but I just can't do it. I can't go to it knowing that I want out of this relationship. Hence the packing up all of her belongings. She's actually on her way over, and I'll be ending things for good with her.

As I finish stirring the Cinnabon creamer into my coffee, there's a light knock on the door followed by Heather letting herself in. I can hear her remove her shoes and place her bag by the front entry as she is smothered by Guinness and Chip.

"Hey," I say casually as I walk toward the living room where I place my coffee on the coffee table. "Do you want a coffee or tea or water or anything?"

"Umm, yeah actually I'll just grab some water, thank you." Heather makes her way to the kitchen and fills a glass with water and ice before joining in me in the living room. She sits on the same couch as me, but we have a cushion of space between us (not intentionally, but because the dogs are laying there).

We sit for a moment before I build up the courage to say what I need to say. Although I know deep down this is what I want, and what is best for me, and possibly even Heather too, it doesn't mean that breaking up with someone isn't difficult. I take a deep breath before starting. "I mean there's no easy way to say this Heather, but this isn't working for me any more. I really wanted to make this work, to move on from past hurts to re-kindle what we once had, and I just can't get there. My head, and my heart is no longer in it. I'm really sorry."

I'm pleasantly surprised to see Heather looking at me with a look of understanding, relief. She also takes a deep breath before responding, "Okay. I wasn't really expecting that, I thought we would always be together the way we keep coming back to each other. But I appreciate your honesty, and I'm glad you told me so that we aren't wasting our time. It just still sucks," she wipes the start of a small tear before it has the chance to fully be exposed.

"I know, I feel the same way. I just have been thinking a lot, and that's exactly it, I don't want to be wasting either of our time. I'm glad you can understand. This way we can just move forward, and at least have things end on a positive note."

"Yeah. Ugh, I'm really going to miss these guys," Heather motions to Guinness and Chip as she pets them both. "Okay, well I don't think there's any point in me sticking around so I should get going. I can come back in a few days for some of my things."

"I actually gathered everything and have it in a small bag here," I stand and get the bag from the kitchen and hand it to Heather. "Feel free to look and see if I've missed anything."

Heather looks through the bag as if it's made of porcelain and carefully peruses her items. After what seems to be an eternity, she looks at me to say, "I think that's everything, thank you." Heather walks toward the front door and puts on her shoes, she grabs her bag from the front table and looks like a wounded puppy. I walk toward her and embrace her in a hug. Nothing romantic, nothing sexual, just a comforting goodbye hug. After a few moments, she turns without looking at me and walks out the door.

I breathe a sigh of relief mixed with sadness. I'm relieved to finally be done and have closure, no more of this 'are we together or not purgatory,' but I'm also sad to be ending this chapter. Heather and I did have some great times, especially in the beginning, so I think it's normal to somewhat grieve the relationship that we once had.

I make my way to the living room to clean up her water glass and remember that I have that concert tonight with Riley and what was supposed to be Heather and her friend. Now I need to either find two people to go with us, or I'll be having a guys' night.

My mind suddenly jumps to Blake. How can I ask her to come, without making it seem like it's a date, or like I'm suddenly on the rebound? Maybe I'll see if her and her sister want to go with Riley and me. Just a couple of neighbours going to a concert. Innocent. Harmless. No big deal. No hidden agenda.

My heart quickens as I pull out my phone to text Blake. I realize we haven't spoken much since the night she revealed her mom's opinion of us. We have had random small talk about hockey and the dogs but nothing serious, and nothing to address that night.

I type something out and erase it about three times before settling on something simple.

Hey, Riley and I have tickets to see Walk Off the Earth tonight. Our friends had to cancel last minute, so do you and Audi want to join?

There. Simple enough, I've made it clear that it's not just me asking Blake out, it's a group hang. Do people do group hangs any more?

Within seconds I receive a text back,

Sure. Audi doesn't work today so I'll double check with her but that sounds fun. Not gonna lie, I'm surprised you're not taking Heather.

Okay, now to figure out how to break it to her. Short, simple, then divert.

We have officially broken up. It starts at seven-thirty, come over around five-thirty, Riley is meeting me at my place, and we can all drive together. We can grab a quick bite to eat and a drink beforehand. See you girls soon.

I place my phone on the kitchen island and take what seems to be my millionth deep breath. I can't believe I just did that. I don't know why I feel so nervous. I hang out with Blake literally all the time. But this time it's different. This time I'm hanging out with her knowing that we are both single, knowing that I want to pursue these feelings welling up inside me, but the nervousness comes from not knowing how she feels. Maybe she is coming because she's used to hanging out as friends and thinks it's harmless because Riley and Audi will be there too. Maybe she isn't even giving it a second thought. Maybe I'm the only one over thinking this. Well, whatever, I guess we will see how the evening goes and that'll help me gauge where her head is at.

Audi said she is in. See you in a bit. :)

Well, I'll be damned. There we go. I decide it might be best to exert some of this pent-up energy and to the benefit of my dogs, take them out for a walk. We go to the Beacon Hill dog park and toss the chuck it for an hour while I walk laps around the park. By the time I get home, I'm sweaty and hot so decide to shower. I check the time and it's already four-thirty. I get myself ready and even spray an extra sprit of my best Acqua di Gio cologne (even though this isn't a date, I'm fully aware, but it's more of a respect thing, to smell good for the people around me. It's not just for Blake).

By the time I'm done getting ready and brushing my teeth, Riley is texting me that he is here and walking in. I hear the front door open and Guinness and Chip run down the stairs to greet him.

"Hey! I'll be down in a minute," I shout down the stairs.

I make my way down to greet Riley as he is helping himself to a drink from my fridge.

"Hey, how's it going. So is Heather's friend hot or what?" Riley asks, as he cracks open a Coke can.

"Um, change of plans. So, Heather and I actually broke up, and Blake and Audi are coming instead," I say, a bit quicker than I typically speak.

Riley takes a moment to respond. "You're kidding."

"Nope, not kidding, and they're actually going to be here in a few minutes. Are you okay with that?"

"Yeah, for sure, I'm just thinking that it's about damn time!" Riley exclaims.

"About damn time, what do you mean?"

"It's about damn time that you finally ask Blake out. So of course, I don't mind being your wingman, plus Audi is cute." Riley has seen Audi around just from being my neighbour and he has asked about her before, in which I mentioned her age, and that she has a boyfriend, and that was the end of that conversation. Although Riley is a few years younger than me, I still think he wouldn't want to date that young, plus, she has a boyfriend.

"I'm not asking Blake out on a date. It's a group hang."

"Whatever you say there buddy. But Tod has been calling this one since the day he met Blake, so I'm sure he would have a heyday to hear about this," Riley jokes.

"What are you talking about?" I ask. Tod is one of the older guys from hockey. He's one of the main organizers for our beer league. I've known him for over ten years, ever since I moved here and joined the beer league.

"The first time he met Blake, when she came out to play. As soon as you guys left, Tod made a comment about how much of an idiot you are," Riley pauses to laugh. He sees that I'm waiting for him to continue his thought and explain a bit more, so he then continues, "He said something like 'That girl stares at him like he's God himself. What's he doing with a girl like Heather when the girl next to him is clearly in love with him' or something like that. Everyone in the dressing room sort of laughed and agreed that you were an idiot and then we all carried on. So yeah, Tod would have a heyday right now saying that he called it."

Before I have time to comment, there's a knock at the door. For half a moment, my breathing stops. I can hear my heartbeat in my ears, I can feel it in my carotid artery, and I'm focusing on the lub-dub sound of my heart, Riley interrupts my thoughts as he says with a wink, "Go get her tiger."

Blake Taylor

Well, Alec really didn't give me much time to get ready and thank goodness Audi agreed to come with me tonight. When he texted me, I was not remotely close to being going out ready, so I quickly put on some makeup, straightened my hair, and changed my outfit. I decided on these cute black heeled booties, dark denim jeans, a black tank top and an unbuttoned flannel on top. Casual enough where it doesn't look like I'm trying too hard. Audi looks like a stunner as always. I swear she doesn't even need to try, and she turns heads. She's wearing white denim jeans with a floral crop top and her hair in a messy bun. Not a lot of people can pull off white jeans, but she sure does.

Time feels as though it's in slow motion as we wait at the door for Alec to answer. This is my moment. This is my shot. This is when I can finally make my feelings known. He is no longer in a relationship, so it would not be disrespectful for me to flirt with him. I don't think I am going to come right out and say 'hey I like you' but I will make it very clear based on my flirting and body language that I'm into him. I'll try to get a read on Alec too, if I'm getting total friend vibes, then I'll know to put a lid on the flirting and that he's not into me. But if he flirts back, then that's a whole other ball game.

As we walk next door, I can't help but notice a different vibe from Audi, so I quickly ask her if everything is okay, and if Trevor is okay with her coming out with us tonight.

"Well, what he thinks doesn't really matter. We actually broke up two days ago."

"What!" I half shout.

"Yeah, I mean he has a *lot* of growing up to do, and I think I need to do some soul searching of my own. But we'll leave that story for another time."

I realize that we are approaching the front door to Alec's house, so I briefly stop Audi before continuing. "Just know I'm here if you need anything okay. Now let's have fun tonight!"

The door opens, and Alec greets us with a warm hello. He looks handsome as ever. He's in his modern-day cowboy boots, dark jeans, a button-down flannel (how cute we're both in flannel), a perfectly groomed short haired beard and his black Calgary Flames hat. The facial hair really suits him. Like really suits him. He's never really sported much facial hair before. It's not like a long beard, it's still very short to his face, maybe he's gone three days without shaving, but all the edges are cleaned up, so that it perfectly outlines his strong jawline. Very handsome. I do my best not to gawk and say something coherent. I settle with, "Hey."

Alec and Riley both come onto the front porch and Alec locks up before we all make our way to his truck. Riley says hi to Audi and I and we both return the greeting. I get in the back seat behind Alec, and Audi gets in behind Riley.

"Woooooooooooo! Let's have some fun tonight! You guys are all so quiet and acting like a bunch of tight asses!" Audi shouts as soon as we get in the truck, scaring the living hell out of the rest of us.

"Oh my gosh! You scared me. But yes! Let's have some fun! Thanks for inviting us, guys!" I exclaim.

"This is all Alec's doing," Riley replies.

We drive to Charlie O'Donnell's, (we call it Charlie's), which is a three story (plus a rooftop patio). Irish pub downtown to grab some appetizers and a drink. The waitress, dressed in an extremely short kilt and deep V-neck T-shirt, escorts us to a table on the top floor where it's a little quieter. Audi and I sit next to each other, and Alec sits across from me, and Riley across from Audi.

The butterflies in my tummy settle, but don't completely dissipate. I think they're more of excitement butterflies than anything. I can't believe I'm actually out with Alec right now. Yes, I know Audi and Riley are here, but still.

Every time Alec and I make eye contact it's like there's a magnet that is connecting us. I can't help but feel drawn to him. I get lost in his grassy green eyes, and I can't help but feel warm, safe, seen. It takes everything out of me to break that magnetic pull and look away, because truthfully, it's all to easy to tune out everything around me when I'm looking at him. It's taking everything out of me to be present in conversation with Audi and Riley, so that I don't come across as distracted and rude, but with every moment that passes, an overpowering craving comes over me, in which that magnetic pull drags me back to Alec.

Can he feel it? Can he feel this wave of electricity between us? I've never seen him look at me the way he is tonight. It's as though these past two years of friendship, he has always had this type of guard up, and tonight, that guard is down, and he's letting me in. Letting me see him. As I realize this and realize that he is also not wanting to break eye contact with me, I decide to embrace it. Enjoy it. Relish it. I vow to myself, from this day moving forward, any time I'm in his presence, whenever I am speaking with him, I will always make eye contact, no matter how jittery it makes me, because having him look back at me, the way he is now, is a feeling I don't ever want to miss out on again.

"What is their popular song again? I keep mixing this band up with a different one?" Audi asks, which therefore breaks our magnetic bond.

"They did a remake of a song, and it was sort of acapella and it went viral, and then people got interested in their own music and now they're a pretty big deal. I think the song was 'Somebody that I used to know,'" I reply back. As I finish my sentence, the waitress approaches our table and asks if we would like a drink. I had already scanned the menu and was feeling like a fancy little cocktail, so I ordered the Pink Flamingo.

"Ouu! I want that too!" Answered Audi.

"Actually, that sounds fun, I'll do one too. Riley, do you want in?" Alec asks.

"Yeah, why not. I don't want to be the only one without."

"And actually, if it's okay, do you mind if we order some appetizers now?" Alec asks politely.

"Absolutely! What can I get for you guys?"

"I think we will do loaded nachos with beef and chicken, and then your waffle fries, and two orders of the chicken strip things. Was that everything? I heard you two gals saying you both wanted the chicken strips," Alec says.

Audi and I both respond in unison, "That's perfect!"

The waitress writes down our orders and says she will be back shortly with our drinks. Audi and I continue in minimal conversation as we await our drinks. Alec and Riley appear to be talking about a trade that's happening in the NHL. Riley is a major Toronto Maple Leaf's fan (I have no idea why, considering he isn't even from Ontario, but hey). Audi keeps making googly eyes at me and gesturing at Alec. I keep trying to signal to her to cut it out. I'm anxious as it is, I don't need my little sister trying to embarrass me.

Our drinks arrive and as we are about to do a table cheers, Audi stops us all, "Wait! It's bad luck if you don't look each person in the eye as you cheer them!"

We all sort of chuckle but do as we're told. First, I look at Audi and cheers her, then Riley, and cheers him, and lastly, Alec. We make eye contact, and believe it or not, I think smoke may be coming out my ears as my head feels as though it's about to pop off with the amount of eye contact, we've had tonight. We cheers, and sip from our drink, still not breaking from each other. I finish my sip, and as I'm lowing the cocktail from my mouth, I let out a flirty smile directed toward Alec. I see that it's well received because he returns a grin. Not a full smile, but a grin that is possibly even more delicious than I could have conjured up in my brain myself.

The evening continues with lots of chatter and laughs. We poke fun at each other, and tease Alec and Riley for anything under the sun. They don't hold back either, making jokes where they see fit. By the time our food comes, my cheeks and jaw hurt from laughing and smiling so much.

We have to eat fairly quickly as the food did take a bit longer to arrive, and we don't want to be late for the concert.

To our surprise, Alec actually takes care of the bill and thanks us all for coming out. Audi taps my knee under the table with a swooning type of look that implies 'what a gentleman!'

We make our way back to the truck and hop in to drive the couple of blocks over to where the concert is being held. It takes a few moments to find a parking space, but we finally do and only have to walk a block to the venue.

Once inside, we scan our tickets and make our way down to our seats. The concert is being held at the Victoria Royals arena. They have the ice boarded up, with the stage at one end, a standing section, and then rows of seats. Of course, there are also seats in the regular arena chairs. Our particular seats are down on the ground level a few rows back from the standing section.

We take our seats, with Riley at one end, then Alec, then me, and then Audi and make small talk as we wait for the show to start. The boys get up together and gesture that they're going to get us beers. We give a thumbs up as they walk off.

Before the boys are barely out of earshot, very excitedly, Audi asks, "So! How's it going!?"

I smile widely as I truly feel happy, excited, giddy even, and I can feel my sister's happiness for me. "I think it's going great! I'm having so much fun. And I mean, we never even spoke prior as to like, what this means. I still don't even know if he likes me. All I know is that I like him, and being with him tonight and laughing and just hanging out feels different. I can't stop smiling."

"Blake, sitting next to you two, is like sitting next to a fireplace. You know when someone has their fireplace turned on, and you decide to sit on the little ledge in front of it, and as each minute that passes your skin becomes hotter and hotter? That's how my whole left side of my body felt at that restaurant as you and Alec's connection was on fire."

"Really? You think so? I kept getting frozen every time I would look at him. It's like I would get filled with the biggest butterflies, and the feeling of those butterflies was wanting me to look away, but there was also a part of me that just couldn't get enough," I explain.

"Yes really! Anyone with eyes could see that you two have some sort of connection that people can only wish for. At one point, Riley and I smirked at each other and sort of signalled at you two, because you guys were so deep in conversation it was as if Riley and I weren't even sitting next to you."

"Oh my gosh! I'm so sorry if we were being rude! I didn't mean to ignore you guys!" I say apologetically.

"No! Not at all Blake, but what I'm saying is that you two make sense together. Oh, here they come, I'll shut up!" Audi quickly changes the subject, "So anyway, yeah, Shayla is going to pick me up after this and I'll stay at her place for a little late night girls' night."

The boys re-join us at our seats and they each hand us a beer. Audi and I say thank you and within moments, the lights start to dim, the crowd starts to cheer, and the strum of a guitar fills the arena.

"Helloooooo, Victoria! Are you excited to see *Walk Off the Earth* tonight!" The crowd roars in response. "Awesome! I'm Shawn Hook and I'll be opening things up tonight! Let's go!" He starts singing one of his popular songs 'Reminding Me' and the concert officially begins.

It isn't long before people are up on their feet and feeling the music. Shawn Hook is on stage for about forty-five minutes and then there's a small intermission where the stage crew sets up for *Walk Off the Earth*.

"Blake, let's go grab a beer," Alec signals to me. A small tingling sensation succumbs my body. It's almost like, butterflies in your tummy, but all over your body. You know that feeling when it's winter, and you're in an outdoor hot tub, and you get out, and that immediate rush of extreme cold floods your whole body, that's how I feel right now. I have goosebumps on the back of my neck, down my arms, all the way to my toes. I've never felt such overwhelming excitement mixed with anxiousness. But it's good anxiousness, it's a moment that I've been excited for, for a long time now. To be alone with Alec, to possibly flirt with him. To have him see me in a different light, not just the neighbour girl, and it's finally here.

I steady my nerves and follow him single file down our row until we reach the end to the open area. Alec signals over to the hockey boards and I give him a questioning look.

"It's a short cut. We can hop the boards here and go around behind where the net would normally be and get to the concession quicker," he explains.

"Uhhhh, you do realize that I'm like three feet tall, and I doubt I can even climb over the boards,

"I say jokingly.

"I'll give you a hand if you need it."

We walk toward the boards that Alec pointed to, and he climbs over first. He waits on the other side, and the independent and confident side of me knows that I should be able to climb over without any help, but the other side of me wants him to help me. Pathetic, I know. I climb over and he offers his hand as support, and although I can manage, I don't want to be rude and leave him hanging, so I take his hand as he helps me lower down to the other side. His hand feels so warm, secure, strong, protective, trusting, and safe. I've never held his hand before, but it feels comfortable, like home. Once both feet are planted on the ground we let go.

The venue is very crowded, so we walk very close to each other, and in high traffic areas, I swear I feel Alec's hand on the small of my back, directing me, protecting me. But I'm too embarrassed to look back to see if I truly do feel his hand, so I embrace the warmth and guidance.

We get to the concession, and we stand in line next to each other. I notice the washroom is right next to us, so I hand Alec a twenty-dollar bill and tell him that I'm going to run to the washroom quick. I do actually have to pee, it's probably from all the nerves, mixed with the drinks from the evening, and I also need a quick moment to myself. A moment to gather my thoughts and feelings. I look back at my reflection in the mirror and see a side to myself that I'm not sure I've ever seen before. I'm not the type to toot my own horn, but I look radiant, as if I'm glowing. There's something different, as though there's a twinkle in my eyes that has never been there before. I take my moment, my deep breath, wash my hands and exit.

Alec is standing around the corner waiting for me, holding a trey of four beers. Our eyes meet and a smile escapes his lips. The tingling returns, the goosebumps explore my body and as I approach Alec, my heartbeat intensifies, and if it weren't for the roar of the crowd, I'm sure he would be able to hear it.

We walk closely once again as we return to our seats. When we reach our little shortcut by the boards, he hands off the drink trey to me so he can descend first. When it's my turn I reach the trey down to him and climb down. Getting down is easier because I can do a small little jump once I get both legs swung over the boards.

We return to our row and re-join Audi and Riley, who are now standing next to each other, immersed in conversation. We hand them both a beer and they continue talking. We make it back to our seats just in time, because as I'm about to sit down, the lights dim so that it's quite dark, and the crowd begins to cheer.

The sound of drums beating fills the entire arena, and it's so loud, I can feel the vibration in my chest. Dry ice smoke fills the stage, and lights begin to flash. The sounds of other instruments come into play and the crowd roars even louder. One by one, black figures emerge from the darkness, standing in position behind their said instruments, continuing to play without missing a beat. Lights then shine at the stage, illuminating the band members, allowing for the crowd to connect with this talented crew.

A song that I had never heard before begins, and the music fills the arena, creating a vortex of sound. Alec leans in slightly toward me, I can see his lips moving, but I can't hear him. I step closer to him, and I approach his ear, the way someone would if they were telling a secret. Being this close to him instantly kick starts adrenaline through my body. I can smell his cologne. The hair on the back of my neck rises as I inhale his scent. He smells delectable, with hints of salt water, cedar, and manly musk, and it takes everything out of me to not just stand there, gawking over him like he's a scratch and sniff marker. I lean in closer to ensure he can hear me, but instead of whispering as someone would do when they're this close when needing to tell a secret, I have to speak very loudly, almost yell, and inform him that I couldn't hear him.

I take a step back, so that I'm returned to a respectable distance, and this time it's his turn to approach me. I can see Alec move closer, our faces are so close, we could almost give one another a kiss on the cheek, but for the sake of my dignity, I don't. I simply wait to hear what he has to say. I can feel his breath on my ear before he shouts, "Oh, it was nothing important, I was just asking if you knew this song."

"No, I don't! I like it though!" I shout back.

As the band continues to play, the only way Alec and I can speak, is by leaning in so close to one another, to the point where our lips almost touch each others' ears. But we never touch. We never make contact. Instead, we stand side by side, merely millimeters apart, vibrating from the mixture of our two electric circuits bouncing off one another, and the extremely loud music.

I catch myself staring at him. Not in a creepy stalker type of way, but from a lens of admiration and adoration. There's a type of peace that consumes you, when you observe someone when they don't know they're being looked at. Just watching them be themselves. Watching the world through their eyes. And that's how I feel; calm, comfortable, relaxed, at peace, which, paradoxically is surprising, considering this environment is everything but. But Alec is so handsome. The type of handsome where he doesn't actually know just how handsome he truly is. He's so confident in the person that he is. He's so kind and considerate. And he's just standing here, at this concert, watching this band and having a great time. And I love to see that. I love to see him happy, to see his smile, to see him let loose and enjoy. Okay, maybe I am a creep.

We continue to listen to the music, and our bodies sway in unison with the crowd. The energy in this arena pulses through each loud-speaker, and then through each body that is watching the musicians. There's this vibrational hum that overwhelms my senses, as I try to take in the music. And although I'm present in this moment, in this arena, listening to this song, I just can't shake this electricity pulsing through my veins as I stand millimetres away from Alec. I think if our fingertips were to accidentally bump, we surely would feel a small electric shock, the kind you get when you pull blankets out of a hot dryer.

Alec interrupts my private thoughts as he speaks into my ear, sending goosebumps down my spine. "Looks like they're closing down the show, hopefully they do an encore!"

"Yeah! I'm sure they well!" I call back.

Walk Off the Earth leaves the stage as the crowd cheers for an encore. The lights stay dark, but the music has stopped, all you can hear is the cheering of thousands of people. About ninety seconds passes, and the cheering becomes louder and louder until an all-explosive praise erupts as the band takes the stage for a final song.

As the song comes to an end, a small wave of dread consumes me. I'm sad that this means my night with

Alec is over. I wish we could continue hanging out because I'm having so much fun. But we're here with Riley and Audi and we can't just ditch them considering we all drove together.

We all make our way out of the crowded arena and walk toward the tuck. Audi and I walk together and make small talk as we didn't get to talk much during the concert. She keeps shooting me these "so, what's going on with you two" looks, but I keep dismissing them as Alec is within ear shot, and I don't want to gush over him and have him overhear. Although maybe that wouldn't be such a bad idea, because then he would really know how I feel, but I can't seem to muster up the courage.

"That was such a good show! I loved how they did their acapella song, which was so cool I can't believe they can sound like that without any instruments!" Audi exclaims as we all get seated in the truck.

"I know, they're definitely talented. I don't know if it's because I haven't been to a concert in a while or what, but I forgot how loud it gets! I could seriously feel the drums in my chest," I reply.

Riley turns his head back to join in on the conversation before he responds, "I know, it was so loud we could barely even talk the whole time."

"I didn't mind leaning in a bit closer to chat," I say casually, subtly throwing a little flirt Alec's way. As the sentence leaves my mouth, I see his eyes flicker to the rearview mirror making eye contact with me, and then back to the road. Audi then addresses my comment with a little 'ouuuu' sound, and I kick her ankle to shut her up. We both giggle in the back seat like little schoolgirls.

When we get home, Audi and I thank the boys for taking us out, and we all say our good nights. Alec and Audi make their ways into their houses, Riley hops in his truck to drive himself home, and I also make my way into my suite. I'm welcomed by a very happy Merc, and I let him out the back yard to go for a pee and tell him all about my date with Alec. I don't actually know if it was a date, but that's what I'm calling it. As we make our way back into my suite, I hear Alec's patio door close, and my blood begins to heat up. Was he outside when I was talking to Merc, and I didn't notice? Did he hear me gushing over him? Did he hear me tell Merc how amazing he smelled and how I wish we could have been there alone so we could have continued the night? My cheeks flush with embarrassment as I think about Alec listening to all of my feelings that I basically presented to him on a platter.

Alec Kohl

It's been two days since the concert and I had so much fun, and I was having such a great time with Blake. The vibe was different between us. We didn't feel like *just* best friends, we felt like two people beginning to like one another. I was enjoying all the alone time with her, and getting to chat, laugh, and take in the music together. I also totally picked up on her comment in the truck, and I couldn't help myself but look back at her in the mirror. She returned my look with a twinkle in her eye, and it immediately made me soar, so I had to quickly look back at the road to avoid putting us all in the ditch. I do agree with her though, having to lean in so close to her, being able to smell her coconut hair and, in return feel her so close to me when she had to speak to me, was enough to make my spidey senses tingle. I definitely am interested in this girl.

I guess, all this time, I haven't wanted to let my brain go back there. I told myself it could never happen between us, given how close I am with her family, how she is younger, the reality that we're neighbours so if it doesn't work out between us, then that would be so awkward. Not to mention the fact that we have both always been in relationships. But tonight, we were both single. And ever since that night that Blake told me about what her mom had said, I haven't been able to shake it. I've been thinking about it a lot actually, more than I care to admit, and Kara is totally right. On paper, Blake and I would be perfect together. We have so much in common, we get along so well together, we truly have such a close friendship, and this mutual respect for one another that I'm not sure I've ever had with another female before. She makes me laugh, and I could talk to her for hours without getting bored. She's confident and knows how to hold her own, and I love that she loves hockey, beer, and dogs. And, as much as I hate to admit it, she's extremely good looking. I never really allowed myself to admit that before because I've always been in a relationship but seeing Blake last night with a 'single lens,' I can't help but be attracted to her. Okay, yeah, I'm definitely interested in this girl.

I haven't seen Blake since the concert, but we have texted a little bit. She thanked me once again for taking her and Audi out and told me that she had a great time. She also asked how I was doing with my break-up with Heather, and I told her that I'm totally fine. This break-up feels different. Although Heather and I have gone back and forth a few times, I've always been the type of person who has to give it 100% and try every single avenue before giving up, that way I can always look back and know I tried my best. When I finally decided that things were over with Heather, it was as if a door closed and locked, in which I could never re-open it again. I feel at peace with my decision and I'm happy to be moving forward.

It's funny because I'm actually helping Heather move into a new apartment this evening. Normally I would think it's weird to help your ex out, but she only has a car and needs help moving some furniture and she said she had a few of my things, so I agreed to move her couch and bed for her. I'm happy to end things on good terms, considering we have definitely had our moments of toxicity.

I did make it clear to Heather though that I'm just doing this to be nice, and I don't mean to come across as conceited, because obviously I don't know her intentions, but Heather is known for the 'let me try and get him back,' and I wanted to make it perfectly clear that I'm not interested in getting back together, and that I can't stay long because I do have plans afterward. Heather's text response was a bit defensive (fair enough, I did basically imply that she was trying to get back with me), but she said no problem at all and that she appreciates my help.

Riley texted me this afternoon to ask if I was going to Charlie's Pub tonight with Blake and Dan. I totally forgot that was tonight, so I'm glad he texted me, so I had an excuse for Heather as to why I had to leave. I told him yes, but that I could be late considering I'm helping Heather.

I drove to Heather's cousins' place and noticed her couch and bed frame on the front porch ready to go. I knocked on the door and Heather came out shortly after.

"Hey, thank you again so much, I really appreciate it. I didn't have anyone with a truck able to help me on short notice," she says as she greets me.

"Yeah, no problem. Why don't you grab that end of the couch, and we'll move that onto the truck bed first."

Heather follows my direction, and we continue working well together for the next twenty minutes as we load up her mattress and bed frame afterward. Heather texts me the address to her new place in case we get separated, and I follow behind her as she drives in her SUV.

We arrive at her apartment and once again, work well together to move the furniture in. Once we get everything in, she asks if I would help put her bed together and set it up. I check the time, it's five-forty-five. I'm supposed to be meeting everyone at six. I decide that it's better to be the bigger person, and so I agree to help.

Heather is acting weird. She's sort of flirting, I think. I don't know. But she's being overly nice. She keeps thanking me and is awkwardly staring at me, and sort of twirling her hair. It's weird.

"Do you want to stay for a drink? We can order a pizza and I have some wine in my trunk?" She asks, with flirty eyes.

I finish securing the last corner of the bed frame before responding, "Uh, I can't, I told you I have plans."

"I know, I just thought maybe you'd want to skip them to spend time with me," Heather pleads.

"I'm sorry Heather, I meant it when I said I was just trying to be nice, to have us end on good terms, for this to be a nice piece of closure. I'm not interested in anything more, and I should get going." I look down at my watch and see that it's six-twenty, that took longer than I thought. "Plus, I'm already late."

"Where are you going anyway, what's so important? You seem like you're in such a rush?"

"I'm going to meet some friends, and yes I am in a rush, I was supposed to be there twenty minutes ago," I respond.

"You're going to meet with Blake, aren't you?" Heather asks harshly.

"Yeah, and a few other people too, not just her." I don't know why I'm even explaining myself right now.

"I knew you'd be going to meet Blake. You've always had a thing for her. I wouldn't be surprised if you were sneaking around on me with her this whole time!" Heather yells, her tone becoming more and more angry.

I stare at Heather directly in the eyes, not breaking before I say, "Don't project your shit on me. I'm not the one who cheated, that's your department." I turn and walk out the door, and as I begin to walk toward my truck, I can hear something smash.

So much for taking the high road.

I manage to find a parking spot only a block away from Charlie's, and as I walk the short distance to the pub, excitement consumes me. I'm actually excited to see Blake. I'm always happy to see her, there's a reason why we're best friends, but after finally acknowledging my feelings, it's different this time.

I walk in the main doors, and immediately notice Riley in a booth on the right-hand side with Dan seated across from him. As I approach, I notice Blake is no where to be seen, however there is a beer on a coaster next to Dan, which I'm assuming is hers.

"Hey, sorry I'm late. That took longer than I expected," I explain as Riley scoots into the booth further, leaving me a spot to sit. Moments after I sit down, the waitress comes by our table.

"Hi, I saw you just joined, can I get you anything to drink?"

"Yeah sure, I'll take a Guinness, thanks," I respond to the waitress.

"So how did it go then, you said it took longer than you expected, was it a nightmare or what? I still can't believe you were even helping her after everything she's done," Riley says while sipping his beer.

"Yeah, I don't know. It was actually going fine at first. I made it clear I was just doing this to be nice, and so we can just go our separate ways on a good note," I start. As I'm about to continue, the waitress drops off my beer, I quickly thank her, and then continue. "And then she was trying to get me to stay once we were all done. Wanting to order pizza and have a drink. I told her I couldn't and was already late meeting friends. Then she got all Heather-like, asking a million questions and if Blake would be there, blah blah blah. Then she started going off about how I was probably cheating on her with Blake, which obviously pissed me off because that's the farthest thing from the truth. So, I got pissed and said something nasty and left." I take a long sip of my beer while the guys' process.

"Well serves her right. She shouldn't have said that about you, and I don't blame you for getting mad," Dan says.

"Yeah. Like I said, I still can't even believe that you went there to help her in the first place, so for her to say something like that after you just helped is ridiculous," Riley chimes in.

As I'm about to respond, I notice Blake coming down the stairs toward us, and I can't help but stare. She's wearing tight black jeans, and this v neck tank top thing. Her hair is curled (which she never does), and she has a bit more makeup on than what she typically wears. It looks like she spent some time getting ready tonight, and it really shows. She looks incredible. I notice my pulse quickening as each step she gets closer and closer. I know that I'm staring, but I can't help it, I can't seem to pull my eyes off of her. She looks up and notices me sitting in the booth and smiles at me, sending a jolt of electricity through my already amped up body. I stare at her the whole time she is walking up toward the booth, until she finally reaches our table.

"Here's a napkin Alec, you look like you could use it for that drool there," Blake says jokingly with a wink as she takes her seat across from me. Fuck she's witty.

"Trust me, I wasn't drooling, I'm just not used to you having your hair and makeup done, I'm so used to you looking like a guy, that I wasn't sure it was you, and I had to do a double take," I reply quickly.

"More like a quadruple take," Dan mumbles under his breath. I don't know how Blake can't see that Dan has the major hots for her, even comments like that make it so obvious. But Blake has always been 'one of the guys,' so she probably doesn't pay much attention to it.

"So, where the heck were you anyway, why were you so late?" Blake asks me as she sips on her beer.

"I helped Heather move over some of her big furniture to her new place," I can't even finish my sentence before Blake makes a shocked expression and interrupts me.

"Are you serious? Why would you even do that! Oh my gosh just cut the cord already."

"Yeah well, I was trying to be the bigger person and end things on a good note. Anyway, it's done now, I don't have to see her again, plus I was quite rude to her at the end so I'm sure she won't want to see me anyway," I say defensively. I have to admit, Blake sure is one to talk, I mean, didn't she go through something

340

similar with Colin? Didn't he want to get back together with her, and didn't she have to have one last conversation to end things and have closure? It's really not that different. But for the sake of the guys being here at the table too, I'm going to let her sharp comment go, and try to forget about Heather and enjoy the night.

It isn't long before we're all ordering another round of beer, and we're all laughing and shooting the shit, as we normally do when we all get together. This group makes it easy to just forget about the troubling things in life and just unwind. We all have so much in common that it's easy to talk about hockey and other sports. Sometimes they ask me about work, and I fill them in on some of the cases I've been working on, which always seems to excite them and create in depth debates and conversations.

After my second beer, and still no food, I decide we should probably order something to eat as I'm already starting to feel light-headed. When the waitress comes by, we order five different appies to share and another round of beers. It's probably a good call to order the food, because I need to sober up a bit as I've also noticed myself subconsciously staring at Blake again. Maybe not staring but glancing at her more often than I normally would.

Sitting across from Blake is like sitting next to the ocean. The way she looks at me, she truly pulls me in, the same way the tide rakes in the sand. The sand has no choice but to be swept up by the wave. To be consumed by it. And when she looks away to make eye contact with the other people at the table, it's as if the ocean tide has gone back to sea, leaving the sand on its own. The magnetic pull of the ocean keeps crashing into me, forcing me to continually steal glances at Blake, grasping at every moment I can to make eye contact with her, to feel our energy collide. As the tide goes back to sea, it's only for a few moments, before I'm engulfed with her once more.

"Earth to Alec. Hellooooo," Blake says jokingly, trying to grab my attention.

"What? Sorry I was in my own world there for a second." I focus in on Blake, her eyes twinkling, and I try to pay attention this time.

"I was just asking if I were to have another beer or two, if I left my car parked outside, could you drive me home later?"

"Yeah, for sure, I'm going to have to slow it down here if I want any chance of driving, otherwise we will have to take a cab," I respond.

"Yeah totally. Okay thank you. Oh, perfect timing!" Blake says excitedly as she moves a few drinks out of the way to make room for the appetizers being dropped off at our table.

As the four of us begin to devour the appetizers, an old friend of mine Mat and his friend Luke, who look as though they may have had one too many beers approach the table.

"Well, well, if it isn't Mr. Kohl, I haven't seen you in a while! How've you been buddy!" Mat says as he leans in for a handshake. Mat was cousins with an ex-girlfriend of mine, and he is actually part of CP Police, so I see him around. Oh, and every once in a while, he comes out to play hockey when he can. Luke is a friend of Mat's who I've met only once before. Don't know much about the guy.

"I know, what can I say, I'm a busy guy. Hey, Luke, how are ya? Did you guys want to join us. You came at the perfect time." Everyone shimmies in the booth a bit deeper to make room for the guys. Mat sits next to me, and Luke sits across from him, next to Blake. "Mat, Luke, this is Riley, Dan, and Blake," I gesture to each person as I say their name. In unison, they all say hi back.

The waitress notices two new people join our table, so right on cue she approaches, collecting their order. They both ask for a beer, and we continue eating our food. I can't help but keep an eye on Luke, he seems two sheets to the wind, and seems like he might be annoying Blake a little bit. Every time I look over, he is immaturely trying to tickle her. Who does that? What grown man does that? Maybe he's just too drunk to notice that she is getting annoyed. He really needs to work on his pick-up skills if he's trying to land Blake.

"Hey Blake, Mat was just showing me one of his new tattoos, why don't I switch you spots so you can some see, and show him yours," I say somewhat convincingly. Yes, Mat was showing me one of his new coy fish tattoos on his arm, but I'm fully aware that Blake could see his tattoo from where she's seated, I'm just trying to help her and pull her away from Luke so she can have some space.

"That's okay, I don't want to rearrange the whole table, I can see from here. Let me see Mat. What shop did you go to?" Okay well that didn't work. That flew right over Blake's head. Whatever, I tried. If he's bugging her enough, she will tell him to stop.

About an hour goes by before Mat and Luke decide that they're going to call it a night. Which is probably a good call considering Luke is slurring his words. We wave them off and shortly after, Riley explains that he too is going to head home. Dan, Blake, and I decide to hang for a bit before calling it quits.

"Oh my gosh you guys, that guy was so annoying. Did anyone hear me asking him to stop touching me? Who tickles people they've never met? So creepy." Blake says.

"Blake! I noticed, and that's why I said the whole Mat tattoo thing. I was trying to give you an out so you could move away from him, but it went right over your head. Then I was trying to make eyes at you to try and signal a switcheroo, but again, you were in your own world. Next time just straight up ask me to switch spots and I will," I respond.

"Yeah, I thought that was weird too. He was super drunk though. Not that that excuses it, but he could barely see straight when he came to our table," Dan adds.

"Yeah, that's true. Whatever, he's gone now, and I don't think I'll ever really see him again. Mat was nice though. He mentioned that he played in a tournament with you a while back, Alec? I didn't know he played hockey," Blake commented.

"Yeah, he's pretty decent too. I'll have to remind him about Friday nights. He hasn't been out in a while."

The waitress comes by for a final time asking if we would like our bills. We agree and split everything pretty evenly.

"Well guys, thanks again for tonight, that was fun," Dan says signaling the end of his night.

"Yeah, are you ready Alec? Is it still okay if I jump in with you?" Blake asks.

"Yeah, for sure, I'm parked a block down."

The three of us walk out of the pub together, and after Dan signals that he is parked in the opposite direction, Blake gives him a hug goodbye before walking with me to the truck.

"Well, that was fun. I'm glad you made it out, it would have sucked without you," Blake says looking over at me. Static courses through me. I'm starting to be able to read her flirty statements. To pick up on when she's feeling a moment.

"Thanks for inviting me. I wouldn't have missed it," I respond, not breaking her gaze.

The sky is dark, but the streetlamps expel the perfect amount of light to be able to see Blake's big doe eyes looking up at me, and the shine of her radiant smile. Tonight, was perfect. I don't want it to end.

Blake Taylor

I step up into Alec's truck and I don't want the night to
end. I had so much fun with the guys, but I especially
enjoyed Alec's company. He smells so good; I could
smell his cologne from across the table. It's wild to me
too, that now I 'know' his scent. I never paid attention
to that before, but ever since this crush of mine has
become unbearably difficult to live with, I can't help but
become enthralled with every aspect of him. And did I
mention how handsome he looks tonight, dressed in
dark jeans that hug all the right places, and a burgundy
flannel button down shirt. Lord, it was hard to keep my
eyes off him. But in my defence, I also saw him
checking me out a few times, which only encouraged
my urge to want to flirt, and confidence.

"Tonight, was fun, I'm sort of not ready to go home
yet if you're not. Want to grab a take-out pizza or
something?" I ask.

"Yeah, it was fun. I'm not even hungry, but we
could just go for a drive if you want?"

"True. I'm literally not even hungry, I just wanted
an excuse to keep hanging out," I say forwardly. I catch
Alec's lips curl up into a small smile.

We sit in silence for a few moments as Alec steers us to the outskirts of town. He mentioned that there's a spot just outside of town where you can catch an amazing view of the city lights at night.

The vibe between us is different tonight. Even the air between us feels different. The looks that we keep shooting each other are different. The electricity, the sparks that keep flying between us are enough to preserve permanent goose bumps all over my body. I don't know if it's the combination of a little liquid courage, or the fact that I know for certain that I caught Alec checking me out, but something tells me I'm not the only one who is crushing, and that tonight may be the start of something new between us, where we can give in to those feelings, and stop pretending that we're just friends.

"So, when is it that you leave for California again?" I ask casually.

"In a month I think." Alec and Heather were planning on doing a road trip down to California. They rented one of those van things with the exterior painted in bright colours and funny sayings, where you can live out of it. I wonder if she will still be going.

"Is Heather still going to go?"

"Hell no. I told Riley a while back that I had to pay in full when booking the van, so if Heather and I broke up, that I would be taking him, and he was down for it. I guess in the back of my mind I had a gut feeling we wouldn't work out hey," Alec says with a smirk.

"Dang, well you should tell Riley never mind and that I'll go with you instead," I say with a flirty smile.

"There's only one bed."

"I don't bite…" I look over at Alec and I can see that he's considering my offer. I don't know what is going through his mind right now, but I can literally see the hamster running on the wheel as it reviews an imaginary pros and cons list to me joining him.

"I don't know, I already mentioned it to him, and he was pretty excited about it. But it would be fun with you. But I sleep naked so I wouldn't want to scare you away," Alec responds playfully.

"Oh yeah? Do you plan on sleeping naked with Riley? Because you might give him the wrong impression," I laugh.

"Well, no, I guess I would have to wear underwear."

"Well then, I guess you could with me too then. You're just choosing not to. I see what you're doing there Alec. Dirty dog," I tease back.

Alec smiles and lets out a light chuckle. His face then turns toward me, and suddenly he's serious. "I wouldn't want to ruin our friendship by doing a trip like that Blake. Although, I know it would be so much fun."

Hmm. So maybe I was wrong. Maybe he doesn't have a crush on me. Maybe when Alec is single, he just likes to flirt with girls. Maybe I've been blinded by my own crush that I've just been imagining him checking me out and imagining him flirting with me. Maybe I've been wrong all along and I have no idea what the hell to think any more. Or maybe he does like me, but he's scared that if we date it could ruin our friendship. Either way, I've got nothing to lose, so with an imaginary encouraging pat on the butt to myself, I blurt out something that could either be really smart, or really dumb.

"I get that. You know, we could make this a lot easier on ourselves. Why don't we just kiss. We can make an agreement that if one of us isn't into it, then we forget that it ever happened, and continue on as best friends like we always have been. If we are into it, then even better. It's a win, win."

"You're crazy!" Alec exclaims.

"Hey, maybe I am, but at least then we would have our answer. Oh, are we here?" I say changing the subject as Alec pulls over to the side of a dirt road.

"We are. You can see the whole city from up here. Pretty hey?"

The view is breathtaking. We don't have to climb out of the truck to take advantage of this gorgeous spot. Plus, it's more comfortable in the truck anyhow. I have never been up here before, but it's like a little secret gem, one that I feel grateful that Alec is sharing with me. Which then leads me to wonder if he's brought other girls up here before. I'm sure he has. It doesn't matter, I can't control what he did in his past, I'm here now and that's what matters. I want to soak in every moment that I get with him, and I'm just happy to have him to myself.

I'm not going to lie, I really thought Alec was going to put the moves on, considering we're in this romantic, very secluded, very private lookout point, but he doesn't. He stays planted in the driver's seat and doesn't cross the center threshold. He's either very respectful, or a bit shy. Both of which I suppose are equally possible. But that's okay, being up here, taking in this view and talking openly is another form of intimacy I didn't know I wanted – no, scratch that, I didn't know I craved from Alec. There's something special about having someone's complete undivided attention. Knowing that you're both breathing the same air, conversing in conversation in which they're intently focused on what you have to say, and actively listen to you. Humans want to be heard, they want to feel understood, and Alec always makes me feel heard. Like there's no one else in the room. I guess right now that is quite literally applicable, but still.

We spend about twenty minutes talking about everything and anything. Conversation always flows so effortlessly with Alec. We can talk about everything, and nothing at all, and we still seem to never run out of things to say. There's never awkwardness with Alec. Some people get uncomfortable in moments of silence, but being in Alec's presence is anything but awkward. He has this ability to exude comfort, protection, and tranquility, as if there's no rush, and so even in those moments where we have that instance of silence, I welcome it, because I know I'm in a safe place. A place to be myself. A place to let my mind wander and be free. A place where the man sitting next to me would never judge me, but simply just enjoy me for exactly who I am, unapologetically. I know this for certain because that's how I feel about him too.

"Ready to head back?" Alec asks, cutting through my thoughts.

"Yeah, for sure. This was nice. Thanks for showing me this spot, I really liked it. It's so peaceful."

As we approach our houses, I decide to make a move. If I don't, who knows if Alec ever will, and I've got nothing to lose, so why not. It's not a big move, but at least it will propel us one way or the other. I take a deep breath, "I've had a lot of fun tonight, and I still don't want it to end. You're welcome to come to my place, have a beer, and we can watch a movie or something." And then I wait in silence. Somewhat holding my breath with anticipation. Either Alec will agree, and then this will actually, possibly even be considered a date, or he will deny, therefore leaving us as just friends. Pressures on. What's it gonna be.

"Yeah, that sounds good."

My body breaks out in a cool sweat. Not the kind that you get when you're standing outside in the heat all day, but the kind that you get when you're nervous, or anxious, or excited. In my case, all of the above. I can't believe he agreed. Okay, so this is it. He must like me too. He wouldn't agree to come over if he didn't like me. In all our times as friends, we've never hung out this way before. Ever.

We park in Alec's driveway and walk over to my suite. He looks a little shy, nervous maybe. Maybe he doesn't want my parents to see him, I don't know. But I unlock the door, and Merc greets us both with a flying leap.

"There's glasses in the cupboard by the sink, help yourself," I point toward the kitchen and then motion to Merc, "I'm just going to let this guy out for a quick pee, and I'll be right back."

Merc and I run to the backyard, and I try to shake out the nerves of excitement before re-entering my place. Alec is standing at my island. A sight I've never seen before, but one I could get used to.

"It's nice in here. I've never been in here before, but it's a good size."

"Yeah, that's true, I supposed you haven't been in here before. Except that time, you helped with Merc, but I guess that was super quick and you were focused on him, rather than looking around." Merc makes his way over to Alec for some love pats and scratches before I continue. "I mean I like it and you can't beat the price. I would give you a tour, but you can basically see the whole suite from right here. It's already midnight. If we want to watch a movie, we should probably start it soon, or I may fall asleep." I gesture toward the living room.

Alec sits in the corner of the couch, and I grab the remote off the coffee table and sit next to him. Not touching him, but also not far away from him either. I turn on Netflix and start to peruse. We decide on 'No Strings Attached' with Ashton Kutcher and Natalie Portman. I was looking for something light-hearted, not too romantic, and not too cheesy, and so we settled on this.

As the movie begins to play, I can't help but make small talk with Alec, because when we aren't talking, then I'm alone with my thoughts, and when I'm alone with my thoughts I start to feel the butterflies that begin to swarm and erupt in my tummy, which then leaves me feeling completely nauseous with excitement, anxiety and nervousness. Excitement that I'm on a date with Alec. Anxious because I have no idea how he's feeling. Nervous, because I want to be closer to him, to cuddle, and I want him to kiss me. But I'm nervous to make that move and get rejected. So, I sit. And make small talk.

After about ten minutes I go to reach for a drink on the coffee table and realize we never even grabbed ourselves anything, so I get up from the couch and walk to the fridge to grab us a beer. I ask Alec if he wants one and he says sure. As I return to the living room, I notice a very relaxed, very sprawled out Alec laying on my couch, with a sly smirk. I look at him, then at the couch, then back at him, realizing that I'll have to actually *lay* with him. I place our beers on the coffee table and can't help but poke a jab at him.

"Wow, make yourself at home, why don't ya. Where am I supposed to go?"

Alec taps the cushion area in front of him, gesturing for me to lay and join him. So, I do. In a heartbeat. He doesn't have to ask me twice. Alec is somewhere over six feet and I'm a whole five foot nothing, so I actually fit perfectly nestled in against him. He has his lower arm dangling out in front of him, which acts as a pillow for myself. My back is pushed up against his chest, and we are curled up together. His other arm rests on my thigh, in a respectful spot, and I feel so comfortable. You don't realize how much you yearn for something until you actually get it, and then you realize that you don't ever want to go without that again. That's how I feel about being close to Alec. Now that I've experienced it, now that I know what his touch on my skin feels like, the warmth of his breath behind me, the feel of his heartbeat against me, I don't ever want to go a day without this feeling of closeness. This feeling of home.

We watch the movie with such enjoyment. We actually don't even really watch the movie at all, we just talk, laugh, sip on our beer, and laugh some more. That's one thing about being with Alec, is that we have been friends for so long, and we have always been our true authentic selves with each other. We were never trying to impress one another, and we just thoroughly enjoy each other's company. That's why we became best friends so quickly. Because even something as simple as watching a stupid movie, feels like one of the best nights of my life.

Alec keeps his hand secured on my hip, never wavering, never trying to push boundaries, he just rests it there, comfortably, and respectfully. It isn't until the movie is over, and the credits start rolling and the upbeat tempo of *Rhythm of Love* by The Plain White Tee's starts to play, that I make some sort of joke that entitles Alec to give my sides a squeeze tickling me which forces me to let out a squeal. I roll over to face him and return the playful gesture. He also lets out a small laugh as I tickle him hard under his rib cage. We're merely centimeters apart. Laughing, smiling. Alec's eyes are sparkling, here it is, the moment I've been waiting for is about to happen. However, the instant I think he's about to kiss me, he squeezes my sides again, tickling me more fiercely than he had prior, forcing my body to squirm, in which he pulls me in closer to him, so I don't fall off the couch. As I'm laughing, we make eye contact, sparks erupting between us, electricity coursing through our intertwined bodies, and Alec moves in, closing his mouth over mine. His lips are warm, soft, tender. He's gentle and slow, not rushing this moment we've waited for so long.

Butterflies somehow travel from my stomach up to my head, forcing this feeling of light headedness, the kind you only feel when you're truly on Cloud 9. My entire body is buzzing as shock takes over. Alec is kissing me right how. Alec's lips are moving against mine. It does not feel weird. At all.

After a few minutes I pull back and lighten the mood. I need a breather. "So, I guess kissing me isn't weird at all, is it?" I say with a smirk.

"I don't know what you're talking about, that was awful," Alec replies playfully.

I respond with more of a steamier kiss just to prove my point, which in turn is met with passion. A hungry need envelops Alec's character, and there's flaming heat between us.

Hours pass before I take a moment to look at the time, "Oh my gosh, I didn't even realize how late it was. I don't mean to kick you out or be rude, but I work in the afternoon." It's nearing five a.m. and I swear on my grandmother, all we did was stay up, talk, and kiss some more. There's something so natural, comfortable, and easy with Alec. Time literally flew and I still want more time with him.

Alec looks at his phone to check the time and his eyes widen. "Holy shit. Yeah, where did the time go. I should get home and try to get some sleep. I'll text you tomorrow," he says as he starts to stand from the couch.

I walk Alec to the door, and he leans down to kiss my forehead. Sometimes, a kiss on the forehead can be more intimate than a kiss on the lips. I look up at him and smile. I'm so unbelievably happy right now. And tired. But it was so worth it.

"I had fun tonight," he says looking right at me.

"Me too. I'm glad I convinced you to kiss me," I say laughingly.

Alec makes his way over to his house and while I'm brushing my teeth, I get a text from him that reads *sweet dreams*. A smile forms at my lips and just about touches my eyes. I'm glowing and radiating with sheer happiness.

I just hope that when he wakes up tomorrow, he won't regret it. Because I know for me, after just one night with him, I don't ever want to go without him again.

Boom, boom, boom, boom, boom, boom. It might sound crazy what I'm about to say... Startled, I click my phone so that Pharell Williams stops singing. My alarm sounds at eleven a.m. and I feel like I could sleep for another twenty-four hours. Last night was like a dream. Oh my gosh, was it a dream? I lay silently reminiscing on my night. To any possible onlookers, I must look like a fool lying in my bed grinning from ear to ear, but I can't help it! Alec is so incredibly wonderful, and I'm just so happy. I'm ready to be his girlfriend. Call me crazy, go ahead, it's fine, 'cause I know to many people, I would appear crazy. But when you know someone for so long, and when you have such a deep friendship with that person, and such a foundation of trust, loyalty, and companionship, it just doesn't seem all that wild to me.

I roll out of bed and make my way to the coffee machine to get a brew going. I decide to text Alec to say good morning and ask if he slept okay. I make my coffee and realize that I should take a shower now to try and help wake myself up. Still no text from Alec. When I get out of the shower, I start my face wash routine and my phone vibrates, indicating a new text from Alec, and a wave of warmth passes through my body, with sheer excitement.

Good morning. I slept well. Not long enough though...Somebody kept me up all night ;)

Another wave of electrifying heat courses through my body. Okay, so last night was real! And Alec is flirting, so clearly, he is happy about it.

Hey now, no one was forcing you to stay against your will!

Our light flirting goes back and forth as I get myself ready and have something to eat. I work at two, so by the time I get things done and take Merc for a walk, it's already time to make my way out the door.

Alec and I text my whole entire shift. The store is very quiet, and the other girl Jenna who works here is also very quiet. She is in high school and has a big test next week so because I was the most senior staff, I sort of get to make the rules. I told her she could keep her textbook behind the counter and look over her notes so long as there were no customers in the store. This turned out to be a win-win for me because it allowed me to walk around and text Alec non-stop.

Our texts to one another already make it feel like we're boyfriend and girlfriend. Isn't that wild? We just feel so comfortable with one another, and we're both relationship type people who don't play games, so I think it goes without saying, that we're wanting to pursue this *thing* between us. Actually, I guess it does go with saying, because Alec asked me to hangout after work, and now I'm having an even harder time getting through this already painfully slow shift.

By the time Jenna and I count the tills to close up the store, my heart is racing with anticipation and excitement to see Alec again. I race home, driving slightly over the speed limit (don't tell Alec that), and run inside to freshen up. Merc is waiting for me by the door, and I let him out quickly to do his business.

As I'm changing my clothes and adding a dash of makeup to my face a text comes in from Alec.

I saw your car parked out front. Come over whenever you're ready. You can bring Merc too.

I love that he also loves Merc and is fine with me bringing him. How sweet is that. I send a quick text back saying I would be over in ten. I finish applying my mascara and spray a sprit of my favourite perfume, *Light Blue* by Dolce & Gabbana and make my way next door.

Merc tails closely behind me as he's not used to going out toward the road, he's used to going out the back gate. I cut across Alec's driveway and make my way to the front door. I knock gently. I wait for what seems like forever, but I know is only like five seconds, as he was expecting me.

"Hey!" Alec says with a giant smile as he opens the door. "Come in."

I walk in and I'm about to be greeted with a hug from Alec when Merc paws at him instead. Alec bends down to pat and hug Merc and shortly after Guinness and Chip are all over Merc, therefore freeing Alec. He moves toward me and wraps me up in one of the best hugs I've ever had.

"That was one of the best hugs I think I've ever had," I say out loud.

"Get used to it then. Want a drink? I'm just making lasagna does that work?"

"Yeah, that sounds delicious. And I'll have water and whatever you're drinking." Lasagna. Hmm, that's like an adult dish. I couldn't cook an actual adult dish if my life depended on it.

"I'm having a beer, but I also grabbed red wine 'cause I know you said you like it, so you pick," Alec says, gesturing at both options.

"You didn't have to get wine just for me! That was so sweet. Thank you. Of course, I'll have a glass."

"I don't mind wine, but I couldn't buy a bottle and drink the while thing to myself. I like a glass here or there. So, this works out well, because you can help me finish it," Alec says with a smile.

"Oh yeah? You plan on having me over lots to help you drink it?" I say flirtatiously.

"Absolutely."

The dogs are running through the house with more energy than I've seen them have in a while. I'm sure it's because they have a new friend in their home, so we decide to put them outside to play. We turn on the hockey game and sit at the kitchen island in between cooking together. Alec already did the heavy lifting, and the lasagna is already in the oven, which smells delicious by the way. But we decide to make a salad together and some garlic cheese bread. I don't know what it is, but there's something about preparing a meal together that is connecting.

After about twenty minutes dinner is ready and we seat ourselves at the dining table. Alec fills my wine glass a bit higher to make up for what I already drank, and also pours himself a glass.

"Oh my gosh Alec, this looks and smells so good. Thank you for having me."

"No problem. Hopefully, it tastes okay," Alec replies as he takes off his hat before having his first bite.

"Mmmmm. Yep. Delicious. Good job."

"Fuuuuuck!" Alec exclaims, completely scaring the hell out of me.

"What!? What's wrong!?" I yell back.

Alec starts laughing realizing how scared I must look, and how silly I must sound, matching his yell with a yell. "Sorry," he apologizes. "The Flames just got scored on," he says pointing to the hockey game on the TV.

"Oh my gosh, you really are a di- hard fan hey?" I ask playfully.

"Just a tad. I didn't mean to scare you; I just hate when they blow their lead. Gaudreau turned the puck over again. I get so tired of him. Sometimes he's great and can put the puck in the net, but he's not a well-rounded player, he turns the puck over a lot," Alec says in a frustrated tone.

"To be honest, I grew up a Sens fan, so I don't even know all the Flames players off by heart, but I guess if I'll be hanging around you, I might need to learn them."

"You got that right," Alec says with another smile.

We eat dinner and chat about the game, and how my shift was, and how I let Jenna study, which was nice of me, but also was a win for me to be able to chat with Alec all day. We talk about our night last night, and how happy we are. This seems like the perfect opportunity to sort of ask Alec what he wants with me and what his intentions are.

"I had a lot of fun last night too. I've had a crush for a while, so it didn't feel real. I kept pinching myself," I say brightly.

"I did too. I wasn't sure what to expect, but I'm glad we're here."

"Same. But to be blunt, what do you want exactly? I don't sleep around, and I don't hangout with multiple people at once. I'm an exclusive monogamous type of gal. I like you, and only want to be with you. If that freaks you out, then let me know now so I don't waste either of our time."

"That is blunt," Alec responds with a grin. He takes a sip of his wine before continuing, "I feel the exact same way. I don't sleep around; I'm scared of STDs, and I think that's disgusting. I'm a serial monogamist. I like you and only want to be with you. If that freaks you out, then let me know now so I don't waste either of our time," Alec says with an even bigger grin as he mocks me. But I know he means every word.

"Okay, smartass, no need to mock me."

Alec laughs and it's a sound that I could just bottle up and keep. Alec has been known to many people to be tough to crack, hard to make actually laugh, so when I succeed, it feels like a silent victory. "Well, for the record, I guess this means we're boyfriend and girlfriend now then. Are you sure that doesn't freak you out?" I say toyingly.

"Not at all, now you're stuck with me."

Epilogue
Blake Taylor: Six Years Later

My hand flows through the wind of my open window in the truck as we drive to Summerland. Alec and I are spending a weekend away, at the beautiful bed and breakfast on the lake where we were married five years ago. I can't believe we've been married for five years. My mind is filled with all of the wonderful memories that we have created together both as a couple, and, you guessed it, as a family.

Our relationship moved quickly after that very first night that we kissed. I'm sure any outsiders would feel as though we may have been moving way too quickly, but anyone who actually knows Alec and I, knew that it actually couldn't have happened sooner. The night after we kissed for the first time, we had lasagna at his place and decided we would be boyfriend and girlfriend. Only a month later, I moved in with Alec, which is a funny story in itself. Remember that van trip to California that Alec was going on, and he was taking Riley with him? Well Alec asked me to house, and dog sit for him. He asked that I stay at his place and look after everything. On the night before he was leaving, we were playing *Rockband* in our underwear and I will admit, I was slightly drunk, when I blurted out, "Hey, so when I stay here to watch your place this week, I think I'll just keep my things here and just not go back to my place." Alec had looked over at me with wide eyes, and laughed and said, "Did you just invite yourself to move in?" I replied with a 'yep' and continued playing the game. He didn't disagree, he didn't argue, in fact he welcomed it.

Two months later, Alec had a large family reunion back in Alberta and asked me to join and meet his whole family. I was so excited and flattered. We packed up all the dogs, had Riley house sit for us, and drive the long fourteen-hour trip. We spent the weekend at his aunt's house out in the country. Everyone brought their own tent or trailer and camped out on their property. I met all of Alec's family, both his parents, his sister and brother-in-law, his brother and sister-in-law, and his younger brother and sister-in-law, as well as his seven nieces and one nephew. On top of that, a bunch of his aunts, Uncles, and cousins were at this reunion, so needless to say, it was a lot of people to meet. But everyone was so welcoming, and I fit right in. I had a blast getting to know his parents and siblings, and even had fun with the kids. I remember thinking to myself, how much of an honour it would be to be apart of such a beautiful family.

A smile stretches across my face and Alec briefly looks away from the road to ask me what I'm smiling about. "Oh, I'm just thinking about your family reunion years ago, and how much fun it was meeting everyone.

I remember thinking how badly I wanted to be part of your family and look at us now."

"Yeah, that was a lot of fun. There were so many people there, I'm surprised you weren't overwhelmed," Alec replied.

"Nah, you know me. I'm not shy. I love meeting new people."

Alec returns his focus on the drive ahead, as I continue down memory lane.

Not long after the family reunion, in September of that year, we went back to my hometown outside of Ottawa for my cousins' wedding. I was so excited to introduce Alec to my cousins and Aunts and Uncles. We had so much fun at the wedding, and the day after the wedding, Alec had a little scavenger hunt planned for us. He said he wanted to get to know the town where I grew up, so thought this would be a fun way. I was so surprised and excited, (and very hungover), and couldn't wait to show him around. The last stop on our scavenger hunt was my childhood home, where I have the happiest of memories growing up. Alec knew that this home was very special to me because it was such a symbol of love, happiness, and growth.

This home sat on the corner of two quiet residential streets. We were able to walk along the sidewalk and then sit down on the sidewalk out front. I told Alec stories about my childhood and where I would build tree forts, and swing on the tree swing out front, and the trees that I would climb, and the games I would make up. As

I was reminiscing and looking over my shoulder, when I looked back at Alec, he was down on one knee with a stunning ring. I still remember what he said to me. With a wave of emotion, he uttered four simple lines. "Blake, you're my best friend. I will always take care of you. I love you. Will you marry me?" I must have been in a ripple of shock because I began to kiss him and reach for the ring before even saying yes! I said yes, a million times over and we called our parents right away.

One year later, the following September we were married, and surrounded by our closest friends and family. We were married at a gorgeous bed and breakfast on a cliffside overlooking a gorgeous lake. (Hence the reason we are returning this weekend to celebrate our year wedding anniversary, because it's so beautiful and holds so much meaning). I'll never forget that feeling of walking down the aisle and seeing Alec waiting for me. His eyes lit right up as I approached him. I remember feeling so warm, so incredibly happy, so absolutely certain, and so safe. When I had to sign our marriage certificate with my new last name, I felt like I was in a dream. A happy dream. I remember taking a moment to look up and see all of our family and friends smiling at us and feeling so grateful to be surrounded by so many loved ones. It was as if Alec could sense this, and he planted a kiss on my neck as I signed my new last name. It felt right. Our first dance song was 'Overjoyed' by Matchbox twenty, and still, every time

I hear that song, I get goosebumps all over my body. It was truly a day I'll never forget.

Three days after our wedding we set off for an adventure of a lifetime. We spent our three-week honeymoon in Italy and Greece. I truly believe this was the happiest time of my life. I was in a constant state of bliss. Such joy and excitement. Our love was overpowering and ever consuming. We took in so many memories and adventures during those three weeks, and I'm so glad that we took plenty of photos and that I wrote in my journal everyday so I could remember every little detail.

Breaking my moment of reminisce, I look over to Alec and say, "Honey, remember on our honeymoon, when we were in Santorini, we got to ride that quad everywhere and we even got to see people riding on their donkeys to get up and down the tight stairways like you see in the movies?"

"Yeah. Santorini was really cool. I loved all of Greece. I would definitely go back," Alec replied, keeping his focus on the road.

"Yeah, me too. Maybe we can go again for our ten-year anniversary or something," I say hopefully.

"Yeah, that would be nice."

A month after we got home from our honeymoon, we found out we were pregnant after a short amount of trying. We were over the moon excited, and nine months later we welcomed a beautiful little girl. When she turned one, we bought our dream property out in the country and embraced the hobby farm lifestyle.

It's amazing to me, that I always wanted to live in the country, have as many animals as I wanted, and raise my children to appreciate the outdoors and animals, to learn responsibility for caring for animals and doing farm chores, and then to be able to find someone who also wanted this type of life, also solidifies that we're meant to be.

Six months after moving in, we welcomed a second beautiful little girl, and two years after that we welcomed a gorgeous little boy. Our family of five is complete, and now, on the eve of our five-year wedding anniversary, I can truly say that we are so blessed.

They say that everything happens for a reason, that fate will bring two souls together to be bonded, soulmates if you will. Some believe that God has your life planned out for you, and people will be put in your life for a reason.

I know from the bottom of my heart, that Alec is meant for me. That fate, the lucky stars, God, they all worked together to bring us together. I have never felt so certain, so peaceful, so at ease, so comfortable, so at home. Because that's what Alec is to me, home.

We pull into the familiar parking lot of the beautiful bed and breakfast, and we check in to our suite. We set our luggage down and take in the view from our balcony, atop the cliffs looking down at the lake.

"Can you believe it's been five years? We've accomplished so much already, I'm excited to see where we'll be in another five," I say to Alec lovingly.

'I know. Some days it feels like longer… In a good way. It feels like I've known you forever, and as if we've been married forever. And then some days, our wedding feels like yesterday. But yeah, now look at us. Three kids, five dogs, a farm, successful careers. What's there to complain about hey," Alec says as he plants a small kiss on the top of my head.

I step back inside to grab the bottle of champagne that was waiting for us and two champagne flutes before rejoining Alec on the balcony. Alec pops the champagne and pours us each a glass.

"To trouble," Alec says, proposing a toast.

"What?"

"I always knew you'd be trouble when you moved in. And boy was I ever right," Alec says with a chuckle.

"To trouble. Happy Anniversary. I love you."

Printed in the USA
CPSIA information can be obtained
at www.ICGtesting.com
LVHW041411011123
762333LV00004B/11